THE LAST
TEMPTATION

THE LAST TEMPTATION

A novel by

GERALD K. MALCOM

Q-Boro Books
WWW.QBOROBOOKS.COM

An Urban Entertainment Company

Published by Q-Boro Books
Revised edition.
Copyright © 2005, 2007 by Gerald K. Malcom

ISBN-13: 978-0-9777335-9-0
ISBN-10: 0-9777335-9-9
LCCN: 2006935890

First Printing April 2007
Printed in the United States of America

10 9 8 7 6 5 4 3 2 1

*This is a work of fiction. It is not meant to depict, portray or represent any
particular real persons. All the characters, incidents and dialogues are the
products of the author's imagination and are not to be construed as real.
Any references or similarities to actual events, entities, real people, living or
dead, or to real locales are intended to give the novel a sense of reality. Any
similarity in other names, characters, entities, places and incidents is entirely coincidental.*

Cover Copyright © 2006 by Q-BORO BOOKS all rights reserved
Cover Layout & Design – Candace K. Cottrell
Editors – Candace K. Cottrell, Melissa Forbes

Q-BORO BOOKS
Jamaica, Queens NY 11434
WWW.QBOROBOOKS.COM

Dedication

Carmen and Bianca

Prologue

"It's been ten years, Traci?" Pause.
Traci jumps up in her bed. Sweat races toward her belly button. She clamors for air as she searches the dark for light. She tries to respond, but her voice won't let her. It betrays her desire and sticks up for reality. She mutters, "H-h-huh?"

His response is the same. Nothing changes. "It's been ten years, Traci?" His pause is lengthier. "I can still call you Traci, right?"

She nods.

He can't hear the nod. "Right?"

Her 'yes' is weak.

"Do you know who you're talking to?" he asks.

She drops the volume. "Yes, I do."

"Well?"

"Well I can't talk right now."

"It's important."

"I know it is." Traci hurries the phone to its base. She wraps the blankets tight around her face and falls into the sheets. She closes her eyes tight and makes the voice disappear.

"Are you OK, baby?" Jordan asks. He is still half asleep as he puts his hand on her blanket and rubs her arms. His voice is softer than the other.

Traci flinches at the purpose of his touch. He is consoling her at two-thirty in the morning. If it wasn't a full blown conversation now, it will be in the morning.

"I'm OK. I couldn't quite catch the voice on the other line." She was quick. Almost too quick for her own good. She never professed to be the greatest liar, but she could make up a story or two if she had to. Her mother always told her she should've written a book.

Chapter 1

Traci

Jordan props his feet up on the ottoman and watches *SportsCenter*. They ordered room service, and according to him, she seemed to want him to stay all day. In reality, she wanted him out as soon as possible. Not that she was tired of him; she was scared. The phone call had opened up a box that had been sealed shut, forever. Or so it seemed.

Jordan wanted to make love earlier, but her thoughts were on the call. She was in tune with her body, so it was hard to turn off her brain and allow her body to experience pleasure. She knew ways to divert his attention from sex. Today's diversion was migranes. She also didn't want to throw up on him. That would cover his other request too.

Jordan finishes watching his show and turns the television off. He checks his watch out of habit and asks, "Did you get that call last night?"

Traci freezes. Suddenly the voice replays over again. "It's been ten years, Traci." The voice was thick and throaty. It meant harm. It meant purpose to be placed at two in the morning. It meant that she had to deal with some stuff that no longer existed.

She turned blond. "A call?" The covers were now keeping in the heat. She didn't care. She wouldn't let him see perspiration. He knew she never sweat unless she was nervous or sick. She hadn't quite learned how to throw up on command, so she kept the covers to her chin.

He rubs her back through the blanket. "Yeah. The call from your agent?"

She shakes the cobwebs out and turns to face him. With all the tension, she had forgotten that even though Jordan spoke to her last night, he probably would never remember that he opened his mouth. He slept heavily.

"The agent from the insurance company?" she asks.

"No, the agent from the James Bond movies?" he quips.

She laughs like he is the funniest comedian she has ever heard. She hopes he can't decipher between her nervous laugh and her laugh that is genuine. She always marveles herself an actress. She slaps him in jest.

"Yes." She allows the covers to fall from her face and neck. "She said she would call me tomorrow about some possibilities for the upcoming week." She sits up and props two pillows and leans on them. She loves the hotel she's in, but she doesn't love it enough to pay one hundred and fifty dollars every night to stay in it.

Jordan pulls her near. "You can always come stay with me."

She loved that he was so attentive. He always put his best foot forward, even when she did things to push him away. It was her defense mechanism. If it was too perfect, she would deem it destructive and blow it away before it blew her away. She spoke with her girls about her bizarre behavior, but they couldn't help because they shared her ideas. They joked that they should go to therapy together.

"I can't stay with you. You live too far. You know that. And, are you going to wake up at five in the morning and bring me all the way to work?"

He slips, very noticeably, back into the bed. He rubs her spot. She loses composure. He sings underneath his breath. The words are inaudible, but the melody isn't. It was Luther without the voice. Jordan could carry a melody, but he needed help with the tone. He draws tiny circles on her thigh. His slippery fingers snap the light off.

Most mornings he lacks passion and gives her fury. He would turn over and show her why he was the king of their jungle. He would already be strengthened by the time he spread her legs. She always accepted him with open arms. His hug was always tight; his intensity always bold. He was a beautiful brown. Also, he was lovingly wild in the morning. She didn't and wouldn't have it any other way. She wanted him to thug her sex in the morning. No questions. No hidden desires. She didn't want him to wait for her to climax first. This was his chance to run with the wild and let her know that dick was king. He told her few things in the morning when they had ferocious sex. "I'm not waiting," was one. "Better get there before I do," was another. His voice was always bold, his attitude brass. Morning sex brought out his killer instinct.

He massages her head and kisses her cheek. She forgets about her headache. She wants to open up and let him in. She slides underneath the blanket and waits for him to crawl underneath.

The room is dark. Noise is unobtrusive, and he wasn't

going to allow a headache to disturb his groove. He makes the first mistake seconds later.

"Did the phone ring late last night?" he asks.

She isn't going to allow him to make another mistake. What he doesn't know is that nothing can overtake a woman's headache that is real.

Sharlana asks every question she can within two minutes. They're coming fast and furious. The fire. Jordan. The undesirable insurance agent that dragged her feet. And the hotel.

Sharlana offers Traci an opportunity to stay with her.

Sharlana sits on the edge of Traci's borrowed bed, wide-eyed and far from innocent. Sharlana is a five foot-two, one hundred forty-five pound ball of fire with an auburn weave that falls to the middle of her back. Her dark-skinned complexion enhances her high cheekbones and full lips, and whenever they went out, she would get most of the attention. Not that the tight jeans she wore to accent her perfectly rounded ass did much to deter most, not even the white guys. Traci often wore heels to stay a full head and shoulder above Sharlana. Her style is classic with earth tones to match her cappuccino complexion. Sharlana fancies weaves, while Traci chooses the Halle haircuts. Traci's beauty is a combination of Dandridge and Horne. Sharlana is impressed with fashion of the moment. Her friends joke that Sharlana has that special something that attracted everyone. Only Sharlana doesn't understand why white guys also felt comfortable approaching her.

"There is no such thing as a little fire. Are you sure you're OK? I had to leave work early."

Sharlana is always finding reasons to leave work early.

She works at one of the biggest telemarketing agencies in the city selling headstones, of all things. As much as she talked, it was a wonder she didn't sell out of the headstones. Who in the hell wanted to talk about the possibility of dying over the phone? Traci was convinced that people often bought the headstones just to get Sharlana to shut up. But if anyone could sell a microwave to the devil, it was Sharlana.

"Damn, Lana. I'm glad the whole house didn't burn down. You would've taken off the rest of the year."

"You're lucky I came to support your evil ass. Have you spoken to Jordan?"

"He just left."

Sharlana jumps from the bed and sniffs the air. She dusts her pants and sits on the dresser. "Did you request he wear a condom?" Her laugh is jovial; the underlines are serious. She held nothing back when she spoke about Jordan.

"Not today," Traci snips. She's growing tired of Sharlana's remarks about Jordan. They pause, take a breath, and laugh hysterically. They know when to stop. She knows Sharlana wants nothing but the best for her, but Sharlana doesn't know when to allow someone to grow on their own. Sharlana is a woman who knows that systems were made to be broken. Traci, on the other hand, is predictable. Their schedules reflect their personalities. After the nine-to-five, they both go in different directions. The moon dictates where Sharlana goes. Kickboxing, school, Jordan, and her girlfriends dictate where Traci goes. It seems as though everyone has their scheduled day.

Sharlana's revelation is that Traci should stay with her. Traci's response is in a different hemisphere. Sharlana argues the point of needing someone at a time like this. Traci debates that she may need space because of her crankiness.

"What are sisters for?" Sharlana answers as she heads for the door.

Traci picks up the phone and decides to give State Farm one more chance before calling the higher authority to pitch a bitch. She knows the squeaky wheel gets the oil.

She gets the operator, again. She leaves a message for Ms. Braxton that lacks decorum.

Chapter 2

Jordan

Deanna's head slides through the crack in my door. "Mr. Styles, Traci Johnson called about two hours ago."

Noticing my mood swing, she quickly follows with, "I'm sorry, Mr. Styles. I answered the phone and then I went to lunch. By the time I returned, I had totally forgotten."

If she wasn't the boss' niece, I would've gotten rid of her "amnesia ass" a month ago. "That's OK, Deanna."

Deanna is fine *and* forgetful. Even in my old age, my memory ain't that bad. I remember my conversation with her uncle as if it was yesterday.

Mr. Amsterdam barged into my office, pushing aside papers so he could sit. "You need someone to help you get your shit together."

I finished my thought on paper and gave him a blank stare. He hated the stare, "I don't need anyone. And if someone came in here messing around, I wouldn't know where to find anything."

He coughed up what sounded like two lungs, swirled it around, and gulped it back down. "I'm from the old school, and I say you need a woman to come and help you get your shit together, and that's that!" By the twinkle in his eyes, and the slow swirl of his cigar, I knew he was up to something.

I waved my white flag in defeat. "All right, we'll place an ad tomorrow."

His laugh was hearty. When William F. Amsterdam was a young man, he came from Kentucky with two things: good credit and a dream. He and his wife of twenty-four years started the computer business from scratch. He hired me because he said I had the same fire in my eyes that he used to have. His eyes didn't possess that flame anymore. With his wavy hair split neatly down the middle, he reminded me of the fast-talking street guys hanging in the D.C. bars looking for young love. He wasn't very tall—five feet six inches—and he weighed about one hundred and eighty pounds, with a love for racquetball and a good Scotch. I watched him as he cut the butt of his cigar and searched for his lighter. He rocked back in his seat and eyed me curiously. After lighting the cigar, he blew three perfect halos in the air. I could smell the familiar scent of old black wood, reminiscent of my grandfather's cigars.

"I'm glad that you agree with me Jaw-don," he drawled. I tried correcting him before but it never sunk in. "I have the perfect person for you." This smile revealed beige and orange-colored teeth.

"Who?"

"My niece!"

Stare. "All right, Mr. Amsterdam. Is it OK if I meet her before you hire her?"

He got up and walked toward the door. I heard the laugh and watched another halo shiver toward the ceiling. "Too late. She'll be here tomorrow."

I watch Deanna search her belongings for a pen to take dictation. She is the same height as Mr. Amsterdam, but her weight is distributed quite differently. Hers is *equally* proportioned. Her face is oval, and the mole on the right side of her lip is sexy. She's attractive, but not overly pretty. Her smile more than compensates her attitude. Her cleavage merges in the middle of her chest and seems to discuss ways to break free. Her breasts greet me every morning, shouting, "Help! We're overcrowded." I can't do a damn thing for them.

She begins taking dictation with a slow lick of her lips. She invites me places I don't want to go. I shake it off and think of Traci. She was the first woman in quite some time that made me happy. I was content, even though she withheld sex like it was a prize.

I sit back and watch her finish. "That'll be it, Deanna." She stands and walks toward the door. The extra switch is for my benefit. "And hold all of my calls."

She forgot to take all of her scent with her. I exhale.

Remembering the previous evening, I decide to give Traci a call. I don't know if it was part of my psychic behavior, but something suddenly struck me. *She was talking to someone.* She picks up on the second ring.

"About this morning—" she starts.

"Never mind this morning. Did you get a call last night?"

"Huh?"

"Did you get a call last night?" I repeat.

"Yes."

"From?" I know something's not right. I can't put my finger on it.

She pauses.

Scalp massages soothe me, so I do it myself. "You there?"

She chimes in with her phony voice. Her voice doesn't glow. "I'm here."

"Well?"

"There was a call last night." Her pause is too long. Her phone disconnects. Knowing her need for time, I wait for her call. My phone rings a minute later.

"You there?" she asks.

My laugh was full of pity. I would've thought she would come up with something different to bide her time. Hang ups are too easy. I laugh harder at her inability to speak up about something.

"What's so funny?" she asks.

"You."

"Meaning?"

Between more chuckles, I get out, "I don't know. I can't quite put my finger on it. Something just doesn't seem right." Pause. She needs inducing. "Who was he?"

Her tone changes. Her voice is softer. "Why would you say 'he'?"

"Don't know. If it was a woman, you would've said her name by now."

"For your information, it was a . . ." she pauses and shouts to someone in the background. "Tell them I'll be right there." She comes back to the phone and speaks about an incident involving a kid falling down the stairs.

That's a much better way out of the conversation. After a quick thought, I decide to let her off the hook. I tell her that she should get going. We decide to meet for drinks later. Before she hangs up, she asks me why am I still laughing.

Chapter 3

Traci

Not being a true morning person, Traci rolls over and slams her hand against the alarm clock. Today is Friday and her last day at Sharlana's house after three sleepless nights. The dragging of the feet by her insurance company and her squeaky wheel got her into a nicer hotel when it became available.

Traci can hear Sharlana yelling through the doors. Sharlana offers French Vanilla coffee and a fresh bagel. Traci tells her that she has one more hour before she has to get up. Every morning goes like this. Traci needs every ounce of sleep while the vampire in Sharlana only needs three hours of sleep and a fresh cup of java mocha caramel something with five sugars and one cream.

Her journey from work is filled with dreams and high hopes. She hopes her room is ready at the hotel and she dreams of what her house will look like once it's completed.

Luckily, she walks through the process of obtaining her room when she arrives. Within thirty minutes she is upstairs in her room sitting on the king sized bed with the extra plush pillows.

Room service brings her a bottle of Sangria and a tray of cheese and crackers. She sets up her station on the bed and turns on an old movie with Cary Grant.

The phone jolts her from the superb dialogue between he and his wife while he shaves in the bathroom.

She immediately thinks of the last call. She stares at the phone that sits next to the bottle of wine on the night stand. The ring is irritating. She feels sweat beginning its slow trickle from under her arm.

She picks up on the fifth ring without looking at the caller ID.

Silence.

She hears a shuffling on the other line and then she hears music. Teddy.

"Turn out the lights and light a candle . . ."

A voice interrupts. "You remember this?"

Sharp pains jab her heart. Traci doesn't want to remember this. She doesn't want to hear the song. She hates the melody. She hates the way the song interrupted her mood. Simple words blending in with a simple beats leave her with contradiction. She always loved Teddy, but she hates him now. She loved all the songs he sung except this one. It was their song. It was *the* song. It was all they played for a year.

She hangs up.

The phone rings again. She is more accepting of the annoying ring because she knows it's purpose.

It takes a rest. A minute later, it erupts. She snatches it and brings it to her ear.

"What?"

"I need for you to listen to what I've got to say," Solomon says.

"Talk!" she demands.

The music returns. Force MD's. *Tears.*

She hates them too. The melody is beautiful. That was year two of their relationship, if you could call 'fucking and eating' a relationship.

Solomon was the man with no plan. Their initial meeting set the tone. The girls around the way called him AJ, for Action Jackson. His body was like his name: strong, powerful, and large. Solomon was the only man who made Traci drip with his lips. He was six feet, seven inches and black. A shiny black that made his skin glisten.

She was having a party for one of her girlfriends at her house years ago. She left to get ice, and when she returned, Solomon stood on the porch. They both stood with their guns drawn.

His eyes told hers that she was beautiful. They slid down her neck and carefully licked each nipple. Her jeans were next. He paused at her zipper and nodded with a slick grin. "You're dripping."

"Excuse me?"

"The ice," he replied. The twinkle in his eyes didn't fit his thugged out persona. He stood with his legs spread shoulder length apart like he had the best shit known to women.

Sharlana rushed outside to check on Traci. "What took you so—" Her voice trailed off. "I see you've met Mr. Solomon Jackson." She warned, "Don't look into his eyes."

Traci's look informed Sharlana that it was too late. Traci eased by him with shakiness. He smelled like a hot shower sprinkled with lavender. A young lady behind him yelled for him to wait up.

The rest of the evening was filled with drinks and stares. Mentally, Traci made love to him every time she looked in his direction. She loved when a man was a man. She loved the smell of work, the dirty nails, and the grungy beard. All of her life, she was attracted to men she could never bring home. Why should tonight be any different even though her friends had informed her that Solomon was there with Patricia?

Mona, Celeste, Sharlana, and Traci sat on the couch planning their next move. Mona was overly aggressive with her plan for Traci to nab her man. She wanted Traci to jump up and get her rent-a-thug. Celeste told her to remain calm and keep her cool when she approached. She always preached dignity before everything else. Sharlana, on the other hand, was the go-getter. She went toward the kitchen to see what was going on.

Peer pressure got the best of Traci as she guzzled the rest of her drink. "Anybody else want something to drink?"

Celeste laughed, "I'm good. Go get your rent-a-thug."

They all laughed and gave high-fives.

Hanging onto what dignity she had, Traci wheeled around and began her journey. On her way, she kept reminding herself that she really was thirsty. Her heart pounded as she neared. She kept her breathing short and sweet.

Just as she applied pressure to the door, Celeste bumped into her. "Excuse me, Traci."

Traci grabbed Celeste's arm. "What are you doing?"

Celeste shook her arm free and whispered, "Just trying to get this bitch out of your way."

Solomon and Patricia stood near the back of the kitchen. Without warning, Celeste bolted toward Patricia. "Excuse me, Pat, I think you left your lights on."

Patricia thanked Celeste for being so nice and left to get her keys. Celeste followed her trail.

Solomon watched the whole situation unfold. He was impressed. As she approached, he remained on the counter. She laughed to herself at the nerve he had to be sitting on her counter. She had consumed only two beers, but it seemed as though she couldn't walk without instructions. Her feet were like her emotions: tangled and confused. On her eighth step she realized she was still a foot away. He didn't get up to greet her, but instead remained on the counter waiting for her to finish her approach.

"Hello, Solomon."

He jumped down, landing with a loud thud. She was so close that she could see every hair on his chin. She embraced his scent.

His lips were full. "Ms. Johnson."

To Traci's dismay, her nipples greeted him before she had a chance to. She toyed with her empty bottle. "I'm fine, Solomon." She stared at his curled chest hairs. "Are you having fun?"

"It's pretty nice." He looked around. "Nice atmosphere, too. I gotta thank Mona for inviting us."

Traci's epiphany had Solomon's date all over it. "I told her to invite some people she knew. We really like Patricia."

Solomon loss of air was out of exasperation..

Traci's eyebrows furled . "Aren't you—"

He moved close. "Aren't we what?"

Traci backed up. "Um . . ."

"Did you want to ask if we're *together*?"

"I g-g-guess." The air between them grew thicker. Obsession cologne and stale beer mixed unsuccessfully.

He picked up a bottle cap and brushed against her

on his way up. He noticed his nipples were erect. "Cold? I could turn up the heat for you."

Traci loved his cockiness, but to her he was probably just a good lay. She wondered what would make him think she would even want him. They were on two different levels. BET screamed for her. Who screamed for him? She thought maybe desperate women. She noticed how he thugged himself out. It was a nice appearance. He wore everything well. Nappy Afro. Grungy beard. Clothes that fit just right.

Solomon extended his hand. "Can we go somewhere where we can talk?"

Without thought, Traci accepted his hand and let him lead her somewhere in her own house. He walked toward the kitchen so no one could see them escape. She loved the fact that he respected privacy.

Traci's sitting room comfortably fit a desk, chair, a couple of bookshelves, and small couch. Solomon found his way to the burgundy leather couch, sat down on the edge, and pulled her close. It didn't bother Traci that she had only spoken to him twice. She didn't need to be there, but she wanted to. She was tired of the married but single executives pushing up on her. She needed a strong man to take her.

He stood and began dancing to the music that played in the distance. As Traci's heart thumped faster, his movements against her became more aggressive. It was like he had a connection to her feelings and he was doing everything to keep her engine going. He was sculpted from granite. His thighs. His stomach and his middle.

He massaged her lower back and pinned her against the wall. In the background, the girls talked. In the forefront, Solomon applied more mental pressure. She could feel herself moisten. She inhaled and smelled his scent again. Slight perspiration and his essence mixed to form heaven. She was happy that he wasn't trying to feed her corny lines.

For a minute, they rocked so close and so slow that she could feel every pulsating throb of his manhood.

He spoke softly. His accent was thick and reminded her of Jamaica. She had gone once and the men from the island treated her like a queen. She exposed her neck and closed her eyes. She could hear the birds and the ocean. He grabbed her breasts and fondled hard. After being with men who only made love to her, she welcomed his aggression. He groped her body going up, and massaged her gently on the way down. He lifted her shirt and unsnapped her bra expertly with one hand. Her breasts fell and bounced back to their perky position. After a few minutes she realized that he was definitely a breast man. She tried to kiss his neck, but his lean away from her lips let her know that she was to do nothing. She fell into the wall and let him have his way. She loved his way. More kissing was followed by more touching, and then he unbuttoned her pants. His fingers played in her hairs as his lips and tongue continued to probe her mouth. His fingers walked toward her clit. They rested and then danced on her spot. While his tongue moved in and out of her mouth, she breathed heavily into his. Seconds later, she came.

Solomon clears his throat and tries a different approach. This time much softer. "Look, Traci. I think—"

"What do you want?" she interrupts. Her eyes close as her temples throb. "I mean, you call me out of the blue and expect me to listen to anything?"

"Fucking right!"

Traci looks at her phone like it's a foreign object.

Solomon voice eases back in. "Sorry about that."

Traci jumps at the chance of ending the conversation. "That's why I don't want to talk. It's the same old shit, Solomon."

He knows Traci better than most. "I said I was sorry. What more do you want?" Pause. His voice darkens, "I'm trying."

Traci sits on the phone hoping he'll give up the little fight he is putting up.

"What do you say we talk?" he says.

"Now?"

"No. Later." His mannerism shows irritation with each passing syllable. "Of course I want to talk now."

"I need time."

"You've had time. Don't you think you've had enough?"

She gives no response.

"Don't you think you've had enough *fucking time?*"

Traci's cell phone hits the floor. The battery jumps from the back and bounces to the wall.

Solomon wasn't going to boss her around. Not anymore. After massaging her hands, she puts her phone back together. As soon as she puts it on the desk, it rings almost immediately. She ignores it. Massages more of her hand. Her pace is stubborn.

She couldn't call Sharlana. She would hit her with twenty-five 'I told you so's.'

The phone rings again.

She storms over.

"What in the hell do you want with my life?" she shouts.

"Everything?"

Traci's blood rushes from her face. *"Jordan?"*

"I believe I am. What's wrong with you?"

"Nothing."

"Nothing, hell. I ain't heard you this mad since the Fugees broke up."

She laughs. "You didn't know me when the Fugees broke up."

"Shit. I don't seem to know you now. You are a crazy chick after dark," he jokes.

Traci explains that a telemarketer called her and continued to call and that was why she was so angry. Jordan asks why a telemarketer would call a cell phone. She makes up an excuse to be joking. She can tell he doesn't believe her. She cops to a lesser charge.

"An old friend found my number lying around and he decided to give me a call."

"Must've been a good old friend for you to react like that."

"Not really."

Jordan grills her about her grumpiness as of late. He throws a couple of excuses for her. She grabs the first one that fits.

"I do think it's the fire. Do you know what it's like not to sleep in your own bed for two weeks?"

"I know exactly what it's like not to sleep in your bed for two weeks."

Traci loved that about Jordan. He was always able to make light of a situation, even if it meant him forgetting about his own anger.

Traci's other line beeps.

"Hold up for a . . ." She pauses. She decides that the person she is talking to is much better then who was calling. "Never mind. What were you saying?"

Jordan loses enthusiasm. She felt that he could sense

the sudden change in her tone. She tries to keep it even keel. After the small talk about the weather fails, she decides to open up.

"I've got something to tell you, Jordan."

"What?"

At the last minute, she chickenes out. "Nothing, really. I've got a surprise for you."

Jordan probes. He is unsuccessful. Traci is clever in that she knows he loves surprises. She knows how to throw the dog's scent off. Her question is for how long?

Chapter 4

Jordan

Deanna yells through the intercom, "We're ordering Chinese food, would you like to order, Mr. Styles?" My coffee spills as I spin quickly. I attempt to wipe French vanilla from the most important proposal I had written thus far. Knowing my boss was going to go berserk, I shook my head as I unsuccessfully moved coffee around my vowels and consonants. My job required tons of paperwork, but I welcomed moving up from computer analyst to head of *Computers for Change*. It was an exciting new program where I went from company to company assisting with the change from the old systems to the new ones. I got a piece of the action through bonuses and stock options.

Deanna rushes in and asks if everything is OK. With a sudden wave of my hand, I dismiss her. She buttons up the top two buttons on her shirt as if to insinuate that I didn't deserve to see her cinnamon cleavage.

I watch her until the door closes. After my barrage of silent curses, I turn my attention to my drenched proposal and try to salvage what I can. Coffee is everywhere, and my new suit is stained.

As I clean the desk, Deanna buzzes me to let me know that Traci is on the other line. The phone reaches my ear in a hurry. "Yeah!"

"*Yeah?* You don't sound too good. Everything all right?"

I fall deep into my chair. My mood is indicative of my ongoing day.

"Everything is all right. I just spilled coffee on all the work I just completed." I know her next question.

As planned, she says, "You saved it on disc, right?"

I shake my head at her predictability. "You know I can't write on the computer. I have to see it in front of me. Actually, I was about to enter it on the computer when Deanna yelled through the intercom about some damn Chinese food!"

"Your temp from hell, right?"

I remind Traci that she was the boss' niece and there was nothing *temp* about that.

"I didn't call to irritate you, Jordan. I was just calling to let you know I really enjoyed the other evening we spent together."

My mind raced back to the other night. Traci was like an animal. We've had some beautiful sex before, but the other night was different. "I remember. I don't know what got into you."

"Was it a problem?"

"Not at all." I didn't know where the newfound Traci came from, but I was going to cash in on this sexier model. "What are you wearing?"

"Huh?"

"Huh, hell. What are you wearing?"

"C'mon, Jordan. You know I'm at work."

"I know you're at work, but do I ask for much?"

She pauses. "Let me get up and close the door," she mutters.

"That's my girl," I whisper. I prop my feet on the window sill, put my hands behind my head, and lean

Traci picks up the phone and hastily replies, "A red suit with a cream blouse."

"Not like that. Go a little slower," I coax. "Like you did the other night when you did that seductive reverse cowgirl position."

Embarrassment fills her voice, "Stop."

"OK. Let's start over. What are you wearing?"

Traci speaks slowly, "I'm wearing a crimson-colored top with a matching skirt."

"Yeah?" I position Sambuca, the name I affectionately dubbed my penis, to the left. He yawns.

She continues, "I'm also wearing a cum colored silk blouse."

I shoot up. I love the sudden nastiness of my queen. "What color did you say?"

She plays her part. "I meant to say that I was wearing a cream colored blouse. What did I say?"

"You know what you just said."

"Is it OK if I open my blouse, Mr. Styles?"

I want to let her know she is doing well, but I don't want her to think she's doing too well. "Sure. I wouldn't mind that. Tell me what else you plan on doing."

"I'm putting my hands on my breasts. Shall I take the bra off, or would you like your mind to imagine what they look like?"

"I like the mental thing. Keep it on for right now."

Her mouth makes noises as she does something mysterious on the other line. She asks how she's doing. I tell her to keep going.

"Keep going, who?" she asks.

"Huh?"

"Huh, hell!" she barks. Her voice takes on an odd tone. She is taking her acting to an entirely different level. "Who do you want to take the bra off?"

She wanted me to bow down and give her the answers she wanted the way she wanted them, so I appease her. "I want Traci to take it off."

"I kicked Traci's ass out," she responds quickly. "Ms. Johnson is taking over. Now, who do you want to take it off?"

My tone reaches a higher octave. "You, Ms. Johnson."

"Ms. Johnson is playing with her nipples. Would you like to taste?"

"Yeah."

"Where are your hands, Mr. Styles?"

"One is on the phone and the other is resting on the desk."

"You don't need both hands. Unzip your pants and rub Sambuca until he comes to life," she directs.

I feel awkward stroking myself, but I know it pleases her. I don't know how much pleasure I was going to get out of it, but I give it a try. "I can do this," I assure her. "Keep going."

She moans. "I'm wet, Mr. Styles."

"Touch yourself, Ms. Johnson," I command. I have to regain control of my own fantasy.

A few seconds later, her voice returns. "Like this?"

"Like what? I can't hear you. Taste your fingers," I order.

She moans and begins to slurp her fingers. "Like this?"

I drape my arm across the desk, using it as a pillow while envisioning her slurping on everything from her fingers to Sambuca.

My imagination runs wild. I know exactly where she is located. She is sitting behind her desk, a few feet away from the door. Her head is leaning on the desk while she bends over so no one could hear. They had thin walls and nosy women. She had two pictures on her desk: one of her mother, and the other is of us at the beach. There is a computer to the right, and above her head, on the wall, is a picture that I bought for her of two people straddling each other at the park. The picture was made up of deep browns, golden yellows, and bright purples. There is a huge window on the left that let in the same warmth I feel.

"Mr. Styles?"

"Yeah?"

"Pull Sambuca out."

Without hesitation I unzip my pants and slowly dig Sambuca out of my black and white striped boxers as though I was freeing him from jail. He yawns again and stretches out. Against my leg, he looks like a smaller extension of my thick brown thigh.

"I want you to rub yourself while I touch myself," Traci adds.

I'm man enough, so I obey her wish. My left hand grazes the sides. Within seconds, I am at full strength. "I'm rubbing, Ms. Johnson. Are you still lightly touching yourself?"

She lets out a bevy of moans. "Can't you tell?"

"I wish I was there, I want to—"

"Shhh," she whispers. "Recite some of that poetry I love while you stroke yourself and think about me circling my spot with my fingers."

I grab myself and pump slowly. I wasn't too fond of masturbation, but when done for the right purpose, it was usually successful.

My voice is deep and slow:

"Damn Sweetheart, I like this

Because your finger becomes my lips as I begin to kiss

You until you become wet, sticky, and moist

I'm on my knees with my hands under you as I hoist that fine, brown, sexy, soft ass in the air.

Do you care

if I indulge?

Don't ask if I'm enjoying myself, Girl I know you see the bulge.

But this feels like Christmas & your sweet love box got to be the Grinch

Because you stole my cum and my man Sambuca, inch by inch.

I'm on my knees & it feels like we're miles apart, as if I was out of town

but I'm like Mary J. Blige's song because," I pause and sing, "I'm going down!"

Traci's phone drops and I hear her whisper, "I'm cumming."

I stop stroking myself and listen to her breathing. She always sounds worn out after releasing, and today was no different. The tip of my head felt silky smooth.

Her phone rustles. "You there?" she asks.

"I'm here. Did you cum for me?"

"I did," she admits. "Now it's your turn. Are you still stroking yourself?"

"Yeah."

She continues. "I'm lifting my skirt up, Mr. Styles."

I thought about her lifting her skirt. I thought about

her undressing and connecting with me any way my wild mind went.

"I'm in front of your desk, facing the door and lifting up my skirt. I don't have on any panties either."

I visualized. "I'm looking directly at you and you're right, you don't have on any panties."

"Stroke yourself while you bend me over your desk and have a little taste."

Mentally, I throw her over my desk and pry her cheeks open. The re-introduction of my tongue is always invigorating. She loves the way I make her back buckle and her mind spew obscenities.

I always wait for her to ask for the lick. Sometimes I make her beg.

"How do I taste?" she asks.

"Like pie."

"I'm getting ready to sit down on you now. Are you ready?"

My heart races as my hand shifts to a quicker pace. I can feel myself ready to explode.

"You ready for me to ride it out of you?"

"Yes." My hand starts to cramp, but I don't want to switch hands and disrupt the mood. "Traci?"

She tells me how she loved the last time we made love in the park. She says that it was incredible the way I pushed her against the tree and didn't care about her mood. She loved that I didn't care what she thought about messing up her good shoes. She loved the way I took control and dismantled her sexuality.

"Then when you had me grab the tree and you almost pushed me through the tree with your deep, penetrating, punishing blows to my orgasm, Jordan. It was incredible. I mean, you were so hard. Then when you told me to reach back and hold myself open. Then I told you that I couldn't and you told me that you didn't care what was comfortable or not. That was the first time that you had ever penetrated with no passion and you left me feeling . . ."

"Traci?"

"Yes?"

"I'm . . . I'm . . . I'm . . ."

"Yes?"

"Cumming!"

My door flies open and Deanna barges in. "Did you say, 'come in?'"

Chapter 5

Traci

Traci sits in the dark. She is in the dark about a few things. She doesn't know what to tell Jordan. She doesn't know how to tell Solomon to back off. And she definitely doesn't want to tell Sharlana anything that transpired. Sharlana was on her side, but she would have to hear about her demons coming back to haunt her. Tonight she was going to get a drink and the demons would have to wait for another evening.

She fluffs up a hotel pillow and leans back. Her memory terrorizes her mental. She jumps from the bed and reaches for her pocketbook. She opens it and lies it on the desk. A pack of Newport 100's stare back. She hasn't touched one in eight months. She keeps the box around to show her how far she's come. Sharlana asked her why she kept them around. Traci told her that was how she dealt with her issues. She kept Newports in her bag. She has a chart of desires for the new year in the bathroom, underneath her desk at work, and in her glove compartment of her car.

Her stare returns to her pocketbook. She could never

forget the way she packed the box before opening. She would inhale, hold it in, and blow it out real slow. The sensation was a couple steps underneath sex.

"Are you ready?" Sharlana shouts through the door.

Traci slams her pocketbook shut and opens the door. They hug and decided whether or not to go out or stay in and watch a movie.

They both agree that a drink would serve their purposes better than an old movie.

They leave for the car, and Traci hates to bring up the subject, but figures it'll be easier to get it out now.

"Guess who called me the other day?" Traci asks as she puts her car in drive.

Sharlana, into her music search, answers nonchalantly, "Sebastian?"

"Sebastian? Why would Sebastian call me?"

"I don't know. I guess it's someone from the past for you to bring it up all dramatically."

"I am not dramatic."

"Weren't you an actress?"

They both laugh.

Traci takes a deep breath and blurts, "AJ."

Sharlana's hand sticks to the radio button. Her head spin is slow and her stare is apprehensive. A horn informs Traci that it's her turn to drive.

Sharlana looks straight ahead and purses her lips. "Damn!"

Traci echoes her sentiments. For a minute they sit in silence as Traci weaves through the crazy I-95 traffic.

Traci thinks about the pains of the relationship. She thinks of long, tortured evenings wishing she'd made different choices. She wishes that she had never walked up to him. Part of it was that she was not strong enough to live her own life regardless of what he didn't do. She knew that if she had met him now and decided against her own better judgment to talk to him, she would've lived her life the way she wanted.

Sharlana thought about the constant conversations with Traci about this man. He ruined her girl's life and she had no love for him. She knew that Solomon wasn't shit, but that wasn't for her to decide. Traci had to see for herself what she was up against. Sharlana only knew what Traci told her and she knew there were always two sides to the story. She also knew that Traci was a Leo and Solomon was a Libra. They would mix, but mix and make what was the question. Traci's stubbornness and Solomon's carefree attitude didn't make for great times.

Sharlana comes back into the conversation. "And what did he say?"

"He wanted to talk."

"And?"

Traci shifts gears and moves into the far left lane to get off the highway. "I told him I was busy."

"Did he mention—"

Traci interrupts, "No!"

"What are you going to do? What are you planning on saying?"

"I'm planning on having a drink." Traci's hands go to her temples and she leans her head against the window. "And I don't want to talk about anything tonight, OK?" She picks up her head and drives to the next corner and takes a right.

Sharlana nods.

Traci continues, "So no bullshit tonight. This is our night of rest, relaxation, and Remy."

Sharlana doesn't answer. She sports a blank stare of

her own. "I'm good with that. I do have something to tell you, though."

Traci's expression tells it all as her eyes roll to the back of her head as if she has the lead role in *The Exorcist*. "What?"

Sharlana fumbles. "I sorta forgot to tell you that someone was joining us."

"Who?"

Still staring into the windshield, Sharlana blurts, "Celeste."

Traci's head whips around. Her body follows seconds later. Her voice was calmer than expected. "Now why would you invite her to eat with us?" She feels her eyes start to water. She has a bad habit of tearing when she becomes emotional. She hates the way people associate crying with a weakness. It is the one flaw that she has trouble correcting.

"Hear me out," Sharlana says. "She called me out of the blue a few hours ago because she's going through some things, and I couldn't turn her down."

Traci wasn't too forgiving when it came to certain things. Celeste had pulled the ultimate gaffe when they were younger. Traci didn't trust many people, and the few she did, had no opportunity to make her distrust them. She was a loyal friend and expected the same from those in her circle.

Celeste was one of Traci's friends who betrayed her for personal gain. Traci, being the giving person she was, allowed Celeste to stay in her house while she went on vacation. She told her that Celeste that she could help herself to anything in the house. She didn't know that Celeste would help herself to her career. Traci was reaching levels in acting that she never knew possible, and trusted to help a friend who was going in the same path as she. Traci had received a call to audition for an upcoming pilot for BET. The pilot stunk, but that should've been her call. Instead of calling Traci and telling her about the message, Celeste went on the audition herself. When Traci returned, she found out that Celeste had a gig in the entertainment industry and moved out. It wasn't until a month after her return that she found out about the missed opportunity.

She went to the set of Celeste's new acting job and was approached by the director. He asked, "Why didn't you show up for the audition? You always told me to call if I had something in mind. I did. You didn't. Your friend caught a good break by at least showing up. She met some key people who knew some key people. That's how she got the audition for this." Traci turned and walked out, never to speak to Celeste again.

Traci pulls down the overhead mirror and checks herself. She tries to calm herself before she steps into the lion's den. Five years prior to now, Traci would've ripped Celeste's ass apart. She knew she was more mature and understanding of what people do to make a living. She would've never used someone else's misfortune as a springboard for her own. She decides to go in and make the best of a bad situation.

Traci smiles. "Let's go."

Sharlana gets out of the car and rests her hands on the hood. A thin breeze provides temporary relief from the heated moment. "Look, Traci. Are you going to be all right when we go in there?"

Traci flashes her trademark fake smile and asks calmly, "Do I look like I would start something in a public place?"

Sharlana watches her with a microscope and decides

that Traci is sincere. They walk toward the club in silence. Traci's strut shows attitude, but her facial expression shows compliance with the plan.

"Table for two?" the hostess asks.

Traci holds up three fingers and smiles. She turns to Sharlana. "Is that how you want me?"

Sharlana doesn't touch the statement.

Traci's smile vanishes as she scans the room. The restaurant is nicer than she anticipates. She expected something small, but as she looks around, she notices that it stretches across the horizon. The walls are expertly decorated with vibrant paintings of jazz greats that breathe life into the place. In front, couples hold hands, talk, laugh, and eat. To the left, an older black couple argues. The man vehemently shakes his hand in her direction. After a second of watching his finger wag, she gets up and walks away. He watches everyone who watches him. The tables are bedecked in lavender and cream with matching candles burning in the center. Dizzy and Ella hang from the walls, watching people who knew them. Cigarette and cigar smoke hangs heavily in the corner where smoking is allowed. In the rear, a young Miles Davis smokes his own cigarette and reads sheet music while people of all nationalities noisily socialize and drink at the bar.

Sharlana leads the way through the crowd. They approach Celeste, who is surrounded by a group of overly eager African males. The pit of Traci's stomach churns. She shakes off the rumbling, but the grumbling remains. She wants no part of the meeting, but knows she had her choice to leave earlier.

Celeste has not changed in the years since they last spoke. She towers over the guys who strain to see her cleavage. She wears a leopard Prada jumpsuit with matching shades, even though the sunlight checked itself at the door.

Traci watches Celeste and Sharlana greet each other with similar hugs they use for each other. Jealousy creeps.

When Celeste and Sharlana finish, Celeste walks over to Traci. Her hand extends and she smiles. "Hello, Traci."

Traci accepts her hand and maintains her firm grip a few seconds longer than necessary. She wants Celeste to know that she was not to be messed with, ever.

"How is everything, Celeste? Still in the business?" She can't help herself. She has to broach the subject in some manner.

Celeste laughs and tells her that she has been working in a different field since then. She is trying a career change. She also adds that she isn't giving up.

The next half hour is spent with Traci at the bar. After freeing herself from the group, she is cornered by a guy she knows from college. As much as Traci tries to let it go, she hates the fact that Sharlana and Celeste are still hanging. She loves that Sharlana is her own person and remains that way even though they are closer than sisters.

Another man appears out of nowhere and asks Traci all the questions that men should never ask. He doesn't know that he's coming at the wrong time. She hits him with a barrage of answers as his questions come out. He seems to have a list of questions that she has all the right answer for.

"Traci," she answers dryly. Pause. "That's right. No last name." *Smile.* Pause. "Yeah, just like Prince, Cher and—" Pause. She looks up and points at the picture. "Miles, too." Pause. "No," she says. "I don't like seafood." Pause. "Yes, I do eat red meat." Pause. "A Leo." Pause.

"I think I've had enough to drink already." Pause. "A director for a daycare." Pause. "I own." Pause. "From Tennessee." Pause. "I cook for the right man." Pause. "With my girlfriend over there." Pause. "No, the other one." Pause. "The other's one name is Celeste." Pause. "You have a great night, Gary." Pause. "I'm sorry. I meant, Grant."

Traci fixes her lipstick in the bathroom mirror when Celeste saunters in.

"You look beautiful," a voice chirps from behind.

Traci's eyes make a beeline from her lips to the spot where Celeste stands. She ignores Celeste and continues to coat her lips.

"I said, you look beautiful."

Traci responds, "Thank you." She stands and continues to look through the mirror. "With all due respect, I don't have much to say to you."

Celeste lets out a nervous chuckle. Her soft facial expression shows she is unfazed, but her shifting posture expresses otherwise.

An older blonde haired heavyset black woman strolls in and enters the middle stall with a huff. She slams the door shut. The lock sounds like the jail doors being closed.

Celeste quickly removes herself from her cool demeanor and gives Traci the personality she remembers. "I didn't come for this shit! I came in to apologize for what I did. If you're not ready, then I don't know what to say."

Traci moves close to the sink to gather herself. She can feel tension hit her shoulders. She counts to ten, slowly.

In the stall, Blondie lets out a bevy of grunts before blessing the air with a mixture of old greens and eggs.

Celeste and Traci both cover their noses. They share a moment of togetherness as they shake their heads at the stench.

Traci watches her once the moment leaves. She sees that Celeste uses more makeup than needed, and she is obviously in a different state of mind.

"Why?" Traci asks.

Grunt.

"Stupidity."

Traci spins around back toward the mirror. "How can you be so freaking stupid?"

"Almost twenty years old? People do have stupid moments when they're twenty."

"Not like that," she spits.

Celeste walks closer. "I'm not saying that I look back and think it was all right. It was wrong."

Traci looks at Celeste through the mirror with evil intent.

Celeste corrects herself, "OK, real wrong. What was I to do?"

Traci faces her. "Tell me. I would've told you to go anyway."

"Then why are you so mad?"

"Because you could've just came to me. You could've called and told me about it. And then you moved out."

"I had to."

"You didn't tell me."

"I couldn't. I was embarrassed."

"You should've been." Pause. "I went through a lot behind that."

Traci sits on the counter and tells her about the years after. She explains how she hated acting and the fighting she saw people going through to get a job. After the incident, she fought hard to maintain great jobs and connections. She tells Celeste about her unmanageable situation with a director once she moved to California.

"The groping for the job was disgusting. He had me read for him in his office. He told me that I would do better if I spoke with feeling. He gave me a part to read from an erotic thriller. He explained how I needed to be in character and the only way to do that was to pretend that he was the lead." Pause. "As I read, he fixed my hair. He told me that my beauty would make me more appealing than others because I had the lips." Pause. "The body." Pause. "And then he told me that I was his first choice. He stated that he did all of the hiring and firing within his company, and he told me how many directors called him when someone's character was in question." Her tone is angrier as she imitates his voice. "I'm who they will call to get references for you, Ms. Johnson. And it would behoove you to be *very, very nice to me.*"

Celeste moves close and rubs Traci's arm. "I know," she says sympathetically. "I went through similar experiences. I mean, acting seems secondary to the directors getting what they want, when they want it."

They sit in the bathroom for the next twenty minutes and talk about different experiences and how it has helped them presently.

Chapter 6

Jordan

My *hello* is strained and barely audible. Traci speaks into the phone softly as I roll to the side and look for the time. She claims frustration has taken over her evening and she needs someone to talk to. I know what nights like this are like, so I prepare myself for the evening with an Advil and a glass of wine.

Traci comes in twenty minutes later and pours her heart out about everything she wants to pour out. Celeste. Sharlana. Acting. Her dreams. Her change in career. Me and the holidays.

My phone interrupts her monologue.

Deanna is frantic. "Hello, Mr. Styles. I didn't mean to call you at home, but I had to call you before I do something stupid."

"What's going on? Are you OK?" I ask.

She starts to speak and the phone goes dead. I tap the line three times and hang up. I'm caught by surprise, because Deanna has never called me after five o'clock. I ask Traci if she'd like a drink. She nods her head and looks at me with reservation.

The phone rings again.

She picks up where she left off.

"I'm sorry. I don't know where to go," she whimpers.

"Did you call you uncle?"

She sobs harder and tells me she cannot get through to him.

"You need to come over and talk?" As soon as the words leave my mouth, I want them back. It's too late, and I can't recant now.

"I couldn't impose on you," she adds quickly, "But that would make me feel a little better. I just need an ear."

I figure Traci would understand my position and relax for a bit while we iron a few things out. I give Deanna my address and we agree to meet up in twenty minutes.

I walk back into the living room and Traci finishes her speech.

She speaks about Celeste. More acting. She begins to speak about the phone call. She pauses and asks who was on the phone. She says that I seemed upset.

I tell her that it was my secretary.

"From hell?"

"Yeah."

"Is everything OK?"

"I don't know. She was crying hysterically and I told her to stop by before she left."

"*Left?*"

"She said she was leaving town and wanted to tell me a few things before she left." I knew it was far from the truth, but I had to make it seem drastic or she would begin her questioning.

Sarcastically, she says, "I didn't know you guys were that close."

"We aren't. What do you expect me to do?" I yell.

"Why are *you* yelling?" She looks at me out of the corner of her eyes.

My disposition screams guilty. I have to change. I take a large breath. I reach over and try to pull her near. She moves back and continues her stare.

"Listen to this," I start. "Maybe you can just wait for me in the bedroom and when I'm done, we can continue our conversation."

Her body reacts to the statement before she can express herself verbally. She sits back in her chair; body bracing for something.

"The bedroom?" she asks.

I laugh. I regroup and come back in a different manner. "Yes. Just to give us a little privacy."

By her reaction, I'm beginning to understand that privacy and another woman don't belong in the same sentence.

She remains calm. "If you need privacy, I can see you another time."

Her ability to stop and digress has me at the edge of my seat. I can't catch her mood. I can't understand what I'm doing. I do my macho thing and tell her, "You have to understand that things aren't always what they seem. You gotta trust me. I am not doing anything that would put us in jeopardy."

"And how am I supposed to believe that you have everything covered?"

"Because I do." I stand up and begin to straighten up the living room. My temper begins to change for the worse. There was nothing more disturbing than being in a situation where I wasn't trusted. I start in argument quickly. "What about the call? Am I supposed to trust you?"

She follows suit. "And am I supposed to be jolly and comfortable with you relaxing with your secretary?"

I know I'm making her angry, but that was the only way I would be able to escape the evening unscathed.

We had many discussions about comfort zones we expected when it came to the other sex, but this situation was different. I'm used to a man maintaining relationships outside of the main one. It didn't always work, but my options weren't usually best for everyone in the relationship. She said that men and women couldn't be friends. One usually likes the other, she said. I spoke up for the men and told her that females had something to do with men stepping out. She said that the majority of men she knew, cheated. I questioned what type of men she knew. She mentioned family members, lawyers, and doctors. I asked, "What about the Indian chiefs?" She said my humor was sometimes ill-timed. "Timing is everything," I said. I know I move to my own drum.

She isn't happy with the direction of the evening, and I can't say that I blame her. I try to lose this fight, but it's hard. I concede, "All right. Just wait here and maybe I'll tell her not to come."

Her gaze is cautionary. She nods her head slowly. Another epiphany that I'll never hear. "I'll find something to do. Have her come over. You say nothing is going on, right?"

"Absolutely.

"And this is the first time she's called, right?"

"Absolutely."

She eyes me and laughs.

I know what's coming. She sees an opportunity to talk. Discomfort travels all through my body. *"What?"*

She stops looking. "Nervous?"

I scratch my neck feverishly "What would I be nervous about?"

"I'm sure you know my next question." Pause. I add nothing to the conversation. She continues, "Who calls you?"

My laughter is nervous. I rub my shoulders. I mention something about the wool shirt. She gives me a look. She repeats her question.

I give my bold answer. "Nobody that you care to know about."

Her head snaps back. "Nobody I care to know about?"

"Yep. Nobody."

"My, aren't we being honest?" she says. "Anything else?"

"Flip it."

She starts to question my question, but she realizes what I mean and she quickly answers, "A few people call."

My eyebrow raises. I want the meat. "A *few?*"

She likes my intrigue. She wants to get a rise out of me. Maybe I pretend to rise like the sun when I joke, "Are you cheating on me, woman?"

"Would it bother you?"

It's a typical female answer, so I give her the typical male answer. "Of course it would bother me. I got feelings." Pause. I scratch my chin as though I play a part in a movie. "What about him?"

Her tone changes. She isn't as playful with her answer. "Him who?"

"The mystery guy?"

She looks for a distraction. There isn't any, so she hesitantly speaks, "I'm not ready to talk about that yet."

"Well leave!"

She turns quickly and her eyes show horror. *"What?"*

My smile comes quick. "Just joking. When you're ready, I'll be ready."

She looks bewildered. "Really?"

"I understand. Patients are a virtue."

"Pa-*tience is* a virtue."

I walk over and hug her. "Yeah. Yeah. Patience is a virtue. I got all of that. We'll talk soon." Pause. "About *everything*. About everything." I know she's ready to escape the conversation with very little damage. The only reason I let her go is because Deanna is coming and that would bring the anger back onto my situation. I was great with letting her feel her own heat. Her shit needed to stink sometimes.

Deanna looks like she's been through hell. Her powder blue sweat suit is furrowed and her ponytail needs hay. The whiteness in her eyes is replaced by a dull redness.

"Thank you very much. I hope I didn't interrupt anything," she says softly.

"You didn't." There is an awkward silence. She strums her fingers and fiddles with the remote control for the television. Outside, a couple argues about the man's tardiness and the woman's declining ability to deal with it. The guy wants her to believe his story. She wasn't buying anything he's selling.

"Want something to drink," I blurt.

"What do you have?"

"Depends. What do you have a taste for?"

Deanna sighs. "All the wrong things."

I know she has something to say, so I sit back and wait.

She shakes her head. "I want things I can't have."

"If you need something, just let me know."

"Thank you." Her first smile erupts.

"Enough with that Mr. Styles stuff outside of work. You make me feel like I'm fifty."

"I'm sorry." Pause. "Jordan."

I shake my head in agreement. "That's better. Let me get you something to drink. I know exactly what you need."

She smiles and stretches out on the couch. She yells that she doesn't like too much ice. I tell her that I've been doing this for years. I explain that I know how to make the perfect Rum and Coke. She tells me that she's been making erotic mixed drinks for years. I correct her and tell her that she means exotic. She brushes my comment off and tells me that I shouldn't be mixing too many liquors together. She mentions Cuervo and high blood pressure don't mix. I sneak back into the room and ask her to quit yelling. She sits up and takes a sip from the drink I give her.

"Not bad," she says.

I take a sip. "What's your story?"

Our legs touch. I move back quickly and apologize that it may be uncomfortable for her to sit so close. She claims that she doesn't mind.

"My story is embarrassing," she adds.

She takes a sip. Her huge gulps make it evident that it isn't her first drink.

"Try me. I'm sure I've heard worse."

She shakes her head again and swallows two more gulps. "There is a guy that I'm seeing."

I sit back and fold my legs and listen as her whole life opens up. Priding myself on being the ultimate peo-ple's person, I watch everything as she speaks. I watch her sip when she speaks of an old boyfriend she hated. I notice how she rubs her hair and grins whenever she speaks of her first love. She sips when she speaks of the trouble she got into when she was younger. I pick my drink up and begin to watch the show.

She rubs her hair and speaks more about her boyfriend now. Real love. Innocent. *Rub.* His generosity. His patience. *Sip.* His wife. *Sip.* A confrontation. *Rub.* She speaks about the boyfriend's willingness to stand by her. The way he got her with his smarts. How she secured him with her budding beauty. *Sip. Sip.* The wife's call. The ultimatum by his wife to her.

"You need to slow down with that drink."

"I'm fine," she says. "I can handle this."

"OK."

Sip. "She kept calling me Dana." Her words aren't slurring yet, but her bloodshot eyes give proof that she is well on her way.

"When did she talk to you?"

"She called me on my home phone." *Sip.*

"And she got the number, how?"

"I don't know. If I knew that, I might be where she is." *Sip.* "Trying to whip her ass."

I scoot to the edge of my seat. "You gotta control yourself. No sense in being in jail. What good will that do?"

She rubs her hair. She throws her head back and lets out a sigh. "I am so tired of this. I need my own man."

I chuckle. I'm not touching that statement. I've had my fair share of dealing with the wrong people and sometimes wished I had someone to lean on. I took it upon myself to help out and guide whenever I could. This was a little *too* personal, but I already have my foot in the door and I damn sure can't shut it now.

"Relax here."

Her eyes pop open.

"You'll be all right," I assure her. "I'm going to get ready to meet up with Traci." I pick up the empty glasses. "We had a little argument."

"Because of me?"

"No. Sometimes people have to get their signals right, that's it." I walk toward the kitchen. "You can stay in the room right here. Take a load off. You can't drive right now anyway." She nestles deeper into the couch. "I'm going to take a shower and take off."

"You love her, don't you?" she asks.

"Yep." I hate to talk about love, instead choosing to let my love speak for itself. "I love her."

"That's what I need." She pouts. For the first time, she looks underage.

I grab a shirt from the closet and throw it to her. She makes no effort to catch it. Instead, she watches it hang from the edge of armrest on the couch.

"Just stay here. You'll feel better in the morning."

"Thanks again." She watches me walk away. I can feel her eyes glued to my back.

Chapter 7

Traci

Traci sits in her car and stares out the window. No cars honk. No leaves rustle. No kids play. The quietness is too thick so she turns on the music and continues to stare. Today, the park is peaceful. She comes often to watch the little girls play hopscotch and boys play basketball. She loves the noise of noise. There was hardly a time she could think of that she was lonely at a park.

"Excuse me, Miss."

Traci hears a sharp bang on the window. Her sudden turn makes the officer jump.

Traci snaps back into reality. She rolls her window down and smiles. "I'm sorry, Officer. Is there a problem?"

The female officer's jaw is long and square. Reminds Traci of a cartoon character. Her eyes are slit like she smokes marijuana, and the length of her nose tells of many lies.

The officer speaks harshly, "Just wondering why you're parked here and no other cars are." The officer looks around to prove that no one else exists. She spins her head around quickly and looks at Traci suspiciously. She wags her finger. "You in here smoking the mari-juanas?"

Traci doesn't choose to respond. If there is any smoking, it clearly came from the officer's direction. Her eyes tell it all.

"I said are you smoking the reefers?"

Traci, who is growing increasingly irritated, spits, "No. Not smoking the weeds, the blunts, or the pipe. Now what about you?"

A call comes over the dispatch. The officer quickly responds with coded talk into the walkie-talkie as she stares at Traci. Seconds later, the sirens launch, and the officer is history.

Traci thinks about the midnight call. Her stomach gurgles as something stirs inside of her. She immediately calls Jordan. He doesn't answer. Her temples throb. It feels like the officer had just come back pistol-whipped her.

On the highway, she calls again.

He answers on the fourth ring. "Hey, baby. I was just thinking about you."

Traci turns onto his street. "Were you?"

Jordan laughs and offers nothing else.

The flight up his stairs go quicker than usual. Her knock is much firmer.

Jordan appears wearing a towel. Water always makes him sexier. Not today. His smile blossoms. "Hey, woman."

Traci peeks around his hug. She searches for any-thing that would cause him to not hear the phone. She can't fake it. Her eyes are intense and her speech slow.

"Why didn't you answer the phone?" she grills.

Jordan's hands travel the length of her shirt and stop

underneath her butt. He squeezes and kisses her neck. "I was taking a shower. About to come and see you." He releases his grip and steps back. "I'll be right back. Make yourself at home. Be right out." He disappears into the back.

Traci immediately begins to search. Her mother taught her how to scan a room effectively when she was younger. She remembered her mother going through her father's clothes. She even saw her mother sniffing the crotch of his underwear. That was one memory that never went away. Sniffing crotches and going through wallets.

Her eyes are drawn to the glasses that sit like twins on the coffee table. She looks back and can hear Jordan's horrible rendition of "Can We Talk" coming from the bathroom. She walks over to the glasses and lifts up the one with the ruby red lipstick on it. She brings it to her nose and to take a whiff. Smells like rum and Coke. She swirls the watered down concoction around and looks back toward the bathroom. To her left she notices Jordan's door. She hurries the glass to the table and eases toward his room. Her heart thumps. She can feel each one of her steps come crashing down. The door is slightly ajar, and the room is pitch black. She takes a few steps and holds still as Jordan stops singing. She listens and can hear nothing but water rain in the shower.

With a slight push, the bedroom door flies open. She swallows her heart. His bed is rumpled. Looks like someone is underneath the covers curled up in a ball. She can't move. Taking tiny gulps of breath, she moves close. Her eyes adjust to the dark. She gets a few steps away from the bed and begins to sweat. She wants to find out, but not like this. Her hands go from a reserved gesture to a gesture used to induce fighting. She can feel her nails dig deep into her palms.

"Looking for something?"

Traci jumps. Her heart flutters as everything goes deathly still. She is caught. Frozen. And embarrassed. She can't imagine what it looks liked from his angle. She wants desperately to moonwalk out of there and get back in her car. It's too late for all of that. She takes a deep breath and spins around with different energy.

She hugs him tight. "Hi!"

He looks around her hug.

Traci doesn't feel any difference in the way he holds her. He just doesn't kiss her neck. He doesn't let his hands travel to her ass. He doesn't even press against her.

"I was just looking for something to put on," she lies.

Jordan lets his towel drop. He walks to the bed and sits down. He applies lotion while watching her suspiciously. Usually he rubs himself and entices her. Today he rubs as he dissects her every movement.

"What were you really doing?" he asks. "I can usually hear you rumbling and rattling."

"I was checking." Traci turns around and looks for someone in the door. No one is there. She wonders if Deanna is somewhere in the house listening to their conversation. It's funny what makes a person make moves. In this case, the younger woman in the house listening to an older, insecure woman makes Traci adjust her attitude. She suddenly gets a burst of courage. Part of her is embarrassed because as much as she doesn't want to look like a young fool too insecure to leave her man for a minute, she does. She blows out three quick breaths that are not visible to the private eye that Jordan possesses today. Today will be the last day of yesterday and the first day of tomorrow. Openness and honesty will take place no matter what. She's made changes at the drop of a dime before. Once, she decided that she would no longer call Terrance after calling him everyday for six months. Another time she said she would no longer give an ex-boyfriend oral sex after finding him in a compromising situation with another woman, even though she loved it. Then there was the decision to stop eating red meat on a dare from a friend. Today, openness and honesty will be her red meat. Her oral sex. And her phone calls.

"I wanted to see where Deanna was. I thought she was in here and I wasn't sure. The room is dark. The door half-opened. The mood isn't right." She smiles. "You need to work on your Fung shui. It's all negative up in here." She walks over and kisses him.

Jordan relaxes and finishes putting on his lotion. "Can you get my back for me?

"Of course I can." Traci climbs up on the bed and kneels behind him and begins to apply lotion. She loves the way his back caves in as it gets lower. He never lifted weights, yet his muscles told another story. They tell of sweaty days and sweaty nights in the gym. They express power when it held him up as he swung down into her. It spewed tales of the night he held her up against the wall. She never fully recovered from that night. If he knew the effect he had on her that night and the thoughts that remained, he would make reference to it. She wants him to read her mind and tell her to quit putting lotion on his back. He'll take her everywhere. Maybe even curse at her and tell her to "Get the fuck over there." All he had to do was point. He had the power to command, yet at times he doesn't seem to want to, or even know that he should. He told her that sometimes he wanted her to come get it. She didn't have a problem with that, but she really got off when she was being told, commanded, or even at times disrespected. When she thought about the amount of time that he has spent commanding, she thinks that maybe he happened to stumble upon it and didn't know the power of it. Didn't know the strength of directing a woman with so much power. Kinda like a great haircut or a good job on the nails. The end product was half the battle. The major part was being serviced and taken care of without doing it yourself. Women ran for the service *and* the product. Sex was no different. Reaching orgasm for her was a common goal, but the how was the exciting part.

She continues to rub his back and dream of him turning around. He sits slumped in front of her with his head dropped. She figures that this is his haircut and his nails done for him. She forgets about her dreams and digs deep, feeling his body succumb to her.

A knock at the door brings it all back.

Jordan jumps and Traci scuttles to her feet.

"Oh shit!" Jordan wraps his towel tight. He rushes to the door. As he touches the doorknob he turns and asks Traci if she is presentable.

Traci looks at him with a blank stare. "Are you presentable?"

Jordan looks down at his towel and playfully slaps himself in the head. He gets a shirt from the closet and a pair of shorts from his dresser. He finally flings the door open.

Deanna stands. No words. No breath drawn. Not even a courtesy blink.

Traci doesn't know what she was expecting, but a half naked chick in her man's house isn't the answer. That wasn't half the story. The other half involved a particular over-sized Georgetown sweatshirt that she bought for seventy dollars and eight-six cents at the campus center. By the way Jordan answers, he has no clue what is to transpire.

"Hey, Deanna," he says. He turns quickly and looks at Traci. She doesn't give him the satisfaction of letting him know what she thinks, so she remains silent.

Deanna moves close to Jordan. Her voice is apologetic, "Look Jordan, I think I should leave."

Jordan moves closer and whispers to her that he might need a minute. She grants him permission with a smile and a backwards walk toward the bedroom without a word.

Jordan gives Traci ample time to digress and calm down. He thinks he knows her. If he did, he would have granted Deanna's request to leave with a swift kick in the buttocks. Instead, he chose what most men choose. To make everyone in the room happy.

Traci smiles. "So, how's it going?"

Jordan pops his hands together and gives a smug grin. It pathetic.

Traci continues when Jordan fails to read his lines. "I see she dresses well. Isn't that the shirt I bought for you?"

His eyes follow Deanna's empty trail. "Maybe."

Jordan's eye contact is elusive. He looks at everything but Traci.

Traci, growing tired of the game of cat and mouse, jumps up and walks into the living room. Jordan knows not to follow right away.

Traci meets the bedroom door with a sharp rap. Her stance is indicative of her feelings. Her nostrils flare for increased breath. Her foot taps to a beat that is nowhere in sight. She hears Jordan creep behind her.

All he says is that nothing was going on. He laughs to himself and adds that she was doing all of this for nothing.

"Nothing?" Traci asks. She wants no part of any answer he plans to give.

As Traci's fist is to pound the door again, the door opens. Deanna stands with the same blank stare she had earlier.

Jordan sits in back and doesn't help out.

Deanna's movement is minimal; her words even worse. "Hello," she says.

"What's with the nakedness here, Donna?"

Deanna hands her the Georgetown shirt. "I'm not." She looks at her own clothing and shakes her head. "No nakedness here." Deanna is smooth. She knows not to go out like a total sucker in front of Jordan. She also doesn't press Traci too much.

Traci knows Deanna knows more about these situations then she lets on. Traci won't let this slide, but she also doesn't want to overreact to this either. She has to make peace with her naive man, while at the same time letting this young lady know her proper position. What they did at the job was another story. She knew she would have her chances, but like her mother always said, "Having a man is like having a child. You got to raise him too, baby. Raise him to where when he's on his own, he can stand on his own. If he's weak with you, then he'll be even weaker without you. Nothing you can do about them except let them free and allow them never to fuck up your dreams. He'll move on and move into another chicks dream."

Traci knows maintaining is key. Maintaining dignity. Maintaining her part of the relationship. Maintaining sanity. Maintaining her own dreams. Setting her own goals. Giving up half of you without giving up yourself. She was reading lately and learning how to keep herself while giving half. Today is no different. It is her first real test.

Traci smiles and extendeds her hand. "If there was no ill intent on your part, Deanna, then I have no problems."

Deanna looks at Jordan. Jordan looks the other way.

Chapter 8

Jordan

Damn! I am impressed. She didn't press the issue any more than she should. It wasn't the usual response I got from women. The one before her was a professional in every sense of the word. Outside of the word, she was one of the wildest chicks I had every encountered. She ate fire and spit venom. Not being too fond of venom or fire, I dismissed her.

Today is the first time I saw Traci in a confrontation of any sort with another woman. It scares me that something so simple like a shower can cause the loss of something good. I mentally check the box that says take care of home first.

Deanna's laughter catches me by surprise. "I'll leave, but I'm not leaving this second, though," Deanna says to Traci. Her calm amazes me more than Traci's resilience.

Words rush from my mouth, "That's not a good idea, Deanna."

She looks at me like I disrespected her by taking Traci's side. I move in her direction.

"Look, Deanna, it's time to go. Nothing more I can do here."

Traci takes a step back and picks the glasses up and walks into the kitchen. I watch Deanna pick up the pieces to her ego. She tried to put her foot down, but this wasn't the place. I'm kinda ticked off that she even went there.

I escort her to the door. "I hope all is well tonight. Sorry things didn't work out as planned."

Deanna's fingers graze my hand. "I know."

I shake my head, shrug off her statement, and lock the door. The venture toward the kitchen is filled with many thoughts. I wonder what Traci will say once the smoke clears. I wonder how she'll feel about the comment Deanna made. All of this doesn't make the work situation too comfortable, but nothing I can't handle.

She finishes the dishes while I stand in back watching. She doesn't acknowledge me or make reference to the previous hour. She just keeps washing.

"How long are you going to continue to wash that one glass?" I ask. I press against her.

"As long as it will take for me calm down."

I remembered how she enjoyed being calmed. Since there was no cheesecake around, I would have to go to part two. I reach around and help her wash the cup. I dig my hand deep inside the cup and rub with her. Her neck tastes sweet.

I whisper, "Mind if I taste this?" My question is rhetorical. She knows. Her head falls forward. I hear her silent moan. She tries to hold it in. I eat deeper. My press against her is stronger. More purpose to my lean. A second later she tries unsuccessfully to snap out of it. She grabs the other cup. The one with the lipstick on it. I acknowledge her pain and raise the cup to where we both can see. Before, I would have tried to wash it quickly or just ignored it. Today the man came forward. Allowed me to raise it in the air as though it was a toast. I take myself completely off of her. I lift my lips from her neck. I want her to see that this acknowledgement isn't induced by anything sexual. I take my other hand and change the water's temperature. She likes it warmer than I. I burn my skin so she can smile. I find out that it isn't that bad her way. I guide her hand to the soap and I tap twice. Silky green Autumn Breeze poured. I massage it into her palm. Now I press against her again. She could feel my security. I get close to her ear and whisper, "Watch this," I say. "We live and we learn."

I massage warm water into Autumn's Breeze and guide her lathered hand to the rim. We wash the cup's rim together. She leans to the left. I deserve access to some of her now. I earned it. Living life and not learning is like existing just to die.

I kiss her neck and wash the glass. Her moan is more vibrant.

Together, we start to rinse. She maintains control of the glass when the water stops. She rubs the spot and opens the other side of her neck. We talk without speaking. I tell her that I will never allow stupidity to rule our roost. She says she is more understanding. Willing to accept my human nature and work with me.

Through the window I can see my neighbor across the street parking his car. His music is always loud, but his beats are smooth. Jazzy hip-hop. No words. Just beats. Like Miles doing the two-step with Lena.

"You still mad?" I ask. I can hear her smile. The music plays. She tries to look into the window to see who exists. I tell her to relax. I partially close the curtain. "You don't trust me?"

She finally speaks. "It's not that, it's just—"

"It's just hell." I know what she wants. Mentally I cross over. Love after the war is not always peaceful, but for some reason it brings serenity. "You don't trust that I would have your best interest."

"I—"

My hand comes crashing down. "I, hell. Boardroom Bully." My laugh is sarcastic. I know she runs shit everywhere else. Not now. Every once in a while I knew this is what she needed. Needed to be told to shut up with dick. She needed the thug love. The unintentional, just-because dick. Mentally I put my Tims on and popped my collar.

"Is this what you needed?" I ask. I apply pressure to her back. Jagged jolts of massage rip upward, while the downslide is softer, gentler, and loving. I want to confuse her sexuality. Not let her know when the R&B would mix with the hip-hop.

"Pull these down," I instruct. I tug at her jeans.

Without pause, she lifts her shirt. She moves in slowly, letting me know that she'll do some things on her time. I allow her victory. I watch her lift her shirt and unbutton her jeans. She slides the belt off. The floor welcomes it.

My words slur. "That's good."

She teases me with the slow, steady pulling of her pants down. She knows too much will get me going. Ten seconds pass.

I move in swiftly. "Move. My time is precious." I laugh again. "The time starts now," I add. I yank her pants down around her ankles. Her head hits the inside of the sink.

"Remain steady. You hit your head, and it's your fault. Got it?"

"Yes, sir."

My fingers twirl rapidly with anticipation of diving into something delectable. I step back and watch her skin glisten in the light. Her ass looks like chocolate mountains. Soft Alps. I was ready to rock climb. Get in every crease she owned.

"Spread these for me." I push her legs open slightly and allow her to do the rest. She scrambles as best as she can, but she knows nothing will be good enough for me. I want perfection. She wants to be slightly imperfect, always leaving room for improvement and room for discipline.

Once again, she moves slow.

This time my hand stings her ass. She flinches. This time her head remains still. She is trying to show her resilience. I test it. I get oil from the bathroom. When I get back, she is in the same stance, same spot and hardly breathing so she can hear every syllable to every order I command. Streams of oil splatter off her mountains and fall to her thighs. Revved my engine. I wanted to turn her around and make love to her on the counter top, but that wasn't on the menu. She ordered dick scrambled hard with a side of aggression.

My buckle makes the same noise hers did. Even drops next to hers. I listen to the music for a second as I slowly unzip my pants. "You ready?" I ask. Another rhetorical question. This time it is met with a head nod from her.

I instruct her to reach back and hold herself open for me. Asked her if she ever thought about this. I told her it was OK to talk. She responded with sweet melody. She told me that she thought about it the other day.

"Where were we?" I ask.

She says we were in an alley. She tells me I wasn't too

nice. Borderline disrespectful. I ask her if it excited her. She asks me to feel. See for myself. I do. Run my finger gently up her slit. Her moisture feels like silk. She jerks when I pause at her spot. I have to. We were friends. I always showed my respect. I leave my fingers on the outside of her lips. I continue to rub.

I enter with one full swoop. Her head hits the sink, and her muscles inside clench me tight. I leave him inside. I tell her to remain silent. She can't breathe without permission. She will have to be sneaky and steal breaths once she clenches.

"How do you feel?" I ask.

She mumbles that she feels crammed and violated.

"Want me to take it out?"

"No."

There's no sir attached to the ending, so I punish her. My hips pop back as I only enter the beginning. The tip of my head plays with the lips as it slides in an inch and back out. I don't want her to find comfort with the beat of my strokes.

"What would you like?"

She tells me that she wants the best. She nods at my pants.

She knows how much it turns me on. Makes me feel like I hold the prize. I don't need it, but it is welcomed. Did something to my stroke. It increases the vigor and gives me more drive as I dive in and out. Give her the business. Her head beats like a drum on the inside of the sink. I am impressed by the way she makes that a part of the sex. She would worry about head trauma later.

"G-g-g-give it to me," she stutters.

I stop. Tell her I would start on my own schedule. I didn't need any instructions.

*   *   *

The next day Deanna acts funny. Her walk is driven by business. Her speech is formal. Her eye contact is elusive. I ask her to sit down for a second.

"Sure," she says.

"Is there anything you would like to say?" I ask.

She shakes her head.

I give her the business posture. I lean back, and the soft leather catches me and pushes me forward.

"I think we should have a talk about last night."

I watch her body language. Her hands clutch the front of her jacket. Her foot bounces as rapidly as her brain appears to be moving in thought. She struggles with turning off pleasure and getting into business.

"There were a few things that came out of the other night. First—"

"I've got something to say about—" she interjects.

"Not now, you don't. I gave you the opportunity to speak, Deanna. Now hear me out. I'll give you time to say your piece." I take a sip of water and gather my thoughts. "I think you were way out of line when you came to my house and—"

Deanna sits up to object. I stop speaking and allow her to find her place. She falls back.

I continue, "I thought you were way out of line when you came to my house and told Traci that you weren't going to leave." I take another sip. "That is never your call. Do you know what I had to go through after you left?" She doesn't respond. I continue, "How would you have felt?"

Deanna shakes her head slowly. It seems as though the words fight to come out when she says, "I understand that I was out of line, but I thought we had more to talk about, and I wasn't ready to leave."

"It was time for you to leave. Anyhow, I don't think it's a good idea if you come to my house for anything. And maybe I put you in a bad situation by inviting you over."

Her eyes water. She takes deep breaths to calm herself. I hope she doesn't cry, but just in case, I have tissue near. That would be the only thing I owned to console her. I know to stay fifteen feet away. She left her mark and her mark almost got me kicked out of my own house.

I tell her it's time for me to take care of some work. She reluctantly gets up and doesn't have anything to say when I ask if she has anything to add. She walks to the door and pauses when she grabs the knob. I stop her confusion by telling her that we'll get the chance to talk again, but now isn't the right time. Here I go again. Leaving room for error through someone else's interpretation.

As she leaves, Mario comes in. Mario is the mail courier who lives in the basement and comes up for air with mail and stories of the hip-hop world. Usually not one to fraternize with staff, I take a liking to him. He is funny, persistent, and a ball of energy. He continued to identify with my heritage with stories of his interaction with the blacks in his neighborhood. He said he even changed his name from Tse to Mario when he came over.

"*Posse* was the best western movie with hip-hop flavor," he always says.

"That's the only western movie with hip-hop flavor," I inform him.

He argued that Mario Van Peebles should've gotten

an Oscar for his role. I told him that Tone Loc was a better actor. We fought about the same movie every other week. I told him that when he knew the lead singer of the Five Heartbeats, then we could talk.

Mario walks over wearing a Baltimore Ravens jersey with blues jeans and a baseball cap. He strokes his goatee that hangs a few inches from his chin. He claimed it was his flavor savor. "What's up with Deanna?"

I look up from my work. "What do you mean?"

He hands me a few pieces of mail. As I filter through them, he puts the rest back and sits on the edge of my desk. "Why don't she try to peep a vanilla brother out?"

I laugh hysterically. "A vanilla brother?"

Mario tugs at his jersey. "Yeah. A vanilla brother. She don't give me any rhythm. She blind?"

My laugh doesn't get a chance to subside. "Why would she be blind?"

"I can give her what she wants."

"Which is?"

"Money, power, and respect."

He sounds ridiculous. I had to do my job as a citizen of the hood by correcting his slang. It was way off and rather disturbing.

"You have to let it flow. And flow has everything to do with the inside as well as the outside. Look at your clothes."

Mario inspects his clothes as though he is seeing them for the first time. He pulls his shirt out in front of him. He lets it fall back onto him. He thinks his clothes will make the man. Women love the idea of a thug, but never the product of a thug.

Mario stands in front of the mirror that hangs over the fireplace. "Every woman wants a man with a little thug in her life. And if she wants that, why not have a little thug in her panties?"

I felt like I was talking to my nineteen-year-old son. I ask Mario to sit for a second. I explain the nature of why women want a thug.

"They want a thug's mentality. They want to feel safe. They want the unknown. They want the excitement. They want the thug love. They want the part time of it. The other part time they want the real man. The one who thinks rationally when the thug goes into overdrive. They love the man in Tims, but respect the man in a nice suit jacket and slacks. And look at what you're wearing. Do you think a real woman wants a man with a football jersey on?"

Mario frowns. His shoulders slump and he puts his tail between his ass. He stands up, feeling pretty bad about himself. My goal isn't to tear him down. I walk over and ask him what he's doing this weekend. He says he isn't doing a thing. I invite him to hang. He enthusiastically chooses to hang.

Chapter 9

Traci

The phone jolts Traci from her blank stare. A car's loud horn brings reality a little closer.

"Hello." Pause.

Traci can't answer.

"We should talk," Solomon says. He doesn't seem hurried or pressured. "Now."

Traci's response is muffled. "I can't right now, I'm about to—"

"No more can't, Traci. You need to meet me at Laguardos Restaurant on the corner of H and 11th." Solomon is stern and abrupt as he hangs up.

Traci pulls to the side of the road, stopping in front of a McDonald's. She turns her music on and listens to the local radio personality talk about relationships. He talks about repairing relationships and the hazards of not closing something off. This was one of the things that had been happening lately. People talk to her even when she isn't particularly listening. She thinks about her most recent call from Solomon. The bastard knew she would go. Some things will never change about her.

She is always ready to be led, even if it was into a burning building. Even if she isn't smart enough to resist, she is smart enough to wear a hard hat and fire boots. Today her hard hat would be a time limit of twenty minutes. The boots are Sharlana. She calls Sharlana and tells her not to ask any questions; all she needs her to do is to call thirty minutes after she goes into the building. Traci hangs up and tells her that she would call her as soon as she entered the building. She feels like Elvis.

An old gray woman walks over to her car with a cup shaking from her tattered-mitten-wearing hands. Traci turns her head the other way as she continues to be spoken to via FM airwaves. The old woman walks around to get into Traci's vision of sight. Traci rolls her window down and offers to buy her a double cheeseburger and a hot cup of coffee. She tells her she'll bring it out to her. The woman throws her hands at Traci and walks off.

Instinct had Traci calling Jordan, but she knows his reaction. It will be cordial, but not what she needs. She needs support. She needs someone to understand and tell her that she's doing the right thing.

Sharlana picks up on the third ring.

"You gotta go. Find out what this man has to say," Sharlana tells her.

Out of the twenty minutes she stays on the phone with Sharlana, that's all she hears. The message is loud and clear. Traci revs her engine and takes off for Laguardos.

Traci enters Laguardos and suddenly wishes she had listened to her own instincts. She should've hung up on him and went to the library to study. Instead, she is being led to a place where she would have to confront her past. Face her almighty demon with Satan himself.

She enters the restaurant and is greeted by a friendly waitress who obviously doesn't bring her problems or issues to the job. She asks Traci if she wants to sit at the bar or wait for a table. Traci looks around the restaurant to see if she sees Solomon. Just looking for him makes her stomach hurt. It churns when she turns left, and gurgles when she pans right.

"I'll just go to the bar. I'm waiting for someone," Traci says. She gathers herself and walks past a white couple who stands in front of the entrance into the restaurant. They don't move, instead choosing to kiss like they are newlyweds. Traci brushes by the couple muttering an insecure "Excuse me."

Once past the old couple, the restaurant opens up. It is amazing how many people cram into the little spot that couldn't house more than one hundred and fifty people comfortably. Black satin drapes cover the windows. Black satin tablecloths adorn the tables. And the walls are covered with a mixture of blues, greens and blacks. As she walks by all the occupied tables, she enters the bar area. Black professionals acting professional. The one thing she didn't miss about New Jersey was plethora of people who have nowhere to go to congregate and be around their own people. She used to travel to the city for the exposure, but here, it was all over. Maryland is infested with areas and places to migrate for conversation that's stimulating. For a second, she forgets why she is there. She looks around and exhales.

A black man with a thick moustache and connected beard stands in front of a group of five black men and delivers a punchline that has them all laughing hysterically. To her left, a woman is given a massage by another woman who looks to be her senior by twenty years. They pay attention to no one. The younger woman's head falls back while the older woman dives into her skin with precision, affecting the younger one's sexuality with little effort. A tall bartender makes a drink for three thirsty women at the bar. He toys with the alcohol bottles, flipping them and concocting a drink that would make a rainbow jealous. Another couple, darker in color than most, stand a foot away and hug. A white gentleman with over eager eyes asks Traci if he can buy her a drink. She declines. She watches more. She wants to tell the man who sits behind her to stop promising things he probably can never give that woman. She could hear him promise her that he could keep up what he started. She asks him could he increase the time and money. Traci turns around and notices the gangly brother in his early fifties has a wedding ring as he speaks to the woman half his age whose breasts burst through her polyester turquoise v-neck sweater. Traci looks closer at her own personal clothing selection for the evening. It was modest at best. Blue jeans that didn't hug. A powder blue sweater that left plenty to the imagination. And lipstick that covered and made her lips glisten, not moist. She was all busisness.

"You still drinking Cosmos, woman?"

Traci's eyes freeze. She stares at the black bartender as he continues to mix drinks. She watches the bottles spin in the air in slow motion. She see everyone around the bar move in slow motion. Their laughs are dawdling. Their hand movements deliberate. Their hurried pace is now forced to a slow leisure.

Solomon moves close. He repeats his statement.

Traci snaps out of her fog and stammers, "Y-y-yes."

Solomon presents a Cosmopolitan gallantly.

For a second, she is impressed that he remembers.

The next second, she is angry at because he remembers. Solomon was never one to forget the minor things like what kind of drink she enjoyed. He never forgot that she preferred red wine over white wine. He never forgot that doggystyle brought out the fight in her. He knew she didn't want to be pushed around by anyone, even though it was her pleasure.

She accepts the drink. "Thank you." She takes a sip and finally looks at him. He looks better than before. Like he finally settled into his features. He has aged around the eyes. His moustache remains the same. It wraps around his full lips and meets around his chin. His hairdo is most youthful. No grays or whites. He wears a small Afro with shiny black curls.

Traci stands there, stuck for words. Confused, the straw remains in her mouth as she takes one long continuous sip of her drink.

Solomon points to his left. "I'm sitting over there." He steps to the side. "After you," he says.

Traci gathers up all of the energy she owns and walks in front of him toward the lone empty table that sits on the outskirts of the room. Behind, she hears Solomon let out a sigh of pleasure. He mumbles something about her not missing a beat. Instinct makes her smile; the thought of who is giving the compliment makes her angry. She gives him what he wants. She puts a little effort in her walk. Makes her back curve slightly as her ass shakes thunderously from left to right. She knows the gift and the curse of having a bodacious behind.

She arrives at the table, and before she can sit, Solomon takes her seat and pulls it out for her. Arrogance allows him to move close so she can smell him. He smells fresh, like he just jumped from the middle of a magazine with a scratch-and-sniff scent of her dreams. Only this dream had nightmare tendencies.

She sits. "Thank you."

Solomon swings around and moves his seat a little closer than it was. Their legs don't touch, but he is too close. She moves away.

The music in the background is antique. Smokey Robinson. The people around her are different. Black. Brown. White. Foreign. Tempting. Exchanging stories. Making futures. Desiring. Drinking. Eating. Staring. Closer than close. Wanting. Following. Leading.

"I said, what did you want to eat?" Solomon repeats.

"I didn't hear you. I was looking over there," she explains.

Solomon turns to see what kept her attention. He sees something completely different. Women. Thick. Slender. Tall. Short. Accepting. Denying. Playing the game. Owning the game. Moving closer. Backing up. Kissing. Winking. Smiling.

"I said, I'll take the fish," she says. "Red snapper. Grilled. Mashed potatoes. Beans and a water with—"

"Lemon," he interjects. "I remember a few things about you. I know you ain't changed that much."

Traci pushes her drink to the side. "Let's get this over with, Solomon. I didn't come here to reminisce or make things worse off. You placed the call."

Solomon puts his hands up. "Whoa. Whoa. Calm down, sista. I didn't come for the drama either. Don't you think it was time for us to talk?"

Traci puts her head down. Her nerves kick in violently. "Yeah."

Right now she wishes she were anywhere but here. It's rattling her nerves that this is their first conversation in almost a decade. It plucks her nerves that he is patient with his information and vaulted with his goal. She wants to shake the reason out of him, but that will push him further back. She has to summon all the things she has learned since him. She is far from a dummy when dealing with men, but this was a different type of man. He is charming, intellectual, and addictive. Mentally, she builds more edges to her Great Wall of Traci and readies herself for the battle.

"How have you been?" he asks. "I see you've been taking good care of yourself." His eyes travel the length of her body. He makes sure he pauses at the important parts and smiles. The waitress comes back and he attempts to impose his mojo on her by ordering their food with a few jokes in between. She giggles as he purposely messes up her name. "That's Cand-ass?"

The waitress smiles. "That's Candace. Cand-is."

Cand-Ass isn't making the dinner go any smoother. If Solomon was her man, Traci would have told her in a few words that she was to take the order more efficiently the next time. Then again, she would have directed her attention to Solomon's comment after the bimbo left.

Solomon swallows his drink down effortlessly and slides the cup away. "Let me start by saying this." Pause. "I love you."

Coughs interrupt Traci's breath. Her heart shifts into the eighteenth gear as she moves her chair backwards. Solomon puts his hand on hers.

She remembers the touch. It is like a comfortable pair of slippers with a hole in the toe. Useless for every purpose, but comfortable to say the least.

"I don't want you to leave. I'm just telling you that I still have love in my heart for you." He remains smooth.

Age took the edge off, but left the sting to the blow. "I will always love you, Traci." He maintains eye contact. Solomon knows the key to Traci is her eye contact. If she feels stronger than her opponent, she looks them directly in the eyes. If she feels inferior to the person or situation, she will never look for more than a few seconds. It's a flaw that will remain with her until she leaves the earth.

Traci tries to look Solomon in the eyes. In this conversation alone, she had upgraded to five whole seconds without looking away. Small to him, but major to winning the war.

Her voice quavers. "Go ahead," she insists.

"I was saying that my love remains. And it was time to come back."

Traci's fist pounds the table softly. "Come back where? From where?" She could feel her blood pressure rising and couldn't remember any of the steps she needed to bring it down, so she breathes.

"You don't think it was time?" Solomon's voice is beginning to change, showing irritation and aggravation.

Traci throws her head in her hands. "I don't know."

Solomon's hand shuffles inside of his black suit jacket. He watches Traci as he searches the inside of his pocket. He takes out a picture and puts it on the table and slides it in front of her. He sits back and watches Traci cry softly. After a second, he leans over and takes her hands away from her face.

"It's OK," he consoles.

Traci lets him. That's the least he could do. She feels comfort as his fingers wipe away a tear that scurries down her cheek. At that moment, all the disgust she has left. He was always her shoulder to cry on. Always her rock. Today wouldn't be any different.

Traci takes sips of cool air as she prepares to look at her future. No more running from her past and hiding behind old decisions. Her vision goes from the oscillating fan above to the hardwood table that holds her future.

Panic sets in as she sees the picture. Sharp jabs puncture her soul. Her fingers tingle. Anticipation causes the earth to tilt. Dizziness rocks her equilibrium. She cries. Usually she kept the soft side to herself, but she's growing tired of hiding out and being strong for everyone but herself. Soft tears stroll down her cheeks and fall to the table. This time Solomon doesn't console. He sits back and lets it rain.

Traci grabs the picture and slides it in front of her. More panic sets in. More pain tugs at her heart. Sweat covers her body. Traci picks up the picture and brings it near. Her fingers trail the edges. She holds her mouth with the other hand. She whispers, "She has my eyes."

Solomon adds, "Yeah. I always tell her that she has Mommy's eyes."

Chapter 10

Jordan

Tony is waiting for me as soon as I walk into the Zan-zaa Bar. Mario trails behind as we move toward the front door.

"What's up, Tone?" Tony walks over and gives me the pound. He looks at Mario and asks who he is when Mario turns around to speak to a young lady who's profiling near the door. Meeting Tony twenty years ago was one of the best things that ever happened to me. He is the only friend who keeps it real, even if it wasn't something I wanted to hear. My other boy Dallas left a year ago with my sister at the last minute. He came to her rescue when her husband was abusing her. Tony tells me to let it go as long as Renee is happy. I tell him that I still don't feel good about Dallas having sex with my sister after knowing everything I know about him and his sex life. Dallas never opposed me, whereas Tony got in my face. Him being six foot-seven and three hundred and twenty pounds doesn't help my case any. The women refer to him as the Satin Teddy Bear. I told

them that there was nothing satin about Tony except
the thongs he wore.

"This is fly, J," Mario said. He walks over to Tony and
extends his hand. "What's up, big man?"

Tony doesn't extend his hand. He stares at Mario's
outstretched arm. "Big man?"

Mario puts his hand down and adjusts his red button-
up shirt. It matches his fire engine red pants. He smiles
and walks closer. "Yeah, big man. It's not an insult. Do
you know what we would do over in China to get some
size like you?"

Tony breaks into laughter and tries to cover it up.
Mario spots it and slaps Tony on the arm.

"You can laugh, big man. The women love a man
that's got a little comedy inside. Or at least that's what J
says."

Tony looks at me and mouths, *"J?"*

I shrug my shoulders and walk into the heart of the
party. Black women are everywhere. There are a few
white and Chinese women sprinkled in the mix. Myself,
not really ever trying the date thing with the white
women, chose to always stick with the sisters. Tony is the
ruler of many, even though I never see him with any. He
is more passionate about women and what they think of
him. I am not so concerned. My theory is, if they liked
me the way I was, then it was great. If they had an issue
with how I was, they could always look around and find
someone who could give them that.

It is relatively early, and people are jockeying for position around the club. There is one couple who chooses
to display their dance skills as people watch. The black
man has very little rhythm, but his suit speaks volumes
of his work. His leather shoes are shiny, his diamond
weights his pinky finger down, and his cuff links sparkle

when he lifts his drink to his lips. The white woman has more rhythm and less style. Her pumps are Payless and her jeans basic. She shakes her big breasts, which try to jump from her silky green blouse with every bounce of the bass line. I tell Tony to go over and do his two-step and go get that white woman. Tony pays no attention to me. He throws his hand in my direction and tells me that I better worry about my broke-ass dance moves.

"I do have something to tell you, though. Got a second?"

"Yeah. What's up?" I ask.

He puts his arm around me and tells me that he needs to tell me in private. I quickly excuse myself from Mario. I tell him that Tony and I had some business to take care of.

I tell Mario, "You can buy the first round. I'll take a Grand Marnier, and Tony drinks Budweiser."

Mario laughs. "Diet Budweiser?"

Tony begins walking away. I follow with curiosity. We relax near the pool tables, which are located in the rear.

"What's going on?" I ask.

Tony looks left and then right. He checks his phone before he begins speaking.

"Come on with this Secret Service shit," I yell. "You always act like you got some secret that will bring down all the super powers in the world. Spill the beans."

"You rushing me?" He stares at me for a second. "I can take my top secret ass back to the bar."

"Tell me what's going on." I hate to beg.

He looks around before speaking. "I saw Traci."

My heart races. I look around. "Where?"

Tony remains calm. "Not here. Earlier."

Tony has my full attention and now is putting his information on cruise control.

"Earlier? Where?" I didn't care if I didn't seem in control.

"Earlier at this bar. Or was it a restaurant? I don't know. It was Laguardos, the restaurant near H Street."

"I ain't never heard of no Laguardos. You sure it was her?"

"Positive. I know your girl when I see her."

"What was she doing?"

"I don't know. Calm down, boy. You acting like a chick?"

I can't defend myself. I *am* acting like a bitch. I *am* concerned about what my woman was doing, and at this point I'm not afraid to inquire further. If I know Tony, I know he will take advantage of my eagerness.

He speaks slowly, "I said, why are you acting like a chick?"

"I'm not."

"Who's your daddy?"

I walk away. I'm not going to sell out completely.

Tony stops me, laughing. "Just joking. You need to relax. She got you all messed up in the game. You want the story, right? I saw her at a restaurant with a guy. They ate. They hung out for a second, then she left."

"That's it? Any more?" I ask. "Were they all close and shit?"

Tony laughs at my ineptness. He says I was showing my weakness. I told him that I didn't care. I just wanted to know the scoop before I made myself look stupid.

"She was acting a little emotional." Tony hangs on to more information. "I believe she was crying."

"Crying?"

"I believe."

"Can I use your cell phone? I need to call and make sure she's doing OK. My phone is in the car."

Tony takes out his cell phone and hands it to me. He stands in front of me and watches me dial the numbers. I turn my back to him.

"Can't a man get some compassion *and some space?*"

Tony laughs. "As long as you can admit it." He goes back toward the bar area.

My fingers shiver as I dial. I wonder who she was with and what she was crying about. Traci was never one to cry, especially in public. In the eight months that I've known her, she had never let a tear so much as fall from her eyes. She was the rock. I often joked with her and called her steel.

Her phone rings for an eternity. I leave a message.

"Hey. Give me a call as soon as you get this. Just checking up on you and making sure you're all right. I'm out hanging with fellas. Talk to you later."

I hang up feeling no validation. I stand in the back of the club clutching the phone. Almost trying to will her to call me.

Five minutes pass and all that happens is more doubt and even more wonder. I call again. No answer. This time I don't leave a message. I go to the bathroom and check myself. A man offers to damn near wash my hands for me. He gives me a paper towel and offers me a host of colognes. To his dismay, I decline. I find Tony at the bar. I grab my drink that Mario bought and await Tony's smart answers or his dry jokes about my phone calling.

"How did it go?" he says.

I throw him his phone. "OK. She wasn't there."

Mario approaches the bar and dances next to us with a young black woman draped over his arm. He grabs her hand and makes her do a pirouette for us. Tony half-heartedly admires her. I pay no attention.

Mario says, "Gretchen, this is my boy, J. And this is his

friend, Tony." Mario waits for us to make a comment. She is cute, but nothing to brag about. Mario adds, "I think she's from Italy or Germany."

Gretchen extends her hand. "I'm Gretchen from Germany."

Tony accepts her hand. "I'm Tony from the Bronx."

I follow suit and shake her hand. "I'm Jordan."

Gretchen smiles at Mario and turns back to us. "Heung has been showing me around a little bit."

"Heung?" I ask. I look at Mario. He doesn't return my look.

Gretchen says, "Yes. He has the cutest name. Heung Lo."

I laugh so hard that Gretchen takes a step back, shakes her head, and walks away. Mario follows.

I explain to Tony that I have to get my bank card from the car. He snickers and tells me that he will be at the bar talking to the short Oriental with the long pony-tail and points her direction.

"You always go after the little chicks that you could carry underneath your stomach," I say.

He rubs his stomach and sucks his teeth. "And you always go after the ones that go after the other ones." Before I can say a word, he's off. A few feet away, he turns around and yells, "And don't forget your phone, play-boy. You might need to check up on the Mrs."

His humor always hits home. I try to hit home as much as I can, but he gives me no opportunity. He lacks the social life for me to barge in and make corrections the way he did. My girls did their best to hook him up, but due to his diverse taste in women, they didn't know what would please him. On the other hand, most of the women were afraid to be with a man so large. I told him

I would have to start looking in the zoo for a compatible mate.

My walk to the car is full of resolutions. I decide that if I get the chance to speak to her tonight, I will be truthful and honest about everything. I don't know why, but it feels like I am losing a part of her. I will be honest, even if it hurt. I knew she wanted to get married, but it isn't for me right now. I will tell her something about allowing her to soar and hope she believes me. I will tell her that just coming out of a marriage, I am not ready to walk down the aisle again.

I knew she wanted kids. Lots of kids. I'm not ready for that, either. I have one. That will have to carry her through until we are ready to make moves. It wasn't a conversation I wanted to have, but when it feels like the whole world is slipping, you're ready to save it by every means necessary.

It boggles my mind to see my growth, or better yet, to see the insecurities of being scared to lose someone. My father never told me the old cliché about if it's meant to be, it'll be. He was real. He sat me down one day. Even offered me a beer. Michelob Light. I didn't care. It tasted like soap, but the message was clear. I was growing up, and he wanted to acknowledge it with his personal rite of passage. A warm beer on the front porch, kicking to your old man about life.

"A grown man is given rules, and it's up to him to make the rules work for him," my father would say.

I had rules. Always did, but I learned how to make them work for me.

He always said, "The white man been doing it for years, son. It's time for us to catch up."

I've been catching up in everything else but the relationship department. My first marriage was a failure and I was convinced that I wouldn't do it again until I was ready. Traci will know tonight that I'm ready, but at the same time, it will still be a work in progress.

I return to the club and look for Tony and Mario. Mario is in the same spot with the German lady. She drinks like a sailor and dances like one. Surprisingly, Mario doesn't have bad rhythm. He moves around her with his hands clinging to her jeans. I ask him where Tony is. He nods toward the dance floor. He declines my offer for a drink. He tells me to come back in a little while and he just might need one.

I walk over to the dance floor and see Tony moving around like he's doing aerobics. His shirt underneath his armpits is wet. He gives me the head nod when he sees me on the edge of the floor laughing at him.

My phone rings. The number is private. I jump up and hurry to the back.

"Hello?"

"Jordan?"

"Speaking." I put my hand over my ear. It doesn't work because all I hear is mumbling. I dive deeper into the walls, near the back door.

"I'm sorry to call you, but I just thought we could speak for a minute."

Deanna has horrible timing. "What's up?"

"Nothing. Just needed an ear. And I know it wasn't the best time the last time, but I desperately need to speak with you."

I thought about Traci. Then I thought about the other man. "I'm at the Zanzaa Bar. Where are you?" The words feel bad as soon as I say them.

"Home. I need to get out."

"I'll be here for about another thirty minutes. Stop by. We'll chat and then you'll be all right." Pause. "And I'll buy you a drink. Do you remember Mario?" Pause. "Yeah. He's here. I'm sure he'll love to see you." Pause. "Hello? Hello?" The signal fades.

I wait by the bar with a drink *and* my phone.

"You see the moves?" Tony asks.

I move back. "No, but I see the sweat." I fake like I wipe sweat from my pants. "I saw you dancing with the young lady. She needed an umbrella."

"And you need goulashes with all the crying you've been doing tonight. What happened? She called you back yet?"

Instinct has my head dropping; pride has me lifting it high. "Not yet. I'm sure she's all right."

Tony and I revisit the past when a beautiful Jamaican woman walks by. He remembers his ex-girlfriend. She left him. He says that he left her. I give him playback on what really happened. We go from high school to college and all the near disasters we had.

Deanna startles me. "Hey, Jordan."

I turn quickly. "What's up, Deanna?" She arrives at the club quicker than I thought she would.

Tony grabs my arm. "Who's that?"

"She's the Sweat Inspector, Big Draws." We laugh.

I introduce Tony to Deanna. I tell her that he's my closest friend. Tony jokes that I won't be if I keep up the whining. Tony offers to buy her a drink. Deanna tells him she wants a Long Island Iced Tea. I don't know if it's a good idea, but what can I say? She's a grown woman. She has on a pair of tight black jeans that leave nothing to the imagination. Her D's damn near doubled in the raspberry sweater, and her face is radiant under the lights.

While Deanna crowd watches, I check my phone. Still no call from Traci. I was moving out of the worried phase and moving directly into angry mode. Tony returns with Deanna's drink. She declines his invitation to dance, and with that, he is off to the next woman.

"Can you dance?" Deanna asks.

I look her up and down. My smirk is proof of my disbelief that she would even ask. "Can you?" I ask.

"Do black people eat chitterlings with smoked hog maws, bacon, and cheese balls?" she jokes.

"Hell no! But if you think you can hang, please bring it." I lead the way to the dance floor. She follows, taking huge gulps from her drink. By the time she reaches the dance floor, she has finished half of it. She's trying to gather courage any way she can.

The music is much older than she, but she knows the words.

"Ain't no stopping us now," she sings. Her moves are sultry. Her hips sway and her fingers pop. For a second, I forgot that we work together. Quite a few people from the bar flood the dance floor. We are forced to close the gap between our dancing. She takes advantage and grabs my hand. I pull back. She doesn't flinch. Instead, she turns around and backs up against me. I try to move farther back, but a heavyset chick with thick eyebrows gives no way. She forces me into Deanna. I accept my fate and dance with no intentions.

As the music switches to hip-hop, the crowd swells. The heat beats down the backs of everyone. It does nothing to deter them from dancing closer than close. A few of the guys pop their collars up and unbutton the top buttons to their shirts. A quick pan to the left shows a six foot Brazilian woman with her hand sliding inside the shirt of Mario. His head tilts toward the air and his eyes close. He stomps his foot twice and spreads his arms like Michael Jackson. Deanna turns back around.

"I want to thank you for the other day," she says.

I do my two-step. "No problem. Glad I could be of service."

"And about the—"

"Shhh. Didn't you say you wanted to dance? Then dance, woman."

She smiles and we dance. For the next five songs, we dance through every generation. We start with the bump. The Gap Band sings "Outstanding." She knows the words. It tickles me to see the younger people who know the words *and* the dances. She turns to the side and softly moves her hip against mine. We laugh and switch sides and bump again. Nice & Smooth rap about the Hip-Hop Junkies. We get close and rap together, "Rickety Rocket was my favorite cartoon. After marriage the honeymoon. I'll be there gag me with a spoon. Who loves Popeye?"

Tony jumps in and yells, "Alice the Goon." He jumps back into his own dancing circle.

We cabbage patch to LL's "Rock the Bells."

"Damn, old man," she yells. "You still got it."

My next dance doesn't go so well. My crip walk is a little crappy. Actually, I look around to see if there are any blue flags in the air.

The DJ switches rhythm and puts on Luther. If This World Were Mine. My guards go up. She pushes them down when she says, "We can dance like this." She holds her palms out. "This is safe, right?"

I put my hands on hers and we dance slow. Only a few couples remain on the dance floor. Luther digs into the soul. I close my eyes and sing, "I'll give you the flowers, the birds, and the bees."

She continues, "And with your love beside me, that'll be all I need."

We sing together, "If this world were mine."

She falls into me. My arms catch her. I pull her close. Dance as I feel my way toward comfort. She wraps her arms around my waist and her head falls deeper into my shoulder blade. No lips. She sways seductively from left to right. I follow. Luther continues to press my subconscious. I think about the good old days in school when a dance was just a dance. There were no thoughts about bills. Who someone was taking home. What time they had to get home. It was just a dance. A chance to feel a real woman's body next to yours. You could concentrate on the particulars of her body. And smile. Remembering the innocence of a dance, I pull her close. Feel the contours of her back as I massage slowly. We stop dancing . . . with our feet. Our shoes remain glued to the floor as we dance with our middle. My hands slide down the side of her arms and around the jut of her hips. They are soft like I imagined the day she walked into the office with a black dress on. The black dress that was meant to tickle and tease. And toy with you until you literally had to shake the thought away. And when I did, she laughed and walked out of the office.

I jump back. "Sorry." I tell her that I just got caught up in the moment.

She pulls me near and tells me it's OK. Moments are made to be spent. Her wit is quick. Mentally, she's sharp. Almost too sharp to be in a position like this, in a place like this. I excuse myself.

"Jordan, wait."

My phone rings. I put more pep in my step and my quest to get away is validated.

I turn around and tell her that I'll be back. "Wait right there," I say. She stops dead in her tracks. First thought I have is that she listened. That will make a great part of her personality if she is consistent.

My voice is over eager. "Hello?"

"Damn! I saw you sprint away. Did you get hard-on over a dance?"

I hang up quickly. "Fucking Tony," I thought. I head back to the bathroom where Towel Timmy remains. I use the bathroom and the bastard tells me he ran out of towels. I laugh and flick my wet hands in his face. In whatever language he speaks, I know he called me an asshole.

Deanna is waiting where I left her. "You all right?" she asks.

"Sure. Had to use the bathroom. That OK?"

"Sure. Was everything all right on the dance floor? You kinda left in a hurry." She snickers. She stands by the pool table, caressing a pool stick. Her movement as of late is always on the seductive side. I ask her if she plays pool. She remarks that she doesn't hold anything she can't handle. I put four quarters in. I rack the balls and watch her line up to break.

"Now that's what I'm talking about," she says enthusi- astically as the white ball slams into the top of the balls, splattering them across the table. She makes one. Noth- ing special. "You wanna make a bet?"

She makes me chuckle. "Of course. What can you handle?" I don't care how she takes it. I take another sip.

"You have to buy me a drink," she says, "if you lose. And then you gotta dance with your shirt off."

I quickly scan the way she holds her stick. I want to

see if she is bluffing or if there is a pool shark lurking inside of her. She gives no indication either way.

"Come on, scary," she says. "We got a bet, or what?"

"What happens if you lose?"

"Everything," she says. She bends over the table and smiles. "Seven ball, corner pocket." The ball slams into the corner pocket. Her eyes never leave the table. She continues, "Didn't know I played a little bit back in the day, did you?"

I chalk up my cue stick. "Yeah. Whatever. Go ahead. Your luck's about to run out soon."

She calls another ball into the same corner pocket. It follows suit. Another ball eases into the other pocket. She laughs as she stands up and misses an easy shot. I laugh. Tell her it was almost twelve and her balls would stop falling. She says it was a gift from her to me that she missed that easy shot. I tell her to keep talking.

I'm confident when I say, "Twelve cross corner." The ball dies right before it goes into the hole. I check the tip.

"Ain't the stick, playa." She hits the next two balls in. She walks over to me and puts chalk on the tip of my stick. I snatch my stick away and tell her that she better start playing *her game*. She did.

"Eight ball over there," she says. She points to the pocket near where I stand. I close my eyes. She walks over. "Before I shoot this ball, do you wanna tell me something?"

My eyes stay glued to the ceiling. "What?"

"Remember the day in the office when you told me to come in?"

My eyes dart everywhere but in her direction. I was waiting for her to bring it up, but until now she kept it hidden. I guess she feels it's perfect timing.

"What about it?"

"I've always wondered about that day." She leans against the pool table and holds her stick between her legs. "What happened?"

I take a sip. "What do you mean what happened?"

"I thought I saw you doing something." Pause. She searches for eye contact but I wasn't in the position to give her any. "Were you doing something?"

"Like what? What do you think I was doing?"

"I thought you were masturbating." Her statement stung.

"I wasn't masturbating," I tell her. My voice is firm and believable. "It was an old college injury." She looks at me in disbelief. "Hamstring," I say. More looks. "Back in eighty-eight," I say. Her eyes squint. She searches for the truth, but she doesn't quite know how I lie. "I played quarterback." She shakes her head. "I was number twelve," I tell her. "Played quarterback ever since I was ten."

"You ain't gotta tell me nothing, Jordan."

I wasn't. I ask her if she is going to shoot the eight ball in or give me the game.

"As much as I want to be nice," she begins. She positions herself behind the white ball and shakes her ass slightly. "I just can't give you the game." Her stick meets the white ball with force, pushing it into the eight ball, which lands exactly where she says it would. Without looking at me she says, "I'll hold your shirt."

I sneer. Watch her watch me. I don't want to take off my shirt, but I never renege on a bet. A minute later I walk by Tony and head for the dance floor.

He stops dead in his tracks. He yells toward me, "What in the hell are you doing without your shirt on?"

Chapter 11

Traci

Traci is livid. It's been over three weeks, and in spite of the quick settlement she received, she feels as though nothing is getting done in a timely fashion. She walks around the house and takes note of everything that has not been done. The living room is the only room that is completely redone. She drops to one knee and thoroughly inspects the hardwood floors. They are smooth to the touch. She exhales at the possibility of being completely done.

"Looks great, huh?"

Traci whirls around and brushes her pants off. "It does look pretty good." She extends her hand. "I'm Traci."

The husky black man in paint-splattered overalls takes her hand. "Ms. Johnson, right?"

"Yes." She accepts his large, crusted hand. His calloused hands press against her palm.

"The name is Larry." He smiles to ease her pain. "I know it looks a mess, but let me show you what we're doing with the house."

Mentally, Traci lets out a loud hmmm.

Larry leads her toward the kitchen and begins explaining what is being done. He bends to show her the new black and white floor tiles, and as he points out the different colors, the crack of his butt is exposed. Traci guffaws.

He immediately stands up, pulls his shirt down, and leads her to the bedroom where the most damage had been done. He points to the wall where the fire had taken out a huge chunk.

"This was sheet rocked a few days ago." He runs his hand up and down the white and gray striped wall. "We're going to paint over the walls tomorrow."

Traci follows and feels the smooth wall. It intrigues her how these men could replace things and make it look as if nothing had ever happened. Memories were replaced. No longer could she see dents and bruises that represented history. She rests on the little ladder that sits in the middle of the floor and realizes that while the downstairs looked a mess, the real mess upstairs was being taken care of. Hopefully it won't take much longer.

"When do you think the place will be completed?"

Larry scratches his chin. "The boss says that he'll be here to do the major work on the outside of the house sometime this weekend."

"How come the boss is never here?"

"He's got a lot of contracts to do, so what he does is hire us out to do the painting, taping, and tiling, then he comes in and does the big stuff. It's kinda like we're the prep cooks. We do the grocery shopping, dice the onions, cut the peppers, and then he comes in, cooks the meal and gets all the glory."

She winks at him. "Well, I appreciate the work you're doing here."

Larry ushers her toward the front room and explains that it will probably be about a week and a half before she can move back. He also explains that she can come and check whenever she wants.

She thanks him and walks out the door.

Larry rushes to the door and yells, "Is there anything special you want done before we complete the job?"

"Just hurry up," she says before turning and laughing to herself. "And you can get rid of all that old furniture."

"So, what happened?" Sharlana asks. She unwraps her chicken salad sandwich and lays her carrot sticks inside the plastic. Instead of staying inside to have lunch, Traci and Sharlana walked a few blocks to the local park where everyone took their boxed lunches. Minus the lunchtime homeless people, it was a perfect place to have lunch. The pigeons were respectful, the homeless weren't. They felt like you owed them because they were in a struggle. Traci was in a struggle herself. She wonders if any of them would come to her rescue if she needed them.

She takes out her sandwich. Today is peanut butter and jelly day. She bites into her sandwich and clears the roof of her mouth with her fingers.

"Damn. You can't eat peanut butter jelly without using your fingers?"

Traci fakes like she's going to wipe her fingers on Sharlana. "I can eat it and be all proper. But who wants to be proper?"

Sharlana ignores her humor and continues her questioning. "Not you, I guess. Now, how did it go?"

"We gotta talk about that now?"

"Would you prefer later?"

Traci stops eating her sandwich. Her head falls simultaneously with her words. "She's got my eyes."

Sharlana puts her sandwich down and pulls Traci near. Traci leans against her shoulders and tries to hold onto every ounce of dignity she owns. She sobs softly. For the next minute no one speaks. Traci knows she has decisions to make. Sharlana knows that she has to be there for support. Her friend would need her now more than ever. Sharlana grabs Traci's hand and rubs. Neither one speaks as they watch the foliage fall from the trees. They marvel at the change in scenery every year. They even went tree watching once. Sharlana is partial to the elm. Traci likes the weeping willows.

Jordan surprises them both. "Hey, baby." The intensity of the conversation overtook their awareness of their surrounding.

Traci shoots up and fixes her hair. "Hey."

Sharlana adjusts her suit jacket and stands up. She dusts her pants off. "Hello, Jordan. We didn't see you come in."

Jordan exchanges pleasantries with both. He explains how he went to Traci's job and they said that she went to the park.

"And this is the only park I know." He takes his hand from behind his back and pulls out a dozen red long-stemmed roses. "These are you for you."

Sharlana nods appreciatively. "I'm leaving, Traci. If you need me, give me a call."

They hug.

Traci looks at Jordan and holds back all of her tears. She summons up the courage and energy to prevent her from breaking down. She knows Jordan wouldn't understand much that was going on. She is still processing the best possible solution on how to get out of the situation with as little damage as possible. She brings the flowers to her nose.

The roses are wrapped in a lime green wrapping paper with a red bow.

"Thank you, baby," she tells him. Her hug lacks passion, but is full of purpose. She wants to compensate him for being there for her, even if he didn't know why.

Jordan pats the bench next to him. "Grab a seat, sweetheart."

Traci sits down, folds her legs, and continues to look at the foliage fall. Her nerves kick in. She steals a peek at Jordan when he makes a remark about a kid fifteen feet away. She wants to tell him about Solomon, the meeting, and the child. Her child. All that comes out is, "How was your day?"

Frustration covers his face. "Fine."

She puts her arms around him and beats him to the punch. "I got your message last night." Pause. "And by the time I got settled in, it was late."

"What time did you get in?"

"Late."

Jordan tries to hide his irritation. "What's late?"

"Ten-thirty."

"Professors keep you guys later and later," he says.

"Sometimes they do." She turns quickly to Jordan. "Look, I've got a confession to make."

Jordan sits up quickly and turns even quicker. "Go ahead."

"I lied," she confesses. As soon as the words leave, she wishes she could reel them back in. She can't. Her stomach moves mountains inside. She opens her mouth with full intentions of telling him about the meeting and explaining the picture, but it doesn't quite come out like that. "I-I-I met someone last night."

She can't dare look him in the eyes. Guilt. Hurt. Shame. They all have a party inside her heart.

Jordan spins her around to face him. His grip hurts her arm. "You met who?"

"Someone," she whispers.

Jordan jumps up and stands over her. "Someone like who, Traci?" He is more than irritated. His aggression shows up to a party that it wasn't invited to.

She finally looks up. His forehead wrinkles. Thousands of lines above his brows show the hurt and pain that she causes. She wishes she could just tell him to run away because what she had to say was too much, but that wouldn't help. She needed her man to stand beside her. Not in front of her screaming and yelling because he had no clue. Her fingers tingle. She tells herself to stand up and man up. Her excuse would be that she wasn't a man. She played tricks on herself at the most inopportune time. She does deep breathing. She even counts to three, three times. Nothing happens. Words don't form. She forces herself up. She puts her arms around his shoulders.

"Baby, I need time."

He shrugs her hands away and paces. "Time for what?" He kicks a bunch of leaves that gather around his feet. They fly about her picnic area. One golden leaf with a deep brown base sticks to his shoe. He tries unsuccessfully to kick it off. Traci bends down and picks it from the toe of his shoe. Jordan doesn't bother to muster a thank you. She knows he is angry, and he has every right to be.

Jordan grits his teeth. "What do you need time for?"

"I just gotta sort some things out."

"Does it have anything to do with this man you saw?"

"Who said it was a man?" She knows she shouldn't have played this game with words, but she is in defense mode and that is the only game she knows.

Jordan wrestles with a thought or two as he looks down at the ground out of anger because she knew he wasn't observing the beautiful foliage that he just desecrated.

"No one said it was a man. I just figured you were talking to a guy." Pause. "So, you weren't talking to a man?"

"Does it even matter? I just said that I need time." She hugs Jordan and holds him tight against his will. He doesn't return her intensity. His hug is filled with pity. She feels him going through the motions. One thing she knew about Jordan was that he couldn't hide his feelings. Everything he did was filled and completed by emotion. His hugs. His lovemaking. His work. His laughter. Even his selection in what he cooked. One hundred percent emotionally driven.

Jordan pushes her back. "I just need to know what's going on. Is something going on that I should know about?" His face shows displeasure in the questions he asks.

Traci knows he wants to shake the shit out of her, but that isn't in his blood. He had raised his voice, but never his hands. She'd had enough of that before. The swollen eyes from crying. The puffy eyes from a right cross. She wouldn't take that anymore.

"Nothing that you should be concerned about right

now." Pause. She wants to tell him something to cure what ails him. She doesn't want to leave things so open. "What I can tell you is that it is nothing romantic." She kisses his lips. "Absolutely nothing romantic. I just need time to sort out a few things." She gives him a hug. She feels a little return. Her smile is smug. "I promise things will be all right in a little bit. Bear with me, please."

"How long do you need?"

"Not long. And I don't need you to leave. I need your support." She pulls back from his hug and looks into his face. He is warmer than before. "Silent support of course," she says with a smile.

Jordan's lips crease to a grin. She knows she's made progress.

She adds, "As a matter of fact, I'll send you an invitation to show you that the only romance I want is from you."

Hand in hand, they walk back to the office in silence. Traci clutches the brown and orange leaf she retrieved from his shoe.

After receiving a call with an invite to her hotel room, Jordan's ready for anything. He begins his journey to Traci's room with wonder about what she has in store. Earlier, he showered longer than usual. He sat with his head against the back of the shower and the heated silky beads hit his back. Soothed his thoughts. Caressed his emotions. Brought him down a level. He needed this evening more than Traci thought he might.

Traci, on the other hand, had some tending to do. She needed to make amends for the argument that never happened. She was able to throw the dogs off again. She was growing tired of hiding from her past while her future stood in front of her. This afternoon she had every intention to tell him what was going on, but he appeared out of nowhere and that killed her spirit. She needed preparation to give him all of the information. With all that said, she didn't have time to put a plan in action regarding her daughter.

Not only did she have her eyes, she had her smile. Traci's teeth were a little crooked on the bottom, and her daughter shared the same. Her long, black, curly hair was thick like Solomon's. Her nose was long and thin like Solomon's. She wondered whose temperament she owned. If she was lucky, it would be a combination of both. Traci prayed she had her drive. Her determination. She could definitely use Solomon's humor. His athleticism. Even his personality as a whole.

Traci stands in the mirror brushing her hair, wondering what her next step will be.

Someone knocks on the door. She jumps from the bathroom and closes her robe. Jordan arrives early to receive his retribution. She felt she owed him. And when she paid up sexually, she opened all doors.

The door swings open.

Jordan walks in and calls her name. She does her ninja thing and disappears into the back.

He smiles and does a slow spin around the room. It's dark, minus the flickering light that comes from the host of candles near the bed. The bathroom door is closed and he can hear water running. He looks into the mirror that hangs near the television. He takes his hat off and fixes his hair with his fingers. Content with his rumpled mess, he falls to the bed. He turns the radio on. Soft jazz flows. Saxophones dance on the ceiling while the bass guitar humps the walls. He sits back and lets the music take over. Traci knows that jazz is like a sedative to him. He listens to it when he is angry, sad, and deep in thought. She always joked that it brought out the man in him that hip-hop couldn't.

"You ready?" Traci yells.

Jordan stands and double-checks himself in the mirror again.

"I'm ready."

"Did you see the gift on the chair?"

"No." Jordan hurries to the chair and retrieves the gift. The box is small, wrapped in satin pink and blue wrapping paper, and has a pretty baby blue bow on it. Traci knew Jordan liked gifts, no matter how small. He opens it like it's Christmas. He unties the bow like he unties his sneakers. He throws the bow on the bed and peels the gift like a banana. He looks at the bathroom door, which remains closed. The water stops, and in between the saxophones cries, he hears nothing. He goes back to the gift and unfolds the box. He has no clue what it holds. He lifts a bottle out of the box and puts it under the light.

"Numb-it," he reads. He turns the bottle around and reads the back of it. "Numbs the throat or the anus."

As if on cue, Traci comes out of the bathroom. With her white robe spread out, she looks like an angel.

"You like?" she asks.

The bottle remaines in Jordan's hand. He turns it around and continues to inspect it. "I think it's different."

Traci spins around. "The robe, dummy."

Jordan laughs. "Yeah. Sure. That too." He smiles and lifts the bottle in the air. "About the Numb-it. Is this—"

"If you have to ask, then maybe you don't need it."

"I wasn't about to ask anything. I was just going to tell you that you made a great choice." He stands up and walks over to her. He shakes his head appreciatively. "I'm impressed."

Traci knows it's time to reward him for his patience. Also she knows how to bide her time. Jordan was becoming more aggressive with his quest for answers.

Traci walks to the bed and disrobes. She knows Jordan isn't used to this side of her, but he deserves it. He has been patient. Now is her turn to turn the switch and be the bitch she he knows he wants.

"Nice collar," he says.

Traci strokes her collar. She touches the silver spikes that jut from the black thick band as she spreads her legs. Her hands travel down her stomach and stop at the top of her lace panties.

Jordan stands in front of her with his mouth open. He raises his hand to touch her.

She steps back. "How much money do you have?"

He laughs. "What?"

Her tone changes to a professional one. "I said, how much money do you have?"

"You're funny."

"Not if you want some of this," she says as she does a dance move and ends up near the ground. She returns eye level with her eyebrow cocked and one hand hanging from her collar seductively.

"You been smoking?" he asks.

"No."

"You seriously want to know how much money I have?"

"Why not?"

"Why?" He was playing a game or biding time.

"You want basic or the value meal?"

He chuckles. "The value meal."

"Well, how much money you got?"

He chuckles again. "You want me to pay for some—"

She stops him short. "Yes." Pause. "Or I can take off the collar and give you the basic." She meant business.

Jordan adjusts his pants. His smile is coy. He appears to be interested in what she has to offer, but pride makes him hesitant.

Traci takes advantage of his hesitancy. She pushes his buttons. "You ready or what?" she asks.

Jordan takes out his wallet and thumbs through a few bills. "I've got about forty dollars." He laughs. "You take checks?"

"No. Money. Forty will get you a little. Not the Numb-it, though."

Jordan looks at the bottle that lies on the bed. It must've appealed to him because he goes through his pockets in search of more money. He pulls out a crumpled bill. "Wait. I got a total of fifty dollars." He turns back to the bed and picks the bottle up. "Will that get me some of this special sauce for my Big Mac?"

Traci takes the money and inspects it in the light near the mirror. "This'll do. Sit on the bed."

Jordan's movement is slow. He acts as though he doesn't want to receive his gift, but the smile he shows tells a different story.

Traci puts the money inside of her collar. The bills stick to her neck and tighten the collar.

She stands in front of him with her legs spread shoulder width apart. She moves close enough for him to smell her. She watches him stare at her panties. She grabs his head and brings him extremely close. "How do you want it?"

Jordan suddenly looks unsure. His words fail to come out.

"How do you want it, big boy?"

Jordan lifts himself from the bed. He's met with a push from Traci. He falls back.

"I didn't say get up," she says. "I said, how do you want it?"

Jordan makes a feeble attempt at asserting his authority. "I want it all."

"Then tell me. Tell me you want it all."

"I told you."

"Grab me. Take control. Do something different."

Jordan jumps up suddenly and grabs Traci by her collar. He pushes her toward the wall and forces himself on her. He can feel the discomfort in her breathing. He doesn't care. If this is how she wanted it, she would get it. "I want to use the Numb-It," he states.

She snickers, amused at his sudden impulse to become aggressive. He takes her laughter as a sign of disrespect. He continues to squeeze harder. "I want you to turn around and give me all that I want."

Traci chortles. "And how would you want it?"

Jordan stops her short. "You got the money, right?"

Traci feels the transference of power. She wants to give way to his manhood, but he'll have to take it. She isn't in the giving mood. Through the mirror she can see him pondering his next move. With his free hand he unbuttons his shirt and slides it off.

"I need you to follow," he says.

"Then do so without speaking," she says. She feels the noose tighten around her neck. She is going to force the man out of him even if it hurts. She plucks more of his nerves. "I'm ready. Did you start controlling me yet?"

He flings her around as her words stumble out. She falls to the bed in a heap on her stomach. His touch isn't loving as he pulls her ass to the air with a giant tug.

She's like putty in his hands. The fight she had is no longer present. Her voice lacks aggression. Her breathing subsides.

What he doesn't know is that she is allowing him to mold her. Dictate to her. Make demands of her. She followed the script of being a good bitch. And all good bitches understand that they *are* in control. And that's what he ultimately wanted.

He asks her to give him the bottle that was on the bed. She reaches in front, and then reaches in back to hand it to him. He pulls himself out of his boxer briefs and lays his lumbering piece in the middle of her cheeks. She flinches. Not quite ready for what he is. Noticing her hesitation, he rubs her collar and reminds her that she has fifty dollars to show for her hard work and pain.

She doesn't mind working hard, but the pain was something else. He slaps her butt twice for her to move up like he was a jockey trying to get his horse to move. She bucks and moves forward like he suggests. He presses the cold cream onto his fingertip and pushes his finger inside her ass.

She gasps.

He asks her if she said something. She puts her head down and ushered a quiet 'no.' He proceeds. Pushes his finger in even more. He puts his ear near her head to see if she's speaking again without his permission. She isn't. Apparently she has learned some lesson.

Traci knows she has to hold in all of her verbal reservations. She hasn't yet tried this portion of sex yet, and figures what better time than the present. She knows she's giving him a birthday present early. Her head presses into the pillow as if she couldn't hear it, it would make it easier to deal with. His commands make it easier to do without thinking. That was the whole trick. Get the mind off of the act.

"You feel pressure?" he asks.

She shakes her head. "Be careful, please," she pleads.

"There's no pleasure if you don't enjoy it," he responds.

She doesn't know if it's just a bullshit line, but it works. Kinda eases her mind to know that he isn't trying to destroy her body with punishing blows to her virgin territory. With that, he begins his assault.

While he massages her back with one hand, his other hand travels around her ass to where he splits her legs. He reaches in between her legs and massages her hairs. He had watched her play with her hairs when she had nothing better to do. He re-enacts her movement and kisses her back. She jumps at the touch of his lips on her mid-back. She moans as his fingers spiral downward toward her clit. His piece remains between her cheeks. Only now it is thicker than before.

"You don't mind if I take charge of this, do you?" he asks rhetorically. She knew she was not to answer, so she doesn't. Instead she nods her head.

He strokes her hair and whispers, "Good girl." She knows this makes him feel better. His fingers remain stuck to her front. He puts his whole hand over her clitoris and lips and presses against them all. She moves her body forward to meet his pressure. He knows how she loves clitoral stimulation. Once he feels her rhythm, he strums. He regains his grip on the back of her neck and presses her deep into the bed. His piece, which is still located between her ass, is no longer lumbering. It feels like lumber. Thick. Hard. Wood. She promises to yell 'timber' later. His head presses the opening of her asshole.

"I'll leave it at the tip. You push back when you feel you can, OK?"

Traci nods.

His grip leaves her neck as he hangs onto the back of her collar. He yanks her head upwards. He tells her that he wants her to rotate her hips and get him in as much as she can. He explains his purpose of just getting the head in. She never fell for that line before, but that was because she didn't want to. Now she feels obligation to at least try. She takes matters into her own hands. She reaches around and takes each cheek in her hands and opens herself wide.

"Is this how you want it?" she asks. She backs up against him and allows slightly more than the head to enter.

He pushes his hips forward. A sharp pain shoots through her legs and back. Her scream is not for the weak.

Jordan

I wonder if I hurt her. She lies there whimpering.

"You all right?" I ask.

"I'm fine."

"You sure?"

"You can try it again. I just need a break for a second, OK?"

I want to try new things, but not at her expense. I wave the white towel in defeat and move to something different. I help her turn around to face me. I kiss her lips and tell her she did well for the first time. Her look is different. She appears to be in a fog. I snap her out of it with a passionate kiss that we hadn't shared in a long while. With us, the first thing to go was the passionate kissing. Every time we kiss it reminds me that we used to love to kiss. I checked the imaginary box so that if we did go that route, her concerns would be heard.

I grab her by her neck and bring her head close. I whisper, "I'll take that money back." I quickly snatch the money from her collar and put it back into my pocket. I didn't know what she was going through, but it had to be heavy for her to go buy something so we could try some anal sex. I whisper to her that I have wanted to make love for quite some time. I meant real love.

What starts out as a simple peck on the lips, turns into five minutes of slow tongue dancing. I remove her collar and we sit on the bed enjoying each other's sexuality while our fingers travel to familiar places. She moans as I find different ways to stimulate her. My hands remember that she loved her breasts to be cupped. My mouth remembers how much she loved to be kissed on the nape of her neck. And my fingers recall times they slid across her clit, causing glands to swell and juice to drip.

Her hands find my chest and slide downwards toward my prize. Her unbuckling is far from expert, but the job is done. Her dig is slow and deliberate. Her cold hands mix with my heat, sending sighs from her lips. She caresses the sides with elongated strokes. A drop of cum forms at the tip to let her know that below, he acknowledges her stroke. Her hand snaps and jerks. She remembers how I enjoy it. I explained before that the hand movements were just as important as everything else. She grips tight at the base and loosens her grip as her hand slides to the top. I respond with back arches and chills. After a minute of allowing her to develop a rhythm, I force her to stand and turn around.

She complies without hesitation. I back her against

the door and take control from behind. She reaches around, fumbles, and grabs hold of me. Her thumb strokes my head. It blossoms. She lets go, wets her thumb, and feels her way back to me. This time her thumb glides across the head. She rubs, strokes, and then puts the tip between her forefingers. She spreads her legs and brings me near her opening. She lets go.

I take over. I cross the line. Entering without permission. She gasps. With one smooth swoop, I fill all of her. Her body tenses, braces, and receives the blow. Her head rests against the door. Her outstretched hands hold her up. I push the extra inch in and hold my position. I can feel the beginning of something new.

"Squeeze," I demand.

Her message is loud and clear. She'll do everything I ask today. I don't get many of these days, so I make sure it's well worth it. Her muscles clench, sending shivers throughout my body. I have to squeeze too. She feels my swelling and shivers.

I want to be nasty, but at the same time I feel the need to make love and reconnect. I decide on both. I make love to her old school style. I love her like Donny Hathaway's hit, "A Song for You." I give her that old time loving that rocks her until her face presses the cold wall. I withdraw from her. Inch by inch. I pause at the head and leave him just outside of her lips. I swing my hips slightly from left to right. With one full stroke, I fill her again. I can hear sounds of wetness as I enter to the max. Her hands are still spread and I can barely see her face. Her back is arched and her ass raises to the ceiling. Sweat forms at her lower back and makes her brown skin glisten.

"You ready?" I ask.

She lifts her head and shakes it slightly.

Her response is not what I was looking for. For the next minute, I create noise. I give her what she affectionately dubs, 'the business.' I grab her hips and tilt her ass upwards and fill her with long, intentional, weighted strokes. I pull back and stop when I get to her opening, then come slamming down into her. A loud smack is heard every time I enter. My thighs hit ass every time I reach back and come forward. Her head slams against the door with every down stroke.

I ask again, "You ready?"

"Yes." Pause. "Sir."

I slow my stroke. She anticipates force, but I meet her with loving movements as I swirl around inside of her. I massage her back and make love. I remember all the things that she likes, and I make her love them. I make love when I kiss her nipples gently, then harder. I make love when I lick the inside of her ear lobe. I whisper things I love to say. "I've been waiting." Pause. "I'm going to enjoy *this.*" Pause. "I thought about making love to you all day at work." My hands rest on her shoulders as I dig in from the left and press deep until I come out on the right.

I stop. "Get on the bed." Without hesitation again, she walks away and follows direction. As she approaches the bed, I give further instructions. "And get in a position I like."

I watch her body shake as she walks away. Sometimes I sit back and am amazed by her beauty. Her skin tone seems made from heaven. Her waist is thick, not fat. Her ass is full, not wide. I want to follow her to the bed and jump right on her, but I have to maintain control. I do. I tell her that she's doing a great job. She lays on her back and slowly lifts her legs and spreads them wide. She holds her legs with her hands and waits.

I turn on different music. I pick one from her collection. Old Prince. *Beautiful Ones.*

My strut is mean. As I get closer to the bed, everything comes into focus. She is even more beautiful than from afar. Her breasts look up at me and speak. I say hello back by kissing them slightly. I lick each one appreciatively. I merge them and eat both. I nibble and pull as I draw away. Never lifting my head, I continue downward. I put my nose in it. She smells like fresh air and she tastes sweet. I run my tongue the length of her lips. She wants me to eat, but that wasn't on the assignment. I did because the energy was fantabulous. I eat her middle. She grabs my head when I slurp. My eating is enthusiastic. Her clit grows and becomes even more sensitive with each passing second that I avoid it. I eat from the inside of one thigh to the next. I bump her spot with my chin as I pass over it. She grabs my head and tries to force me into her. I get up. Everything is on my time.

I lift myself up and dive into her. She wraps her long legs around my waist and puts her arms around my neck. I need more openness. I spread her legs with my arms and hold them up. She's exposed and vulnerable to any blow I choose to give her. I give her my gangsta. I push deep, come right back out and push in again.

"You don't mind, do you?"

"No." She shakes her head from side to side. "Sir. No, sir I don't mind." She braces for the next blow.

I spread her legs even wider. Tilt her more toward the sky. The aggressive down strokes causes the smacking sound I made earlier. This time, her sweat and mines make it louder. Like I was killing her. I let go of her legs and tell her to open up. She does. I calm. Slow my pace. I rest inside. For the next ten minutes, I make love to her for one minute, and the next I fuck her till her pussy aches.

My rhythm goes from smooth long strokes to jagged pumps that infiltrate her soul and stop her breath. She wants me to stop, but continue. I oblige. I rest inside of her and can feel her muscles clamp down.

I want to cum, but not like this.

I pin her hands above her head as our fingers make a perfect fist. She grips me tight and brings me closer. I can feel her heat and smell her scent. It turns me on.

We kiss. Our sexuality joins hands. They act like it's their first time as each tries to hold on. No one wants the feeling to end. The more I slow, the stronger her moan. Within minutes, we barely move. I found exactly where she wanted me to remain while she got hers. Upwards to the left, pressing hard. I brace myself and let her lift herself and get her orgasm. With every grind upward, she twitches. I feel her engine mount. *Grind.* She shakes. *Grind.* Twitches. *Grind.* Grips. *Grind.* Grabs. *Grind. Grind.* Slaps my ass. *Grind.* Locks her legs. *Grind.* Her body locks. She holds me real close. *Pause.* "Give it to me, please," she begs. I know how she wants it. I press hard and move an inch. She begins her shake. I consume her spot. I grab her hair and bite her neck. She lifts her head, allowing me access to her neck.

"You gonna cum for me, baby?"

She nods. She's on the same page. She wants to hear my voice and not hers. I give it to her. My press intensifies. My grip on her hair strengthens. "Come for me," I say. *Press. Pull.* "This feels good." *Press.* "Damn this is wet." *Pull.* "You don't mind if I take some pussy for myself, do you?" *Press. Press.* I eat her neck. Put my hand on her forehead and hold her down as I lift her with a deep, drenching stroke. *Press.* She loses control of her legs. "Cum on me." Her body locks. She holds on for dear life. I put my arms around her and pull her to me. Through me. "I-" *Press.* "Love-" *Press.* "This-" *Press.* "Pussy!"

"S-s-stop," she screams.

I press her orgasm out. She buckles and bucks. Grabs my hair. I pull her hands from my head and pin them down. I toy with another section inside of her, then go directly for the spot. Her tremor is psychotic.

She screams, "Fucking shit!" She loses complete control. Locks her arms around me and presses against me. Her body suffers from great convulsions. She mutters, "I can't take it," and then slumps to the bed. I lay inside of her. My hardness relaxes to a thick limp that lay inside of her until she calmed. I give her a minute. She'll probably need two. We hug. The music no longer exists. The coldness of the sweat is a remembrance of love and war. Pain and pleasure. I know she wants sleep. I know she needs sleep. I'll worry about my orgasm at a later time. For one of the first times, my pleasure was definitely all of hers. I slept.

"I went out with Solomon," she blurts.

I awake, rub my eyes, and sit up groggily. "What?"

Traci sits in silence on the bed. She is pushed up against the headboard with her knees cradling in her arms. Her eyes are red like the sunset. A shadow is cast on the evening that started so bright. Her body language displays irritation, anger and hurt. Her tone is full of defeat. The room seems much different than earlier. The candles don't smell so nice. The darkness is blinding. The truth, which stands a foot away, seems to be ready to move the Alps.

She turns away. "I went out with Solomon."

I can hear her cry softly. Tears always overtake my

anger. I want to move closer, but this name stopped me. Solomon. It flows from her tongue almost too casually.

"Who is Solomon?"

She turns more. Her feet rest on the edge of the bed. Her face still disappears inside her hands.

"Who is Solomon?" I repeat.

I swing to the other side of the bed. I put my boxers on and search for my slippers.

I can hear her turn toward me. "Jordan, I—" she starts.

"Jordan, I, hell!" I scream. "We make love. We connect. Then we talk about a Solomon." I shake my head. I know something is up, but this isn't what I bargained for. I would've been fine with her telling me she's not ready for something so serious. Or even if she tells me that she was dealing with issues involving family. But not Solomon.

I stand up. My pace begins. I can't stop it. The back of my slippers pop against my foot every time I step. "I need some answers."

She walks to the window and opens the curtains. She looks into the night. "It was just dinner." She can't even look at me.

"Dinner?" I walk near. "Just dinner?" She doesn't respond. I feel fire well deep inside. I gather myself as best I can, but it doesn't work. "Then why so secretive?"

"It was hard."

"Hard to go? Hard to tell me? Or hard to keep secret?"

She spins around and throws her hands in the air. "Hard to everything. I wasn't hiding anything. I wasn't hiding anyone. And I'm coming to you now."

"W-w-what, you just wake me up out of the blue and

mumble some other guy's name? And you don't think that's going to bother me?"

"I was afraid to talk to you."

"Why?" I scream.

"Because of that." She backs away as though I was going to physically harm her.

"Because of what?" I ask.

"Yelling." Pause. "I don't like the yelling."

I move back a step. "You better get used to something. You live in this fantasy world. You think we can have confrontations without yelling?"

"I do."

"Yeah, but you throw shit. That is irritating to me."

"Well, your yelling is irritating to me."

"But guess what?" I scream. "It's only yelling. And you call it yelling. I call it raising my voice. I mean, so what I yell? Do I disrespect you verbally?"

She turns back to the window without a response.

I repeat, "Do I disrespect you verbally?"

"No."

"Do I curse at you?"

"No."

"Then you gotta take something. You look at it like I'm starting at the worse level. I control quite a few things around here," I spit angrily. "It would be so easy for me to come at you when I'm mad and curse and scream insults. But I don't," I say in a more pleasurable manner. "You look at me being out of control when I'm giving you a different tone. Or yelling. I look at it another way. I look at it like I'm calming myself by only yelling. Same thing with your throwing stuff around. I can't take that."

"I don't throw it at you."

"You don't have to. I yell. You throw things around."

She turns around and sits back on the bed.

I continue, "You gotta understand that everyone has their own way of getting anger out, and if you think I'm out of control when I start yelling, it's the other way around. I'm maintaining control by not doing a whole lotta other shit I could be doing. All I do is raise my voice with sensible words. For the most part."

She wrestles with how much was correct and how much wasn't. "I can accept that," she half-heartedly says.

"And I can accept you throwing stuff around." Pause. "With that said, what's going on with Solomon?"

"Absolutely nothing." She gathers more strength with every word spoken. "Absolutely nothing."

"Then why the secret?"

"We had to get some things straightened out."

"Like?"

"Like I'm not ready to divulge yet." She stands and walks over to me. "I need you to support me."

"Yeah. Yeah. Yeah. Support you silently, right?"

She shakes her head.

"Wrong," I say. "I need to know the facts."

"I'm not ready right now, Jordan."

My heart punches my shirt. I don't think she is lying, but the truth is hiding somewhere. It isn't on her face. Didn't come out of her mouth. It isn't even present in the room.

"When will you be ready?"

"Soon."

I can't take it. My pressure begins to rise. She isn't giving any answers, and I can't beat them out of her. "Does this man mean that much to you that you put us at risk?"

"We are not at risk," she says.

"We *are* at risk. Right as we speak." Pause. We stare into each other's eyes and for a moment, I don't know her. Don't know who she had become in the last month. Don't know who she would be in the next one. "You just bought a week. But, within the week, we should be talking. About something. If not something, we'll be talking about a whole lot of nothing."

I turn around, get dressed, and slammed the door shut.

Chapter 12

Traci

During the next week, time walked. Traci didn't talk to Jordan or Solomon. She needed a break. She threw herself head first into her work. It eased her mind when little Rahiem Jacobs had to be called in for questioning about his mother's illicit drug use. Not that she was happy for his mother, but it took the pressure off her own life and helped her deal with other people's. It always seemed easier to deal with another person's problem. Then there was Ms. Crenshaw. Always minding someone else's business when she needed to be minding her own business. Namely, the calling out of work two straight weeks in a row. She was always able to come up with a note from a doctor telling of another ailment she had. This week's ailment was gangrene on her big toe. Traci didn't have the heart to ask to see it. Lastly, there was Mama Joseph. She was the surrogate mother to everyone in the daycare. This week she said 'she wasn't nobody's fucking mother.' Traci chalked it up to her age, lack of medication, and her stepfather passing. Traci gave her the week off and told her to come back when she was ready. Everyone was on someone else's schedule. She was on Jordan's. Whenever he was ready for her to talk. Solomon wanted to talk whenever he got ready. It never dawned on Traci that people might get tired of waiting and then they have to get overly aggressive with her for her to move.

The phone interrupts her thoughts.

"Hello, Ms. Johnson. This is Ms. Braxton."

There is a very long pause by both.

"You there, Ms. Johnson?"

Traci clears her throat. "Yes, I'm here. I've been here for the past three and a half weeks, waiting to go back home."

"I didn't call to argue. I just called to inform you that your home is done and you can move back in today." She pauses and waits for a thank you. Realizing the wait can go on forever, she continues, "There will be someone there until about eight o'clock tonight. If there is a problem, you can contact me on my cell phone."

Traci mutters a thank you and hangs up. Her first call is to the movers. Luckily, someone has cancelled today and they can move her things back into her apartment by early afternoon. She immediately calls Sharlana to invite her over for lunch and to tell her the news.

"I'm going to call the girls tonight," Sharlana says.

"I really don't feel like being bothered with a bunch of noise tonight," Traci tries to explain. She knows there is no way to get Sharlana to forget about it.

Sharlana pulls out her cell phone and peruses her contacts. "We won't stay long. I'll just call up a few. You need to be around some friends tonight, anyway."

"You're right," Traci concedes. "Speaking of friends—"

"What?"

"I gotta tell you what happened with Celeste."

Sharlana gives her the face that says she told Traci to talk to her years ago.

Traci sits at her desk and checks her messages for the fifth time. Like the four times before, the service repeats that there are no new messages.

Oh, well, she thinks. *Why cry over spilled milk?* She whips her keys out and heads for the door. Finally, sleeping in her own bed is going to be perfect.

Butterflies dance around the pit of her stomach as she holds her breath and pushes the key inside the doorknob.

She hears the familiar click of the lock, closes her eyes, and takes a huge gulp of air.

She steps into the living room and opens her eyes. Her jaw follows her pocketbook to the floor. Traci looks around to make sure she is inside of her own house. She slowly walks to the front door and looks for her name on the mailbox. "T. Johnson," it reads. She comes back in and shakes her head. *Who . . . why . . . when,* is all she can think as she approaches the living room.

The furniture is beautiful: a chocolate Boerner Model D sofa with matching loveseat and chaise. For as long as she could remember, this was high on her list. Once before she had saved up to get the couch, but things happened and other bills had to be paid. Beautiful, soft, Italian leather upholstery, double topstitched at the seams is a thing of beauty. Her hands sink into the chocolate leather and follow it from end to end.

After sitting for what seems like hours on the new furniture, the doorbell rings. She immediately thinks of

Jordan. The nice in him was surreal. Then she thinks of broke-ass Solomon. Never in a million years. She kicks her shoes off and pushes her feet onto the couch.

Sharlana barges through the unlocked front door with three bags in tow.

Traci lifts herself from the couch. "What's up?"

Sharlana stops short in the living room. "Damn!" She walks over and puts her hands into the leather. "This is some bad shit." Her fingers run alongside the ridges of the sofa. "This is some expensive shit, Tee. Where'd you get this at?"

Traci doesn't feel like explaining. "I bought it."

"So, you finally got it, huh? Now I won't be hearing all the complaints about the black leather crap you just got rid of." She pauses. "As a matter of fact, where is that furniture? I could put it in my study room."

Traci doesn't know what to tell her. She doesn't know where any of her furniture was. Hell, she didn't know where this had come from. "I gave it away to one of my mother's friends," she answers convincingly. "They needed a couch. You didn't need it as much as they did."

"You're right," Sharlana agrees.

Traci has to change the subject. "What's in the bag?"

Sharlana reaches down and pulls out four bottles of liquor. "This is what's up. A bottle of vodka, Kahlua, Hennessey, and a bottle of Chardonnay for the women who like to act like ladies."

Traci laughs and leads Sharlana to the kitchen. After showing her all the work that was done in the kitchen, they go upstairs and sit on the bed. Traci took part of the insurance money and bought a huge oak sleigh bed, giving the movers extra to set it up. Other than two old-fashioned dressers and an old-fashioned night-stand, nothing else touches her floor. She has three large framed Ansel Adam pictures of trees and forests hanging on her walls. This is her way to get away, without actually getting away. On her nightstand is a CD player that plays many sounds of nature. She has a choice of rain, babbling brooks, or other sounds of the night. The sounds comforted her when she didn't want to be alone. Next to her CD player is an old picture of her mother and father holding her at her first birthday party. It is the only picture she has of her parents together.

"Have you thought about your dilemma?" Sharlana asks.

Traci ignores her and turns her CD player to the rain track.

Sharlana repeats, "Have you thought about your dilemma?"

"What dilemma?"

"Uh, duh. Jordan."

"No. I've got other things on my mind besides Jordan," she lies.

In fact, Jordan is all Traci has on her mind lately. Usually he would've called her by now. This isn't like him. Traci begins to doubt herself for telling him anything. She wishes she'd kept quiet about Solomon.

"Do you think he's going to start seeing someone else?" Sharlana asks.

That thought has never entered Traci's mind. Why would he start seeing anyone? After thinking for a few seconds, Traci replies, "No. I'm not worried about that. He should be worried about whether I'm going to start seeing someone."

Sharlana laughs off Traci's comment because she knows that Traci won't bring it to that level. "If you would've listened to me, you wouldn't be in this mess right now. Not everything is meant to be told. You gotta keep some things to yourself."

"And you don't think telling him that I at least met someone out was something I was supposed to expose?"

Sharlana finishes the last of her drink and puts her glass on the floor. Traci continues to glare at her until she removes the wet glass from her newly finished floor.

Sharlana wipes the tiny wet ring from the floor with her hands and holds onto the glass. "Do you think he tells you everything?"

Traci shrugs her shoulders.

"Did he tell you everything about his little secretary?"

"He didn't do anything wrong," Traci defends.

As a matter of fact, why was she defending him in the first place? She was tired of hiding her feelings and wanted so desperately to open up, completely. Now was her time. She sits Indian style on the bed and leans back against the bedpost.

"I really loved Solomon. I mean, I really would've done anything for him."

"I know."

"And the baby just makes things even more difficult." Pause. "How am I supposed to deal with this?" Traci is overcome with grief. Her hands start to shake. Her tears fall one by one to her jeans. And she is desperate to leave the subject alone.

Sharlana reaches into her pocketbook and pulls out a tissue.

Traci dabs her eyes. "I'm sorry, Lana. I'm acting like a big baby."

"Don't worry about that."

"I'm confused about what Solomon wants. What Jordan needs. And—"

"And what about you? What does Traci need?"

Traci blows her nose. "I don't know."

"You know something." Sharlana playfully punches her arm. "You know it's time to have a drink." Sharlana hands Traci her glass of wine. "What does Jordan need?"

"The truth."

Sharlana stands up and holds her hands to the sky. "And the truth shall set his black ass free."

Traci laughs. It seems like such a long time since she shared a laugh with anyone.

Sharlana continues, "So, Jordan just wants the truth?"

"Yes."

"Give him half."

"What half?"

"The half where you tell him about Solomon?"

"I told him about Solomon," Traci reveals.

"And?"

"And he wants to know exactly what's going on." Pause. Sip. "Sad thing is that I didn't talk to him much about the baby. It was an emotional day. I was crying. He was crying."

"He was crying?"

"He shed a tear."

"Then what?"

"Then he had to pop a man pill and admit to there being pollen in the air." They both laugh. "I love Jordan."

"I know you do."

"But what do I do?"

They get up and walk back downstairs. "If I knew what to do, I would have a man."

The doorbell rings as they hit the kitchen.

Twenty minutes later, Traci, Sharlana, Mona, and Precious sit in the living room and reminisce about old times.

Chapter 13

Jordan

The past week was hell. Traci and Solomon had my head spinning. Deanna had me wondering. And Tony was driving me crazy with all of the questions about all of them. For someone who didn't have a woman, he sure had a bunch of advice for me regarding my situations.

"Traci will tell you whatever she's ready to tell you when she's ready," Tony tells me. "Be patient."

He has some nerve talking about being patient when he spent most of the next day calling a female after he got her number. Sometimes he would call more than three times. I told him that it was overkill. He called it being consistent.

"That's why you consistently get no sex," I tell him.

"Fuck you."

"You probably couldn't do that."

I tell him that I'm angry because she was withholding some things that I knew would have a direct reflection on our relationship. I wanted her to come clean. I didn't care if I didn't like it, I just wanted to know.

He tells me to forgive and forget. Easy for him to say. He asks me if she knew some of the things I did in the past, would I think she would still be interested in dating me?

"Probably not. I was kinda nasty when I was younger," I explain.

"No nastier than your mother. It runs in the family," he jokes.

He tells me to cut her some slack. She didn't do anything wrong. I don't think she's completely innocent. I just don't know where to put my finger. It stinks somewhere. I just can't locate the stench. This time I know it isn't on me.

Instead of diving into another woman for comfort, I tried something different. I got back into writing. Wrote for the moment. Wrote for the sexuality while keeping my pants up. Wrote for the memory of the past eight months that were good. Maturity crept. I accepted.

Tony holds up a postcard. "You going to poetry night tomorrow?"

I think hard. It has been a long time. "I might as well. You going?"

"Hell no. I'm not going to be up there reading a poem about rhythm and blues and wait for the ladies in the front to give me three snaps in a circle."

I laugh and snatch the postcard. "They don't do snaps in a circle. That's *In Living Color.* You're ignorant."

"Spell it."

"T-O-N-Y!" I read the postcard. "Join us in celebrating that special person or that special moment. Invite a friend, mate, spouse or that special someone and share 'Black Love!'"

Traci comes to mind. That was our thing. I introduced her to poetry. She introduced me to food. Many nights we swapped a poem for a food. I gave her *Stolen Dreams* one night. She fed me sushi. Another time it was crab rangoons for my self-titled, *Come for Me.*

After picking up the phone and slamming it back down for the fifth time, I decide to call and invite her to the poetry spot. To my luck, there was no answer. I leave a message for her to meet me at the event.

"Mr. Amsterdam is on line four," Deanna yells through the intercom.

Mr. Amsterdam has been on my back about getting this new contract with Webber Construction in downtown D.C.

"This is Jordan."

"Jaw-don, how's it shaking down there?" he slurs.

I know from his slurred speech, he is in the middle of having his daily Scotch. "If this is about the-"

"It's not about the new contract I haven't received yet," he interrupts. "It's about Deanna."

"Hold on," I whisper. I go to the door and check Deanna's whereabouts. "What's going on?"

"Is she acting a little strange?"

I don't like being in the crossfire of anything. I pick and choose what I divulge. "She has been acting a little funny," I admit. "I wouldn't say it was anything to become alarmed about."

"Well, I was just asking because I've gotten a couple of complaints from the office, and being that she's family, I've got to protect her." He pauses and continues, "But if she's messing up, Jaw-don—"

"I don't think there's anything to worry about."

Before he hangs up, we discuss how long it would be before I aggressively went after the new account. I tell him that I need about two weeks before I had something written up and then a serious proposal would go out to the company. Appeased by my answer, he tells me to keep my eye out for Deanna and if anything happens, to let him know immediately.

Minutes later, Deanna appears in my doorway. "Can I speak with you?"

I continue putting my signature on a few papers and invite her in with a swift hand gesture.

She sashays in and sits. Her breasts search for freedom in her navy blue top. She folds her legs and watches me. "The other day when I—"

I shake my head and stop her, without looking up. "No need to apologize."

"Who said that I was apologizing?"

My pen stops. I look up quizzically. My laugh is far from comical. "You should be apologizing."

"For?"

"Your sense of something. You almost got me killed in my own house."

"Yeah. Well, if it'll make you feel better. I apologize."

I go back to signing papers. "Thank you. And button up your shirt."

"Bothering you?"

I knew we should have a conversation now, but I wasn't in the talking mood. "Nope. Professionalism. It's professionalism."

"I enjoyed the other night," she says. "It was kinda nice to see you without the shirt and tie."

I look up at her. "It was nice seeing you, too."

"Do you think we can—"

"No," I state firmly. "We need to leave well enough alone."

"Can we talk from time to time?"

"Talking is fine as long as it's work related. What about your friend? You guys still dating?"

Her head drops. Her voice drops even lower. "Not really."

I snap my fingers cheerfully. "You gotta snap out of this funk, Deanna. You gotta let the dead weight go."

"I know what you're saying," she says. "And believe me when I tell you, this talk is helping. It's just hard to walk away."

"It's better to walk away now than be carried away in a body bag because of someone's crazy-ass spouse."

Deanna looks as if she is about to cry, so I quickly change the subject. "What are you doing this upcoming weekend?"

She methodically massages her temples. Seconds later, her face lights up as if she has just gone through a holy transformation.

"Nothing now, thanks to our little conversation. Listen, Jordan, I'm just going to tell him that it's over and deal with the consequences. And if I need to talk, I don't want you shying away from me, because I know I'm going to need it." She forces a smile.

"I won't." I thought about inviting her to the little poetry slam that I was going to be at, but Traci wouldn't be too fond of seeing her when we were having our own problems.

"How did you finally know that Traci was the right one?"

"Through hard work and failure."

"Do you think she's your soul mate?"

I think about it before coming to the conclusion that I really didn't know the answer. I thought Serene was my soul mate, and then things went sour.

"It depends. Can a man have more than one soul mate?"

Deanna shrugs her shoulders.

"I don't know, either. I know that right now, I'm very much in love with her."

"Would you die for her?"

My heart shudders at the idea of dying, let alone for someone else. "Would I do what?"

"Would you die for her?" she repeats.

"Whoa, Deanna!" The question catches me off guard. I know I love Traci, but dying was another ball of wax. Many questions filter through my head. Would she take care of my son if I died for her? Would she die for me? "I don't know."

Deanna puts her head down and whispers, "I would die for him."

My forehead wrinkles as I shift in my seat. "You would die for whom?"

"The guy I'm involved with," she answers meekly.

I ease back into my chair knowing this conversation could go anywhere. "So, you would die for him even though he's a married man?"

"He's only married in name," she says defensively.

I throw my hands up in the air as if I was getting robbed, and laugh. "Don't get mad at me, I'm just an innocent bystander."

"I'm sorry."

As she begins to open up, it is easy to see that she doesn't have the total control she leads people to believe. The fine young black woman that comes into my office every day in tight skirts, brimming with confidence, now appears to be a vulnerable young woman who can't seem to find love if it slapped her in the face.

Her head remains stuck to her chest. "I love him and he loves me." A few seconds later she dabs the corners of her eyes and sniffles. "Haven't you ever fallen for someone who was in a bad situation?"

I admit, "I did fall for someone once, but you gotta know where to draw the line."

"But it's easier for you to draw the line because—" Her voice trails off.

"Because what?"

"Can I be honest?"

I clear an imaginary path with my hand. "Go right ahead."

Deanna continues, "Because you can be in a relationship with another woman and not really fall for her, because your penis is doing all the thinking."

Her openness is scary. She talks like she had been watching talk shows all of her life. "Damn!"

"C'mon, Jordan. I might be young, but I'm not completely naïve. Men are physical and women are mental."

She hit the nail right on the head. Women definitely are mental!

She continues with a little more assertiveness. Sticking her chest out, she states, "When I give my body to a man, it comes with a lot more than the physical."

Damn freak! "And we don't give more than the physical?"

She gives me a weird look.

"Contrary to popular belief," I say, "not all men are in it for the booty."

A guffaw follows. "You've never been in it for the sex?" she asks.

"I never said that. I was young before."

"Four score and seven years ago," she quips.

"Funny."

"When did you change?"

"When I matured."

She grabs a note pad and a pen and laughs. "Hold up. I gotta write this down." She puts the pen and pad back down and continues, "When men mature, they slow down?"

"Pretty much."

"Please tell me the age they start maturing so I can start dating men that age."

"A man's maturity doesn't have a number."

"How do you tell then?"

"You can't. You have to do a lot of talking and praying," I say with a chuckle. "And you were doomed before you started with him anyway."

"Why?"

"Because you can't build a house on quicksand. The foundation that you're building your relationship on is filled with deceit and lies."

"I know what you're saying, but it's a hard situation to get out of. I don't want to throw away the time we've invested."

"But, everyday you stay, it takes two more days to leave."

Deanna stands and gives generic applause. "I guess I need to sign up for your class, Introduction to Relationships."

"My stuff ain't tight enough for me to be teaching a class."

"Maybe you need more research and on the job training," she says. She closes the distance between us.

My mind starts to race. "You have any suggestions, Ms. Simons?"

She gives me a hug, maintaining her hold a few seconds longer than necessary.

Minutes after she leaves, I hear a sharp knock at the door. A funny feeling hits me in the pit of my stomach and a smile erupts. Women weren't the only ones who knew something about intuition. I know Traci received my call and she was knocking at my door now. "Come in, Traci!"

The door inches open, followed by a voice. "Did you say, come in, Tasty?" Tony laughs hysterically. Seconds later, he barges through the door dressed in a royal blue sweat suit. His cologne is overpowering, and his hair is a mess.

I ignore his comment and continue doing my paperwork.

"Don't act like you were working, Negro! I just saw your secretary leaving with the top of her blouse opened."

We both laugh.

Tony sits down and tries to analyze me while he opens up a Tootsie Roll.

I point to the candy. "Don't mistake your fingers for one of those and bite it off."

"Your jokes continue to be as dry as that eczema caked up on the back of your neck," he snaps.

"Yeah, yeah, yeah. You're late!"

He checks his watch and doesn't say a word.

I look up and watch him watch me. He doesn't say a word. He just stares and keeps popping Tootsie Rolls like they're Flintstone vitamins. After I finish my last paragraph, we leave for the gym. On our way down the elevator, he continues to stare and rub his chin.

"You all right?" I ask.

"The question is, are *you* all right?"

The elevator opens. We walk through the noisy corridor and past a group of people outside smoking cigarettes. I give a few head nods to a couple of co-workers, adjust my jacket, and throw my gym bag over my shoulder as we prepare to walk two long city blocks. L Street is always crowded with people, vendors, and smoke. I cough as a bus pauses in front of us, lets a few people out, and chugs down the street. To our immediate left, the smell of peanuts and smog fill the air that remains damp from the early morning shower.

"I got everything under control, why?"

"Because you're acting a little strange," he says.

I don't like being interrogated about my own business. Tony usually means well, but sometimes his timing stinks. "Are we going to work out, or should we stop at the local coffee house so you can give me some fatherly advice?"

"Cut the shit, Styles. You're going to mess around and lose that good woman over some bullshit."

I was getting tired of hearing about what I was going to miss out on. "What about what she'll be missing out on? You always think it's my fault. I've been faithful!"

We stop at the traffic light and Tony looks at me as if the thought has never crossed his mind that I would be doing the right thing. He shrugs his shoulders and concedes, "You're right. I never looked at it that way before. I'm just so used to you being the one fucking up."

"I know I'm right. You act like it's my privilege to be with her. I wasn't the one caught out there with another man at some damn restaurant talking about God knows what."

He nods his head again.

"Can you believe that since we've been together, I ain't been with no one else?"

"Strange thought," he says. "I never would've imagined it. You guys do need to get yourself together."

"I'm doing that."

"How?"

"By doing what I'm supposed to be doing! I know how to make things right. I'm not new to this game," I boast.

Tony knows that his point is well received, so he abruptly changes the subject. "Isn't Kendal coming next week?"

That reminds me that I forgot to clear the closet out in the spare bedroom. This new schedule of holidays and summers was killing a brotha. Kendal had been down south for about eight months now. He'd be back up to see me for the whole summer and then for Christmas break. Something is going to have to give because I know that I can't raise a child like this. There were a few times when Serene called me to put him on the phone so I could yell at him. I wasn't going to be a hit man to my own child.

"He'll be here in two weeks."

"When was the last time you spoke with Serene?"

Tony has just said the dreaded 'S' word. "She left a message last week, but I didn't call her back. I'm going to see what she wants, though."

Tony lets out a sly grin and asks, "When she gets here to drop off Kendal, are you going to let her stay over?"

"Apparently you don't know me if you gotta ask that."

"You never know."

"I know. I'm not going there and have her breathing down my neck again. I don't care what the sex was like. An hour of pleasure isn't worth another three months of her calling and three more months of her getting adjusted to the fact that we won't be together, ever!"

Tony playfully pats me on the back. "I'm glad you're finally learning all the things I've been trying to teach you over the years."

"Yeah, I'm learning the craft from a teacher that graduated from the school of love with a GED."

"Whatever. What are you planning on doing with Kendal over the break?"

"Nothing much. It's just spring break. Shit, I need a break just as much as he does."

"Don't he get bored just sitting in the house?"

"Just because we aren't at hoop games and going out all the time doesn't mean we aren't having fun. We talk, grab a few pizzas, and play video games."

He shakes his head. "Freaking video games?"

We reach our destination, give our ID cards, and walk toward the rear. "Yeah. He gets to talk his little stuff to me without me beating his ass for talking back. I'm trying to do some things that friends do. I don't want him to see me as authority all the time." The dressing room is empty, but it smells like someone has left stale socks lying around. We sit down at adjoining lockers and begin to undress. "You need some kids."

Tony stands and stretches his arms out and begins a terrible job of backstroking. "I'll leave that to your aggressively swimming sperm. I guess mine back-float and die, but I'm not complaining. I love my free time."

"I bet you do. You wouldn't have so much free time if you got a job," I say, throwing my socks into the locker.

Tony gets up and heads for the weight room without waiting for me.

Chapter 14

Traci

"Traci, I'm sorry about the miscommunication as of late. Something has to give, and I hope you like the little present that I got for you. I know things aren't going great, but meet me tonight at the Soul Kitchen at 6:30 and it'll all be better. I've got some things I want to tell you."

Traci listens to the message over and over again before hitting the save button. The message only confirms what she already knows: he had given her the furniture and he still cared. Traci's heart feels like a weight has been lifted off of it. She knows he isn't going to leave the relationship, and hearing his message gives her affirmation. What has her slightly miffed is what he has to tell her. She always had a problem with was surprises. She didn't know if it was a setup for a letdown, or if he was being genuine. She convinced herself that it was a good thing.

She wanted to convince herself that marriage would be a perfect thing. Thirty approached, stared her in the face, and kept moving. Now thirty-five is only years away. She has had her fair share of proposals by bastards, bums, and beyond, and being that most of her friends were not married, it wasn't as high as it used to be on her list.

Children, on the other hand, was much higher. She wanted to have children. A bunch of them. She wanted two boys and two girls. She even had all of the names picked out. She had more trouble filtering through the wanna-be-fathers. She was also coming to the realization that she already has a child. Many nights have come and gone with her thinking and wishing she were with her own child. Work was satisfying. It helped her deal with the fact that she gave hers up. Literally, gave her child up for a dream. Now she dreams of making a connection, but it's scary. She doesn't know how the child would act. Her child. Doesn't know how the child even feels about her mother. Does she know about her mother? In the perfect world, Indigo would have pictures of her mother on her mirror. She wouldn't have called anyone else her mother, instead, choosing to save it for the right ear.

Traci falls to the bed, clutches a pillow, and rocks. For the many years she was without Indigo, she learned how to forget. It was almost second nature to say that no kids lived with her. After a while, she upgraded to saying that she wanted kids. To now. When Jordan asked her about kids, she said that she always wanted one she could call her own. She fucked with the English language to cover her own ass. When she told Jordan that, he figured she meant that she called the kids at her job her own.

Jumping up suddenly, she does what makes her feel comfortable. She calls Sharlana and begins her transference. "Are you ready to go out? Girls night out?"

Sharlana knows her. Knows that she is up to something. The tone in Traci's voice told the story if you were astute enough to differentiate.

Traci sits in front of Sharlana's house and checks her make-up. This time she keeps it simple, yet magnificent: a touch of foundation to hide the ugly little zit on the left side of her chin, and a touch of new lipstick called Shema that makes her lips glisten.

Sharlana gets into the car dressed in a tight fitting black cat suit with her hair pulled back into a ponytail. Traci looks herself over and thought that between her tight jeans and Sharlana's cat suit, it would be a wonder if anyone would want to listen to poetry.

Traci looks Sharlana up and down. "What's up with the hooker outfit?"

"Need you talk?"

Traci turns up the music as they sped to the café. The ride is filled with both of them performing horrible karaoke renditions of everything from R&B to rap music. When they arrive, Traci quickly parks and informs Sharlana that tonight is her treat.

Sharlana checks the overhead mirror and without turning from it, asks, "What time is Jordan coming?"

Traci shoots her a surprised glance. "What makes you think Jordan is coming?"

"Because I am far from a dummy." She flips the mirror back up and begins to count on her fingers. "One. You ain't got a poetic bone in your body. Two. You are in a much better mood. Three. Your hormones are raging and I know you need some. And four. Why else would you be treating? If Traci treats, something's up."

Traci dismisses her with her smug grin and a playful punch as they walk toward the club.

The poetry slam is held in a cozy little bar located in a shopping center near the stadium where the professional basketball team plays.

They step inside, pausing at the door. Traci's stomach begins to tremble. She hates surprises, so she concentrates on the lights. The bright lights lighten up most of the place, while other areas remain hidden. The dark spots are where people went for privacy. Bright red lights flicker above, and music travels from wall to wall. Traci looks around to see if she spots Jordan, but with all the people in front of her, she can't quite make him out. They do see friends from college and exchange pleasantries before spotting Precious at the bar.

Sharlana waves to a friend a few tables away and leaves to greet her. Traci arrives at the bar, hugs Precious, and motions to the bartender.

"What are you drinking?" Traci asks.

Precious giggles and nods toward a tall brotha with his back turned. "Him?"

"Who?"

Precious nods again. "The guy right there."

"Oh!" Traci takes a step back to admire his broad shoulders, but mistakenly bumps into a man standing behind her. His drink splashes the sleeve of his cream blazer.

The man turns and huffs, "What the—"

Traci turns to apologize. "Sorry."

The man wipes his blazer, continuing to hem and haw.

Precious reaches in her purse, pulls out ten dollars and pushes it into the man's hand. "This should pay for the drink."

He inspects the crumbled ten-dollar bill. "This ain't gonna cover my suit jacket getting all fucked up."

A hand reaches over Traci and grabs the man by the shoulder. Traci turns around, almost spilling her drink.

"I got this," the deep voice bellows.

"I-I-I can handle this, Solomon," Traci stammers.

By the time she comments, Solomon is in between her and the guy, whispering something into his ear. With his arm firmly around the stranger's shoulders, Solomon leads him away. A few seconds later, Traci can see the man nod in agreement. They shake hands and Solomon walks back toward Traci and Precious, smiling that million-dollar smile of his.

Traci's mind is racing and her fuel is low. *What in the hell is Solomon doing here?* How could she have not seen him standing so close? Poor Precious has no clue who he is, or what type of trouble was about to go down. Traci quickly scans the room for Sharlana, who is nowhere to be found.

Solomon grabs Traci's hand affectionately. "What's up?"

Traci cringes and pulls her hand away. She hates to make a scene. "Nothing is up. What are you doing here?" The familiar scent of Obsession tickles the sticky air that hangs over the bar.

Solomon's eyes follow the same places Traci's eyes visit. "What's wrong, a man can't get no entertainment?"

"It's not that. I didn't know this was your style." Her words come out choppy. Her thoughts are mangled. She tries to pick up the pieces with her dignity remaining intact.

"I've been doing a lot of different things." He bends over and whispers, "I'm not the same man."

Traci grabs her Cosmo from the bar. "And I'm not the same woman."

He nods his head appreciatively. "And that's OK." Solomon takes a sip. "So, who's your friend?"

With all the commotion, Traci had almost forgotten that Precious was still there. She doesn't want to introduce them, but they seemed to have already met, informally.

"Precious, this is Solomon. Solomon, this is Precious."

Solomon holds his hand out and allows Precious to make the next move, like they did in the old movies. Precious follows the script of a Dandridge and lifts her hand. Solomon kisses the back of her hand. "Pleasure to meet you."

Traci grabs Precious' hand and then leaves for the bathroom. Traci hopes Precious doesn't turn around and look back at Solomon as they leave, but it's too late.

Traci's pace to the bathroom is brisk. She looks around to see if Jordan is anywhere in sight. He isn't. She hurries inside the bathroom.

Precious is animated. "Damn! Who is that?"

Traci stands by the mirror with her phone in hand. Traci explains that she dated him for a little while when she was younger. As soon as Precious begins to press the issue, Sharlana walks in. Steam blasts from her ears.

"I thought you were coming here for Jordan," Sharlana says.

Traci puts her phone away. "What are you talking about, Lana?"

"Duh," she say, pointing toward the door. "The other guy." Pause. "The big black muthafucka out there." Sharlana never did like Solomon. And with good reason. Solomon did nothing but shit on Traci for years.

Sure, he took their child, but that was the least he could do after he disrespected her in public and to the public. He didn't do what he was supposed to do when he was with her. Selling drugs for years. Fucking other women for eons. The list went on, until Traci decided that acting was for her. She needed Solomon's support even before there was a child. He always told her that she was better off getting a state job. Telling her that she was only years away from getting to a grade eighteen. This dumb Negro didn't get past grade ten, in high school. He was the hustler that didn't really hustle. He was a thug without the credibility. He was a self proclaimed ladies man without the man. He was merely a boy using his good looks and penis to get women to love him. Sad thing was, there were plenty of women around who fell for everything he was selling. And Precious was definitely buying.

Traci knows what it looks like, but it doesn't matter to Sharlana. She has a deep rooted issue with Solomon. And not that it isn't warranted, Traci just wants her to understand the magnitude of the situation. She knows it isn't in Sharlana to understand the magnitude. She couldn't. All she can understand is that she hates this man and Traci should have no parts of him. Regardless of any situation.

Traci stands up to Sharlana. "Sorry to be the bearer of bad news, but that big black muthafucka out there didn't come to see me."

"Well, why is he here?"

"I don't know. This is a free country, you know. People don't have to call me before they come out."

Sharlana eyes Traci suspiciously.

"If there was something to tell, I would tell it." She stops and stares back at Sharlana. Her stare lets Sharlana know that there is nothing else to say, or if there was, she was not budging on any more information.

Sharlana continues to watch Traci with a careful eye, waiting for her to break.

Precious asks Sharlana, "Are we talking about the guy that we were just talking to?"

Sharlana cut her eyes at Precious. "This is personal. Let us speak about this in private." Her cut eyes remain on Precious.

Precious, all of five feet, walks over to Sharlana and stands in front of her with the same eye stare. "Don't let the nice persona fool you, Lana."

"It's Shar-lana."

Traci is getting tired of the sniping. "Listen, ladies, you two can fight later. I'm the one with the issue."

Sharlana leaves the battleground and goes toward Traci. Sharlana's look is still intense, but she is more focused on the facts and helping get rid of Solomon.

Sharlana asks Traci, "What do you need for me to do?"

Three deep breaths later, Traci speaks slowly, "When I decided to come here, it was because Jordan called and said he wanted me to come here." She puts her hand on Sharlana's. "And I needed some support just in case this broke down. I have *never* been in a situation like this." Her chuckle is nervous. "And all of the soaps and talk shows I've watched since we were fourteen would have never prepared me for this. Got me looking around for the freaking cameras," she jokes.

Precious, feeling a bit left out, says she will go out front and if she sees Jordan she will text her. Traci thanks her.

Sharlana, one to always have a plan, begins mapping a few things out. She wants to know what time Jordan said he's coming. She wants to know how Solomon knew to come here. She wants to know what time Solomon arrived.

Traci's look remains foreign. "I have no clue."

"To which question?"

"All of them."

Sharlana shakes her head and grabs a paper towel. She wets it and gives it to Traci. "Wipe your face. It's time to make some moves."

Sharlana holds the door open and awaits Traci to finish dabbing her eyes.

"Close the door. I know you've got a plan, but I need to know what's going on," Traci tells Sharlana.

Sharlana points to herself and then Traci. "You and I are going to go out there and tell Solomon that his services are no longer needed here. And if we have to tell him that your man is arriving soon, then we'll do that."

Traci doesn't like where Sharlana is going with the plan. She puts an immediate stop on it. "No. We are not going to do it like that. Damn! Don't you know anything about men? If I go in and tell Solomon that Jordan is coming, do you think he will leave?" She points to her own head. "Think. We gotta think about this." She looks in the mirror and shakes her head. "How do *I* continue to get caught up in stuff like this?"

Sharlana stands behind her and fixes her hair in the back. "Because you don't have your shit together."

"And you do?"

"I sure wouldn't have this going on at a club I was visiting. Clubs are for pleasure, not pain."

Traci knows this had the potential to blow up in her face. She knows Solomon is temperamental. He has little control over his emotions when dealing with other people. Especially the white man. Solomon hates them.

But more than the white man, Solomon hates other people infringing upon his. The only thing he doesn't understand is that nothing about Traci was his. Jordan, on the other hand, may approach the situation a little differently. He may sit back and watch before jumping in. He might even try to talk about it. The only thing that is certain is nothing. She felt safe around them individually, but tonight she feels fear with them being in the same area.

Traci jumps up from the sink. "I'm ready," she says with renewed vigor. "I'm going to tell Solomon to leave. I'll have me a drink, then wait for Jordan."

Sharlana smiles.

Traci adds, "Just be here when I break down." She gives Sharlana a wink, then takes off.

When she returns to the bar, she sees Solomon on the other side entertaining quite a few young ladies. She inhales forever and swallows.

"What's up, baby?"

The voice causes panic. She heaves. Empties her lungs in silence and turns quickly. "Hey, Jordan." She gives him a hug and peeks around it. "You finally made it."

He peels her away and kisses her cheek. "Ms. Johnson. How have you been?" His smile eases her mind.

She spins him around toward the patio in the back. "Can we get some air? I'm not feeling too good."

Jordan lets her lead him away.

Traci wonders what to do next. She's a fast walker, but she knows Jordan had to jog to keep up this time. She takes two quick lefts and a fast right. Once on the patio, she knows she has some explaining to do. Jordan sits on a stool, watching Traci's every move.

Traci fumbles with her fingers. "What?"

"Something's not right," he says. His stare is intense.

She feels him scanning her for truth. She has to watch everything she says. She chooses her next words carefully. "I need to tell you a few things," she begins.

"Want something to drink?"

"No. I'd rather tell you what I wanted," she pauses, "rather, what I *need* to tell you."

"Which is?"

She watches his eyes. He told many truths and lies with them. Once the blinking begins, she knows that a lie is not too far off. If there was nothing to lie about, the blinking would mean that he was irritated about the conversation. He was a man about his truths. Straightforward and eye contact. She watches his eyes.

"I need to talk about a few things that have arisen in the past few weeks."

"I need to talk about them too," he says.

"You first," they say simultaneously.

A smile finally cracks on her face. She puts her hand on his. "You go first. I'm the patient one."

Stare. He says, "I'm the patient one, but I'll go first." Smile. *Stare.* "I love you. Ain't never stopped loving." His hands caress hers. *Stare.* "I don't think I've ever been in a situation where I've felt so out of control. But, here I am. Out of control. Sometimes even wondering why we're even arguing. I'm not ready for marriage. Not ready for another kid." *Stare.* "But I want you in my life. I want you to come to me for anything." *Blink. Blink. Blink.* "I'll be patient with you, if you can only come forward and tell me. Tell me whatever is going on with you." *Blink. Blink.* "I know something happened. Not saying anything bad, but something happened."

Traci processes the conversation quickly. Finds out he sincerely cares for her. Wants to be a part of her life.

He is either lying about knowing something, or irritated at the thought of her being with someone. That wasn't an uncommon reaction, she guessed. Within seconds, years fly by. *Solomon. Jordan. Indigo. Marriage. Lies. Love. Heartbreak.*

She chickens out. "Why did you ask me to come today?"

Jordan laughs. "I'll tell you when you tell me what you planned on telling me." Jordan isn't an idiot. She has to try.

"I was going to tell you that there are some things you should know."

"About what?"

"About-" The fan spins. A fly walks with bold intentions across a lady's bread. Jordan's hand twitches. Sharlana walks by and winks. "About—"

"About what?"

"About us." She pauses and bites her lips. She places her hands on the table. "Remember when we spoke about kids? About having them, to be exact."

Jordan's eyes roll. He scoots backwards and bites the inside of his mouth. His blinks are rapid. "I remember."

Traci watches him. His body language tells her of his irritation. The darting of his eyes display disapproval of the subject.

"I have been thinking about a few things. And lately, some things have come up that we need to talk about."

Jordan jumps. *Blink. Blink.* "Are you . . ." His words trail off.

"Am I what?"

He stumbles. "P-p-pregnant?"

Traci laughs aloud. Her loud shrieking chuckle reverberates through the air. She can't stop laughing. "Pregnant?"

"What's so funny?"

Her laughing subsides. She gathers herself. He doesn't know her laugh is full of worry. "Nothing is funny," she explains. "Just full of craziness over the past few weeks." She feels delirious. She doesn't feel like herself. She wants out of the conversation once it returned to issues. Laughter, she could deal with. Issues, much harder when they were about her. "I do need a drink, baby," she says.

"What would you like?"

Instantly she feels pain. She wants to yell that she wants a Cosmopolitan and he should know that without asking. Solomon remembered. It is her first comparison. Maybe Jordan doesn't know her the way Solomon did, but Jordan did many other things that she felt were great. He cooks. Sometimes he cleans. Courteous. Charming. And a wonderfully carefree person.

Jordan leaves to get her a drink from the bar in back. As soon as he disappears, Sharlana pops up. Her eyes are huge.

"Did you tell Jordan?"

"Tell him what?"

"Tell him that someone else is here for you?"

"And get the shit beat out of me?"

Sharlana starts to speak, but decides against it.

"I didn't tell him anything. I didn't get a chance to." Traci checks to see if Jordan is returning. "He's been talking to me. Then he asked if I was pregnant."

Sharlana whirls around as soon as she hears the word pregnant. "He asked you what?"

"Never mind. How are things in *your* world over there with *your* friend?"

Sharlana wipes her head. "Girl, you just don't know what I had to do to get rid of that Negro."

"What did you have to do?"

"Promise him that you would give him a thorough blow job."

Traci trips over the thought. "Huh?"

"Just joking, but I had to re-introduce myself to someone who has no love lost for me. Don't get me wrong, he was cordial. He's always cordial. I just don't like him. I wanted to spit in his face when he bought me a drink."

Traci looks at Sharlana's drink. "What are you drinking?"

Sharlana holds her drink out. "Fuzzy Navel." She sucks her teeth. "And you know the bastard had a nerve to remember that I was the Fuzzy Navel queen when we all used to go out?"

"That's a good thing, right?"

"Not really. I don't need no one remembering nothing about me when we were in high school. You remember the glasses."

Traci adds, "And I remember the polyester plaid overalls you used to wear."

"Kiss my ass."

"Only if you wear the pants, baby," Traci jokes.

"Never mind the jokes. The jokes are going to be on you when you got a retarded one arguing with the stupid one."

Traci brushes her comments off. "Did he leave?"

"Sure did. And you owe me big time."

Traci relaxes. For the first time this evening she feels like something is being accomplished. She owes Sharlana for a lot of things, but today's doing is huge. "I'll pay you. We just gotta get out of here. Quickly."

"And Jordan is OK with that?"

"He don't have a choice."

Jordan smiles as he approaches with a couple of

drinks. "Hey Lana. Had I known, I would've gotten you a drink. See you're already making it happen."

Sharlana speaks frankly to Traci when Jordan gets into the circle. She expresses concern for Traci's sickly status. Jordan brushes them off. His agenda is not met yet. Jordan asks if Sharlana was having fun in a place like this. She responds that she wants to meet someone with substance.

"You got any friends?" she asksd

"Only if you like big brothers with curls and pink lotion."

Sharlana ignores his comment. She reiterates the fact that if he did come across one, she will be available. He tells her that his friends wouldn't be her type. She questions the fact that he knew her taste. He tells her that he could tell her taste.

"Tall. Dark. A zest for life. Able to hold their own, anywhere. Talkative. Financially stable. Kids."

"Why would you say kids?"

"Because you don't want one." He nods toward Traci. "But your friend over there would like one." His laugh isn't contagious.

Traci jumps in. "You ready, Jordan?"

He bids adieu to Sharlana and leads Traci away. "We've got a few minutes. Do you need anything else?"

Traci shakes her head as they approach the bar where Solomon stood earlier. She didn't see any man taller than six-foot out there. She stops and clutches her heart out of relief. She grabs Jordan's hand and inspects him as he speaks to another gentleman about half his age. They talk about a basketball league. Jordan is still active and plays for the camaraderie and the fitness. He has lost a few pounds since they met. He wears his weight well. His blue blazer hangs from his shoulders perfectly.

His suits always fit nicely. No baggy pants. Thick neck. His green shirt matches his tie. She loves the way he mixed and matched. Tonight is no different.

A man chimes in over the loud speaker. "Welcome to Soul Kitchen's poetry night. If you can, please find a seat near the front and be blessed with a little knowledge, wisdom, and culture."

Jordan grabs her hand, grips tighter, and leads her to where the poetry is being displayed.

Jordan finds seats in the front. Traci feels safe in his arms, but at the same time, she feels violated by Solomon's earlier presence. She doesn't know how or why Solomon is there, but she hopes Sharlana did something to really get rid of him.

Traci relaxes her hand on Jordan's thigh as they wait for the performance to begin. They are seated next to a couple that doesn't seem to care that they are in a public place. The man, a cutie of Latino descent, turns the front of his black and white Kangol up and winks at Traci as he continues to nuzzle on his girl's neck. Jordan soothingly massages the back of Traci's hand as he scans the room. He silently acknowledges a few people he knows while the place continues to fill up.

Rose colored candles are on the four tables in the rear and on all the ledges that surround the place. There are two rows of five separated by a small aisle. About fifty people occupy the cold silver chairs that surround them. Luckily, they arrived early and got seats in front where they were sure not to miss a thing. A four by four platform with an old-fashioned microphone is used for the stage. To the right sits the local band, Burgundy Jazz. An older gentleman with platinum cornrows blows on the saxophone while a thin, young, white woman plucks the bass. Behind them, a heavyset black man with oversized shades beats on the drums. Jordan nods his head as the saxophonist begins a sultry solo that brings applause and appreciative head nods from the audience. The backdrop is unique: a huge canvas painting of an old New Orleans saloon with a few people sitting at the bar. On canvas, a lady sits at the bar with a huge white brimmed hat, smoking a cigarette, while a man stands in front of the jukebox.

When the emcee comes to the stage, the bass player and drummer bring the volume down as the emcee informs the audience that the first poet is ready.

Traci marvels at how a young poet, Bless, rocks the crowd. The brotha came out on stage and wrecked it. A woman in the back yells for him to do his thing. He smiles and continues to indulge everyone with his words. Even the men shake their heads in agreement with his message of old school, memories, and soul food. After he leaves the stage, Traci turns around to see if Sharlana is still around. Traci relaxes again.

Jordan leans over and kisses her on her forehead. "Want something?"

"I've had enough for the day." He doesn't understand the magnitude of her day. She is drained, relieved, and tired. She wants to hear the poetry, but her mind is on getting out of there and making this relationship work. She needs it to work. This is one of the only things that she wasn't failing in besides her work. Solomon put her relationship in jeopardy by showing up. She pities him for his stupidity. "I'm glad you're back."

Jordan whispers, "Me, too."

Traci feels a slight tug on her shoulder. Her heart stops.

"You scared the shit out of me," Traci whispers to Sharlana.

Sharlana's voice is just as low. "I had to make sure you were all right."

Traci whispers, "I'm all right. Any new situations arise?"

Sharlana looks around. "Not unless you saw something."

"Nothing. Thank God."

Sharlana leans her head near Jordan. "You OK, Jordan?" She wants to see his response. He doesn't budge when he tells her that he is OK. He doesn't seem mad or bothered. She guesses the coast is clear. She tells Traci that if she needs her to call. Traci squeezes her hand for the support. Sharlana leaves as quickly as she came.

Jordan draws Traci close. Security always seems to elude her, but not today. Jordan is doing everything right while she is doing everything wrong. She counts her blessing that she has Sharlana in her corner. Today would've been a disaster without her.

Traci takes a sip of water and turns to Jordan. "On the phone you said that you had something to tell me."

He scratches his head. "I forgot." He massages her inner thigh. That's one of her spots. He's good at locating and dismantling her spots, making her wish he never found them. He was a teaser.

Unbeknownst to either one, the emcee walks over.

She smiles and speaks into the microphone. "Mr. Styles, we were calling your name." Pause. "You were busy laughing with the young lady." She walks back to the stage and informs the crowd, "If you guys don't know this next performer, let me introduce him the right way. This brotha was a regular with us for years, but he got away from the poetry scene for a while. To my surprise, he called the other day to let me know he was coming and he needed a little time to do his thing.

So, without further ado, I bring you the poet formerly known as Wild Style, Freaky Styles but now prefers to be known as Mr. Jordan Styles."

The audience members who know him shout out his name, while the rest give him adequate applause. Jordan turns to Traci. "You wanted me to tell you, right?"

Traci scoots back in her seat, aware of all the eyes glued to her back.

Jordan walks to the center of the stage and peers across the room. He shakes free from his blazer, sporting a tan crewneck T-shirt that shows off every ripple in his chest. He looks into the silent crowd and gives an adoring smile. "Do you ladies mind if a brotha gets comfortable? It's a little hot up here with all you fine looking black women out there." There are a few loud hums heard around the room.

Jordan places his jacket on the speaker next to the band. He whispers something to Platinum Cornrows and walks back to the stage. A few feet in front, there are red, blue, and burgundy lights that hit every part of the stage. He walks toward the front and unscrews a few of the lights until the stage is dimly lit. He slowly climbs back onto the platform, and on center stage stands a perfectly chiseled black god, with a blue light filling the space around him. As if on cue, Platinum Cornrow begins blowing his sax softly in the background, with the drummer and bass player filling in.

Jordan takes a deep breath, looks intently at Traci, and begins:

"I love you, baby.

Freddie Jackson couldn't have said it better that . . ." he breaks off into a cute little off key chorus. "You are my lady. You're everything I need and more." He goes back to his baritone voice and moves closer to Traci.

"Remember the other day, when I tiptoed in and closed the door?

If my memory serves me correctly, your suit had less while mine had more,

I had on black and you had on your birthday suit,

But I, for some reason, thought the contrast was cute.

You looked like an angel; only we can't make love to angels because God says it ain't right,

But somehow you brought out the giant in me even though it's a feeling I tried to fight.

I mean, I love being with you so much that when I can't make love to you,

I grab my memory and my oil and take you anyway.

They say you gotta love the one you with,

Shit, I love and lust after the one I'm with."

Jordan grabs the mic from the stand and turns his attention toward the crowd. "Now, ladies, how many of you would love for a man to be the man?"

Behind Traci, a lady yells, "Preach, brotha, preach."

He continues, "I mean, be the man

By taking command

of your soul.

Keep the heat up so high that your heart never gets cold.

Make you breakfast in bed, but his lunch is under your covers,

He'd be the corporate brotha in the day or throw on a black skullie at night and be that undercover brotha.

That ain't afraid to take you to the park,

After dark.

He'd be the one that knew just how to please you,

His shit be so real, you'd be draped across the chair with small doses of amnesia.

He knows when to lie in bed afterwards until he was no longer soft,

And knew when you had your fill of him and got a warm rag to wipe you off.

See Traci, I am that brotha that no longer wants to be undercover."

Tears stream down Traci's cheeks. Aware of all the stares, she straightens her back and sits proudly.

Jordan continues, "Traci, I don't think you heard me, baby. I said that I no longer want to be that brotha that's under covers, without you."

Traci doesn't know what Jordan is about to do or say, but she can't take it anymore. Before he really embarrassed her, she gets up and hugs him on stage. They embrace for a few seconds before the emcee comes to the mic and shouts, "Now ladies, are we feeling what this brotha has to say or what?"

In unison, the ladies snap their fingers and yell, "Oh, yeah."

Jordan sits down next to Traci and pulls her closer and whispers, "I'm not done telling you what I came to tell you."

Traci dabs her eyes and whispers back, "I knew you weren't, but I wanted to save something for when we got home. And speaking of home, thank you for the gift. I love it, baby."

"It's nothing. Just a little housewarming gift."

Traci thinks to herself that it wasn't just a little housewarming gift. Jordan must've spent a pretty penny, but she guessed they both would be using it soon.

The emcee gets back up and looks at Jordan and warns the crowd, "I feel sorry for this next brotha that has to represent after those powerful words. He grabbed me a minute ago and said he had to go on while the ladies were still hot and bothered. And this is his first time, so please be nice to . . ." she pauses to make sure she is reading it right before continuing, "Mr. Action Jackson."

Traci freezes. For a moment, she thought that the lady had introduced someone named Action Jackson.

Her head snaps back, then to the side. A man smiles. A lady waves at someone in the front. The bass player continues to bob her head as she plucks enthusiastically at her guitar. Jordan continues to bask in their glory. The emcee's eyes remain in the rear, searching for someone. Jordan joins her in her quest for the mystery poet.

The crowd that stands in back against the wall, near the door, part ways. Solomon steps through. His motion is slower than most people's gait, but so was the speed of everyone in there. Sweat maneuvers down Traci's arm. She unknowingly grips Jordan's leg so hard that he grabs her hand.

"Damn, Catwoman."

Traci apologizes. She tells him that she suddenly feels sick and wants to leave. Her symptoms are coming back. She forces a heave. She doesn't have to make up the headache. And her body trembles.

"You aren't looking too well," Jordan tells her. His hand goes to her forehead like he took classes in medicine. "And you feel kinda hot. I think we should get you out of here."

Traci doubles over and clutches her stomach. Jordan rubs her back, bending down to whisper, "You'll be all right baby. We just have to get you home. I'll take care of the rest."

Solomon walks by. Traci's heart thumps so loud that she covers her jacket so Jordan won't hear. Jordan, who remains on the inside, pulls Traci closer as Solomon steps by. Jordan looks up and watches him as he watches all the other poets. No concern, just appreciation at the people who work their craft as he does. Jordan lifts Traci, who continues to heave and tremble, and begins to walk her to the door.

"Don't go nowhere, brotha."

Jordan continues to walk Traci to the rear to escape, not knowing the voice or the intention.

"I said, don't go nowhere, Mr. Stales."

Jordan stops. Traci keeps walking. Jordan grabs her and catches up, whispering, "Hold up for a second, baby."

Traci hesitates, then stops. Breath is shorter than before. Much shorter. She faces the door while Jordan faces the stage. Traci wants to run out, but her feet won't let her. Her body won't let her remain still as it quivers. She blows a head gasket trying to figure out something. Anything.

Up front, Solomon begins his story via prose. His posture is behemoth. He watches Jordan. Jordan watches him. No one but Traci knows the magnitude of the stare. The evil stare between two. Jordan's stare has wonder. He has to know something. Solomon's stare is haughty. He grabs the mic and removes it from the stand. His crumbled piece of paper dangles from his hand as he speaks again.

His voice is deep. His method unusual. His presence great.

"I said, Mr. Stales, I've been watching you from afar
And as sure as I believe in the sun, moon, and stars,

I believe you don't understand the magnitude of what I've got to say.

And against opposition is where I do best, so please hope and pray

That you don't oppose.

Instead you choose to use your words, your poems, your prose

To fight battles. To win wars.

Ever wonder how someone else can come into your door

And kiss your girl.

Fucking *rock her world*."

Solomon's laugh is sinister. Jordan's hands balls into a fist. He begins to understand something about this guy and Traci and the day she went out. Jordan turns to Traci. She turns away. She has nothing to do with this. If this was how it was going to come out, then so be it. Inside, she cries. She is embarrassed that Jordan has to find out this way. Sick that she isn't woman enough to make things happen the right way. But is there a right way?

The crowd starts to mutter. Many in front shift in their seats. Jordan remains still. Traci can see him open his chest and take in breath. He lets go. His chest remains out. He laughs. His concern seems settled. He pulls Traci near and forces her to turn around. He watches her reaction. She is a constant professional. She doesn't react. Her eyes continue their darting. Her foot taps, inside of her shoe. She steals breath every chance she can.

Solomon smiles again. Brings the mic to his lips and begins.

"That's cute that two people can share together a dream.

But, Nigga, all ain't what it seems.

I mean, it's nice when two people can share a dream.

But, Black man, all ain't what it seems.

I imagine the wealth of words I could use to describe
what I see
But believe me
All I can come up with is fall-a-cy.
Or maybe it's just a misunderstanding.
I mean, my landing
Back.
As a matter of fact,
Do-you-understand-who-I-am?
Excuse me, Ma'am?" He looks directly at Traci, who
doesn't give eye contact.

Jordan looks down at Traci, who continues to avoid
eye contact. He grips her arm tight. She raises her head.

Solomon continues, "I said, Excuse me Ma'am,
Does he know who I am.
I am King Solomon without the forty thieves
And you watch me intently, while silently the little
lady grieves
Because *I'm back,* like Chuckie
And brother you sure are lucky
That I'm a changed man.
One with a plan
To get back what's mine." He points to his watch.

"And now it's time." He digs in his pocket and pulls
out loose change.

Solomon throws a coin toward Jordan's feet and
holds one in his hand.

"If the saying is a penny for you thoughts,
What will you do with this quarter?" He digs in his
jacket pocket and pulls out a picture.

"See my man, this is our daughter.
In-di-go!"

Jordan rushes the stage. Bedlam. His hands find their
way around Solomon's neck. Solomon's fist finds the

pit of Jordan's stomach. Traci stands and nearly gets trampled as men and women fight to get to the gladiators that take their differences to heightened levels apart.

"Let him go," Jordan screams. His fists go up. Traci didn't know boxing was in his blood.

Solomon's smirk remains. The sides of his neck bleed. His hands are down. He looks at Traci as a thick man continues to wrap his arms around his chest. The man tells Solomon to relax. "Don't I look relaxed," Solomon tells him. "I'm fucking relaxed."

The band stands cowered in the corner protecting their instruments as the emcee remains in front of them with the mic in her hand. She attempts to quiet the crowd down with a feeble attempt at assertion. Her voice shakes more than her hands.

Two men hold Jordan back. Each of his hands are held onto tightly by the men. Jordan stops trying to fight them. "Let me go," he shouts. His attempts at shaking himself free are unsuccessful. He grits his teeth and taps his feet.

Traci looks around. Chairs are strewn everywhere. Sharlana rushes in.

"Everything all right?" she asks.

Traci shakes her head frantically. "Hell no, everything is not all right."

"You gotta get out of here."

"Lana, I am not leaving this place until everyone is safe."

"Don't you mean until Jordan is safe?"

"Everyone. He is the father of my child."

Sharlana makes an executive decision and forcefully moves Traci from the area.

Chapter 15

Jordan

My head spins. Does triple spins. Dizziness rocks my world. The punch to the abdomen didn't help matters any. I yell into the phone, "I don't know what just happened."

Tony asks, "So you say he mentioned something about him and Traci having a baby?"

I massage my temples. "Yeah. A baby. At first I didn't even think he was talking to me, but after mentioning certain things, I put two and two together. And you know I'm not a fucking dummy, but you wouldn't believe it if I told you. This shit is crazy."

"And you are fine right now? Do you need for me to come down?"

"No. I'm good. Thanks."

"Where's Traci?"

"With all the ruckus going on, I didn't see where she went."

"Where are you now?"

"Outside of the poetry spot."

"And where is the guy?"

"I haven't the slightest clue. I know if I see him again, that'll be more of his ass I'll hand to him." I close my phone. Frustrated that I let someone enter my world and disrupt. Angry that I lost control. A few people I noticed inside the poetry reading walked outside. I saw them look at me sitting on steps and shake their heads. They mutter something about me messing up their evening with my juvenile bullshit. Another person walks near. She asks me if I am OK. I shake my head. She hands me a bottled water.

"Is your lady friend OK?"

I shrug my shoulders. "I don't know where she went."

"I wasn't sure either." She smiles. "The poem you told her was beautiful."

I had forgotten about the poem. Forgotten about the comfort Traci and I had just gotten to after the rough week. This would be yet another week to get over.

"Thanks for the water," I tell the woman.

"Not a problem," she says.

I watch her leave. I wished Traci was as nice as she. She disappears. The memory reappears. Solomon standing on stage spouting off things to me about him and Traci. They deserve each other. I take a sip. I remember the two classes of yoga I took at a conference. My breathing is wrong. I can't remember the technique and I revert back to my anger. I flip my phone open and dial Traci. No answer. My anger augments.

Deanna picks up on the second ring.

My voice is calm. "I need to see you."

She tells me of her low maintenance and gets directions. We decide on a Starbucks five blocks away. As I walk toward the front of the club, the valet approaches me and asks if I need my car.

"I'll be back. It's only five blocks."

For five blocks, I talk to myself. Silently, of course. Discuss my plan of action for this man who is not nearly as much man as I am. I wouldn't have approached him that way. I would've been respectful of his life, knowing he had nothing to do with it. I would have not made my display personal for the world to hear. Then I thought that maybe he was hurting. *So fucking what* is my next thought. Traci sneaks into my conversation. How she can just sneak in without me noticing is strange. In all the action, she was nowhere to be seen during or afterward. I questioned her integrity. She angered me. *A baby.* It was beyond my belief. She was the one always asking me what I thought about having another child. She always said she wanted one before she was too old to have one. Never once in our conversation was there a mention of a baby. No mention of happening to have one years ago. How does one forget that she has had a child? How does one not find the common decency to tell that she has children?

The streets are barren. The weather is warmer than usual or I am hotter than normal. Either way, I sweat.

A few people sit in lounge chairs at Starbucks. Deanna has not yet arrived, so I take a seat near the window and people-watch. I decide against coffee because even though it calms my nerves, it makes me use the bathroom. I sure didn't need anything with tons of milk in it today. The lean against the window is comforting.

Deanna barges in. "You sleeping in cafés now?"

I wipe my mouth and jump up, unaware how long I have been sleeping. "Hey."

"Hey to you," she says. She takes a seat next to me. "You look like you need something to drink. Espresso?"

"Does it have milk?"

"I don't think so." She lifts herself up and gets her

wallet from her pocketbook. "I'll get you something. Are you all right?"

Today is the first time I didn't feel like censoring anything. She was going to get my life as it happened, live and in color. "I'm OK, I guess. Get me something black and strong."

She laughs. "I'll be asking for the same thing," she jokes.

She returns with two coffees. She got me a Mocha Latte with cinnamon sprinkled on the top. She tells me that it'll wake me up. I take a whiff. It is stronger than my usual coffee and tastier. It burns my tongue as I ease a few drops into my mouth.

She sits with her back facing the window. She wears sweat pants and a jacket that hugs. I realize that everything she wears hugs. I wonder if she has any babies that I wasn't aware of.

"What's going on?" she asks.

I place my drink down and scoot closer to the table. Even though we're pretty far away from all the other patrons, I still don't want anyone in my business, even her, but I need some female companionship. Since I cut the rest off, she would have to do. I didn't need her advice. I just needed an ear with some tits.

She reaches over and touches my jacket. "What happened to you? I ain't never seen you look so disheveled."

My suit jacket is wrinkled, my shirt even worse. Someone spilled juice or something on my pants and my shoes are scuffed.

"Got into a little skirmish."

"Where?"

I didn't want to go there, but I did call. I open up and let anything flow. "At this poetry spot."

"It was a poetry slam? *Literally?*" she jokes.

I don't feel like joking and my facial expression makes it apparent. I know she was trying to relieve me. "It was an event that they hold monthly. I went there and someone acted inappropriately."

"And you dealt with it?"

"Sure did."

"How did he turn out?"

"Worse than I did." I don't know how he turned out. It happened so fast that I don't remember anything but grabbing his neck and trying to strangle the living shit out of him.

"Do you need anything? Need for me to do something or bring you somewhere?"

"I just need for you to drink your coffee and relax. I just needed some company. Can you do that?"

She relaxes in her chair and lifts her drink to her lips. "Of course I can do that."

"I need to talk with you. Where are you?" Traci yells.

I put the phone to my chest and excuse myself from Deanna. Instead of going outside, I choose the bathroom. Luckily for me, it's clean.

"Go ahead," I say.

"Where are you?"

"Where are you?" I ask.

"That's not the issue. I was just—"

"Let's not mention issues." My voice can probably be heard at the counter. "We definitely don't need to talk about that."

"I didn't call to argue."

"You called to do what? To ask what? To fucking tell me what?"

"I need for you to understand me for a second," she wails. "I need for you to listen. Please."

"I'm listening."

She pauses before speaking. I can hear cars in the background. People laugh behind her. "I'm sorry."

"No apologies now. I need to hear some things. You've got a few seconds to talk."

"I need more than a few seconds."

"Traci, you're wasting time. Be a woman about your business. What are you trying to tell me?"

She screams, "That I love you. More than you'll ever understand. More than you can comprehend. And yes, I do have a child. A child that I haven't seen since she was four months. A child that I have thought about every waking day that I have lived. Every minute I speak. Every day I go to work and see the kids, I think of her. Don't you understand how much torture that is?" Her voice quiets. "But I did that to myself. I wanted to remind myself of the terrible choice I made. At first it was for only a couple of months while I got settled in, but then it turned to a half a year. Then a year. Then when the acting didn't make me millions, I quit. Quit on her. Quit on myself. Quit on any dream of seeing her again." Pause. *Sniffle.* "When she was two, I tried to come back and see her, but he would have no parts of it unless I went back with him. And trust me, I didn't want any parts of him. He did nothing for me for the years that we were together. Did nothing for me for the years previous to the baby and afterward. I had a life. A full-blown life that had branches. Life. Growth. Excitement. I asked him to come with me and her. He convinced me to give up custody until I was ready to come back. He said that even if I didn't want him, he would never keep me from my child. But the bastard did. Kept me from seeing her. Kept me from gaining custody back. The bastard made me sign over my parental rights before I left." Pause. She weeps openly. "And what was I to do when I wanted the fame, the fortune, and the dream and I was constantly beat up by him?" Her energy picks up. "Do you know that he once beat me so bad that I had to stay in the hospital for two weeks? Eyes swollen. Jaw wired. Teeth missing. He beat me till I damn near died. And do you know how I signed the papers over for my daughter?" Pause. "Do you know?"

At this point, I don't want to know. "How?"

"With a fucking gun to my head. I gotta go, Jordan. Sorry about the incident. Sorry I didn't tell you what was going on. Sorry I didn't make life easy for you. You didn't pay for this. You bought the idea of a single woman with no kids and big dreams. Well, my dreams are killed, I have a child and a crazy baby daddy that won't, can't, and doesn't want to leave me alone right now."

It hurt. As angry as I am, I want to reach over the phone and pull her to me. I want to kiss her forehead and explain that everything in life happens for a reason. I just didn't know the reason at the time. God was the only one with answers. My battery runs low. My spirits run lower.

"Where are you?" I ask.

"In front of the spot."

My signal fades. The anger subsides. There are bigger issues to tackle. She needs help and if there is any compassionate bone in my body, it would have to surface. It reared its beautiful head. I walked into the café area and told Deanna I had to go. She was disappointed, but not as disappointed as I was with the whole situation.

I go back to my car. I drive quickly. Past the dark,

murky streets of the southeast. Suddenly, the lights beamed. The White House. A few stood outside drawing pictures of tourists. Pictures were snapped.

My car slows near the park. Lights are few and far between, except in the distance. The gray and white marbled fixture in the D.C. skyline emits great life to the obscure park that hides vandals, bums, and the nightlife that was merely heard about. I walk with anticipation.

She sits in her usual spot. Underneath the shine of the Washington Monument. Her back is to me. She hears me coming. My steps aren't for the deaf. She jokes that I stomp like a Grizzly. I tell her I would eat her, and then sleep for months. That was our joke.

Her head is held high; her shoulders open. She turns her head slightly as I near. I slow down. Pause. Move slightly. Stop.

Solomon's poem. His fist crashing into my stomach. Traci bent on the ground after a blow to her face. Her child. The phone call at late night. The pain in her voice when she told her secrets. Water finds its way to the corner of my eye. I bite my lips and nod my head. I want to ask her so much, but the need for answers is overcome by the need to console and take care of her. Hours ago, I would've taken this opportunity to strangle her, but now I want to comfort and rub the pain away.

Her shoulders are hard. Her eyes remain glued to the top of the Monument as I press, knead, and dig into her pain. I feel every muscle in her body. Feel every pain in her heart. The higher she looks into the night, the stronger she remains. It's my job to work it all out of her. I know what she needs. A good solid cry. She needs to weep until her eyes cry bile. I dig into Solomon. I grab hold of her right shoulder with both hands and press him from her shoulders to her arms to her hands to her fingers. I do it again. I rub her shoulder near her neck, and then I rub hard. Rub Solomon's fights and arguments right out of her fingertips. Her head drops an inch. I hear her moan deep inside her body. She remains strong as I work her. The night sends tiny waves of cool air that trickle through branches, bouncing against the leaves and it slithers around her skin. Her other shoulder needs me. Indigo's shoulder. I clap my hands together and rub until I feel heat on the inside of my palms. She leans her head to the left. She opens parts of her soul and lets me in. We bond without words. Our sensuality comes together without intention. I mold new shape while I dig into her skin. She exhales, moans, relaxes, and cries as I perform. As I reach the tip of her fingers, I lean on her. Her head falls backwards and lands on my chest.

"I bet she's beautiful," I whisper.

Her body shakes. I continue to lean against her body, letting her know that someone has her back. Regardless of the argument, the world has to stop. I kiss the back of her neck and play with her hair. She's like putty. She loves when fingers rummage through her hair. She enjoys the idea of just allowing someone to delve into her scalp with loving touches. My touch is flawless.

I walk around and sit next to her. I put my arm around her and she leans against me. "And I bet she has your smarts."

"Jordan, I really want to—"

I hush her and tell her it wasn't time for her to speak. She will have it in due time. She nods her head and says she wants to walk. The luminosity always piqued her interest. We hold hands and walk around the long, sleek building that screams classic. We reminisce about how we met. Laugh about her nasty attempt at Cornish hens on Thanksgiving. We even stop at the spot where we made love one night till the grass got tired.

Tony kept his jokes in until he realized I was OK. That's when the giggling presented itself in the form of his boisterous laugh. "So, he did a you, huh?" *Laugh.*

"What do you mean, did a me?" *Evil glare.*

"He did his stage thing. In front of all of the ladies."

"He did his thing." Pause. "But that ain't the point."

"What was he like?"

"What do you mean, what was he like? You interested in him?" I pick through my grits. There must've been a change with the chefs, because usually the food here is always fresh. Today, the grits have lumps, and the bacon is burnt.

Tony bites his bagel and sips his coffee. "I was just asking about the man."

I throw my fork down silently. I don't want to seem rattled over a guy. I know I have to give in to something. If not, Tony will eat me alive every chance he gets. "He was a little taller than me. Dark skinned brother with a goatee. You know, the usual suspect. He was medium built."

"Any tattoos?"

I shoot Tony another quick look. I see him hold his laugh in. "Tattoos? Yeah," I say. "He had one on his butt cheek that said 'G' and on the other cheek he had 'Unit.'"

We fall out laughing. We finish up and talk about the basketball game we plan to attend next week. Tony says he might not be able to go because of work. I laugh harder than he did earlier.

"You can pick up cans anytime," I joke.

"For your information, buddy, I'm about to embark on a situation that'll bring me some cake."

"You mean real cake." I hold the door open for an elderly lady with a floppy green hat that walks in. "Don't order the bacon," I tell her. "What type of job are you getting yourself into, Donald Trump? I mean Donald Dump?"

Tony ignores me and keeps walking. Winter is approaching and these little jackets we're wearing are going to be outdated in about three weeks. We zip up and walk backwards against the howling winds. "I'm going into investment."

My smirk is killing him. "You mean going into the investment building to do—"

"Regular work," he informs.

We turn the corner and spin back around and walk like regular citizens. "I told you I could get you into the job where I'm at."

"Computers? My ass. The only computer I play is Playstation."

"You gotta grow up," I tell him. "But I definitely would continue the job you got on the twenty-fourth of December. Sliding down chimneys ain't a bad thing."

"And what about you and your nemesis?"

"Big word," I say.

"I called some people you know. They gave me a fast track. Shit, maybe I'll start spewing words of wisdom."

We stop at a red light. Cars whiz by. An old man coughs and spits. A little girl in a red coat stares at Tony.

I bend down. "And if you're a good little girl, he'll bring presents." She and her mother smile.

Tony holds his hands out and recites words off the cuff.

"I've got no time for shit!

You just seen the old man spit.

And the little girl laughed when you made a joke.

Like wheels on a spoke."

"Like wheels on a spoke?" I ask. His rhythm is messed up. His word selection is even worse.

"Never mind my word selection. What are you going to do?" His voice becomes very business-like. "What did Traci say about the situation?"

We hustle into the entrance of the YMCA and present our cards.

"We spoke. We didn't talk about anything in particular."

"She mentioned nothing of it?"

"She tried."

"You stopped her?"

"Yeah. I got caught up in her story about the man."

Tony listens as I continue to tell him what Traci told me. I tell him how she explained the pain she went through. The swollen eyes. The sleepless nights. The baby. The career. The present time. The future.

"That's a lot of stuff to deal with. You ready?"

"Man, ready as I'll ever be. You ready to work out that pudgy ass stomach of yours?"

"Only if you're ready to work out them tiny ass toothpick arms."

Chapter 16

Traci

A sharp knock at Traci's door startles her.
"Who?"

Sharlana yells. Traci peels herself from the couch and opens the door. As soon as Sharlana gets into the house, she hits Traci with a barrage of questions about the evening.

Traci asks Sharlana to give her a few minutes.

"Give you a few minutes," Sharlana exclaims. "You have me drop you off at a park, and then you turn your phone off." Pause. *Stare.* "I need for you to give me a few minutes. This man has got you going crazy." Pause. "Again."

Traci shakes her head in agreement. She doesn't want to agree, but has no choice. Sharlana is right. Solomon was in her life for six years before and now less than two weeks. Each time he disrupts. Each time he lived and shined off of her gold. He didn't want her to succeed, so he did everything humanly possible to prevent it. His misery loved her company.

"I know what it looks like, but don't you think I've grown? You don't think I can handle this man now?"

Sharlana doesn't sound too confident. "I think you can handle the situation now. It's just him. I hate him."

"I know."

They walk into the kitchen where Sharlana sits and watches Traci make a fresh pot of hazelnut coffee. Traci loves her drink light and sweet, and Sharlana loves hers black. She always claims the blacker the berry. They sip by the window at the high table. Traci switched the whole kitchen to white. After the fire, Traci needed change. She wanted something that gave off pure bliss. White was always the color that meant beginning. It was her neutral. Her mums always stood out in the kitchen. It gave it flavor.

"I can handle him," Traci reassures Sharlana.

"I know you can. But I just don't feel right about it."

"What would you like for me to do, Dr. Shavers?"

Sharlana stands up, grabs her coffee, and walks around the kitchen as though she is Traci's therapist. She goes to the curtains by the window and pushes them back so she can look out. She sips and speaks profoundly, "What can you do differently?"

Traci plays her role of the despondent patient. She stretches her feet out and puts her hands behind her head. "A lot of things. I would first start out by telling him that it is completely over."

Sharlana's eyes remain glued to the outside. "That's good. Very good. What else?"

"I would tell Jordan what he needs to hear."

Sharlana lets the curtains fall back into place. She spins around. "Need?"

Traci corrects herself. "Need. Want. Has to hear. It's all the same."

Sharlana nods her head, encouraging Traci to continue.

Traci does. "Jordan needs to hear that I love him. He needs to understand that no one comes before him. Hopefully after him either. He needs to see that this is merely a situation that I am completely lost in. And if he can't or won't understand." Pause. *Sip.* "He'll just have to understand. I want to marry this man." As the words drip from her mouth, Sharlana's mouth opens.

"Marry?"

Traci moves close to Sharlana. Their noses almost touch. "Just as I said. Marry." She moves back to her seat and falls back into her normal self. "I want to marry him, Lana. I want to have kids. More kids. I want him to want nothing better than to build a future with me. Is that wrong to ask for?"

"Not wrong, but sometimes far fetched."

"You need to find some love."

"I've got love. Did I tell you about the young lady I just met?"

Traci picks her cup up and returns to the living room without the slightest acknowledgement of what Sharlana had just said.

As Sharlana barges in to continue her story, Traci raises her hand to quiet her.

Traci scurries for her cell phone that chimes. She looks at the number, takes a breath and then speaks very casually. "We need to talk, Solomon." Pause. Her eyes dart nervously left to right. "I don't care what you have to say right now. I need to talk to you." Pause. "Now!" She puts the phone against her leg so he can't hear what she has to say to Sharlana. "The fucking balls," she whispers. Her voice rises as she puts the phone to her ears and reconnects with him. "I don't care what happened." Pause. "Who?" Pause. Deep breath. Her forehead wrinkles. "It's Jordan, not Gordon." Pause. She checks her watch, never looking Sharlana's way. "We do need closure." Pause. She stands quickly and paces. She stops near the kitchen and screams to the top of her lungs, "I don't care what you say, ass- hole!" Her phone flies across the room and slams against the wall. Sharlana ducks. Everything remains still. Nei- ther Sharlana nor Traci let a breath out. Sharlana looks at the phone to her left while the battery lays against the wall to the right.

Sharlana lifts herself from the chair softly. She walks over to where Traci stands in the hallway. "You OK?"

Traci slides down the wall and sits on the ground. She acknowledges Sharlana with a turn of her head in the opposite direction. She, too embarrassed, looks away

She mutters, "I know what you're going to say. It is out of control."

Sharlana slides down the same wall and sits next to her. "It's OK to be out of control sometimes. Just don't remain stuck." She puts her arm around Traci. "You've got the strength. That's the one admirable quality that you have that most lack. Even me. You have the ability to get out, unscathed."

Traci folds her knees and wraps her arms around them and rocks. "I don't leave unscathed," she whis- pers. "Ever."

"You show strength by taking your lumps and moving on."

"Sometimes I don't."

"Sometimes you do. Most of the time you do."

Her voice remains no louder than a whisper. "I'm not as strong as I appear sometimes."

Sharlana rubs her back. "Sure you are. I look up to

you. Always have. You and I are closer than me and my sister."

Traci stops rocking. "And you and I are closer than me and my sister, too."

Sharlana takes her arm from around Traci. "You ain't got no sister."

"I do now."

Sharlana laughs and speaks proudly. "Since we're taking out the trash. I'm coming out. Full blown."

Sniffle. "You already been out."

"We never really spoke about it."

"Did we have to? Men were just something to do until you came around."

Sharlana holds her laugh in. Her body shakes slightly as she did. "Well, I've come around. I'm not afraid. You cool with that?"

Traci pats Sharlana's knee. "I gotta be. I might need a big bitch to protect me when the shit hits the fan." They both laugh. Traci's demeanor changes. It's odd. "Ten years ago wasn't a mistake."

Sharlana's turn is sudden. "What?"

"Ten years ago wasn't a mistake," she repeats slower.

"Oh my God!" Sharlana shrieks. Her hands start trembling and her body trembles as she opens her arms and pulls Traci close. "Oh." She rubs her back. "My." She pulls her closer. "God," she whispers.

Traci's head falls to Sharlana's shoulder. Her hands wrap around Sharlana's waist. The pain is intense. A second later, everything stops. It feels as though someone scoops out her soul and leaving her hollow. She half-cries, half-coughs.

Sharlana rocks her left. Then right. Stopping for not more than a second, she rocks her like a baby. She rubs Traci's head, pressing it further into her shoulder. She wants to rub the pain she feels. They're sisters. Sharing hurt. Sharing pain. Sharing love. And dreams. And fantasies. And souls. She would die for her.

Traci sniffles. "The first one was for the headache."

Sharlana continues to rub her hair. Stroking from the top the bottom of her neck.

"The second was for the bullshit job that never came through."

Sharlana rubs harder and slower.

A moment of silence slithers by. It's uncomfortable.

Traci's voice weakens, "The third was for my," she imitates herself in earlier years through sniffles, "big old dreams." Her normal voice returns, "I mean, who was I to think that Little Ass T from Hawthorne Street would do anything in Hollywood?" Her head remains on Sharlana's shoulder as she wipes her eyes. "I didn't have support. My mother told me I wasn't chasing a dream. I was running from responsibility." Her voice is evil. "So I popped another one for her. I knew she don't know CPR, so I wish I would've passed out in front of her. Let her feel incompetent. Let her allow my death." Her body shudders. She whimpers and breaks down inside Sharlana's arms.

Sharlana barely moves. She leaves her hand on the back of Traci's neck and digs deep.

Traci sniffles. Her hands fall to the side of Sharlana. She remains inside her hug, limp. "And then I popped one for the *All-Mighty fucking Solomon*. Yeah, he would see me and wonder what the hell to do." She pounds her fist to the ground out of frustration. Venom fills her speech. "I hate him. I hate him." Pause. More uncomfortable silence. She speaks softly, "But I love him. I hate the fact that I love a man that ain't shit. Hate the fact that I can't get him out of my system so I had to get rid of him by *all* means necessary." She cries again. "By *all* means necessary," she whispers. Her body is flaccid. "Then I popped one for Indigo. I . . . popped . . . one . . . for," her voice is barely audible, "my daughter." She loses control of her body. "For my daughter," she cries.

Chapter 17

Jordan

I arrive twenty minutes early. Considering I refer to my timing as always fashionably late, I know it's nerves that make me early. Pacing in front of the ticket counter, I was growing tired. By now, I could've directed anyone anywhere on the east coast. I walk back to the ticket counter.

Diane, who has her name scrawled on the front of a sticky nametag, interrupts before I can say another word. "I checked for the bus, sir. Still no answer. There is a spot on the road where coverage is crappy. Luckily for you, the spot is near. He's in good hands."

I spin around and begin my pacing. "He's in good hands," I mumble. She don't know about good hands.

A bus pulls up and patrons begin piling off. First is a Hispanic couple with a little girl. The heavyset woman takes more time than normal to get down the stairs. An impatient black woman behind her shouts for her to hurry. The husband mentions something incoherent in Spanish to her. The daughter cries once her father starts speaking faster and faster. After the unusual suspects leave, a few college students trickle off. They speak about sharing a cab back to the university. The ring leader is a tall, thin Oriental with thick black glasses and more book bags than his hands can handle. He directs as the rest follows, dragging along their belongings.

I watch each and every person leave the bus, and there is still no Kendal. I go back to the ticket booth and ask Diane is there another bus coming. She says that the bus that just pulled in is the last one for the evening and if he was not on that one, he wouldn't be coming tonight.

The bus driver hustles into the station rolling his luggage. He tips his hat to the baggage handler that stands inside.

"Excuse me, brother," I say.

His rolling stops. His reaction is as though I am interfering with his time. At this point, until Kendal is found, his time is my time.

"My son was on the bus. Did you happen to—"

He points to the bus. "Younger black man." He scans me and continues, "A better looking version of yourself?"

His humor isn't amusing.

He continues, "He was in the back with a young lady. They talked the whole time here. Loudly."

I rush by him as he continues to describe the bus ride. I push the door open and stand by the door. I hold my breath, scared of what I was to find, as I run up the stairs.

"Kendal!"

Kendal jumps up; the girl hits the ground with a thump.

"Hey Dad." He extends his hand to pick the girl up.

She ignores his hand and stands by herself. She doesn't
appear to be much older than Kendal.

"What's going on?" I ask.

"N-n-nothing," he stammers. "I was just talking to—"
He snaps his fingers to jog his memory of the girl's
name.

"Tranika."

Kendal smiles. "Yeah. Tranika and I were talking
about the way the schools are down here." He moves
close to me and whispers, "I told her I might be moving
down here."

He tries. I have to give him that. I'm just not ready to
see him dating anyone at thirteen and a half. Way too
early. At sixteen, maybe I could stomach the dating, but
now is not the time.

I turn around and tell him I will be downstairs. I save
him the embarrassment of making him leave right
away. I hear him tell her that he'll call her before he
leaves. She wants a hug, and it sounds as though he's
hesitant.

"Let's go now, Kendal!" I have to do the father thing
no matter how tacky he thinks it is. We walk to the car in
silence. I don't know if he's mad or embarrassed. I
don't care, I don't want to be a grandfather already. I
just know that during this summer trip, he and I will
definitely have our sex talk.

He had grown a few inches since I last saw him. He
now towers over me by at least three inches. As usual,
his pants are neatly pressed and hanging off his butt.
He has on a navy blue New York Giants football jersey
with a gold chain dangling from his neck. I wish we
would've started the day off another way, but what is
done is done.

I take three deep breaths and change my mood. I put my arms around his shoulder. "You hungry?"

He rubs his stomach and grins. "Starving."

He throws his bag in the trunk and we whisk down I-95. On our way, he tells me about his new friends, new neighborhood, and his new basketball team.

He eases a tape out of his pocket and pops it into the car stereo. We both bob our heads to the beat until someone in the song raps, "Bitch betta have my money."

Wide-eyed and without missing a beat, Kendal ejects the tape, turns the radio on, and adjusts his head nod to a different beat. For the rest of the ride, we chitchat about my new job, where I live now, and how I have been practicing for the past few weeks so I can beat his butt in basketball. He laughs, jumps out of the car, and runs into McDonald's.

"You got a girlfriend yet?" I ask in between fries.

Two quick slurps of chocolate shake and his attention goes to a fly that walks on the outside window like he owns stock in McDonald's. "Nope."

I move closer and point to his chin. "You getting a little fuzz underneath your chin. The girls liking that?"

More fly watching follows more slurps. His cunning grin erupts. "I never said that."

"So, what's going on with the girls? I see you had one on the bus just that quick," I prod.

His twisted lips go in the opposite direction of his eyes. He pause, leans over, and tilts his head toward me. "You didn't say anything about my hair." It is neatly twisted in cornrows.

"It's nice."

He smiles and nods in agreement.

"What about the girls?" I ask.

His eyes go back to the fly as he munches on a few fries. He mumbles, "Some of them look good."

"Yeah?"

"Yeah." His answers are short and sweet, and if I want details about what's going on, I will have to step up my questioning game.

I pop a fry in my mouth and chew aggressively. "You having sex?"

He freezes. My breathing stops, my heart drops below my stomach, and everything seems to move in slow motion. I didn't want to hear the answer, but I had to.

Another quick no escapes Kendal's mouth.

Quick answers from him always mean there is something else going on. I don't want to bring up the subject as soon as he gets here, but after the whole bus ordeal, it has to be done immediately.

I take a quiet gulp of air and let it out even quieter. "We need to talk about sex, Kendal."

He takes a few creases from my forehead and puts them on his. "While we're eating?"

"As opposed to when? When you're sleeping?" He isn't making this any easier. I reminisce about my sex talk with my mother when I was a little younger than Kendal. She brought out a thick book that had pictures of cartoon people having sex. My older brother gawked, and my younger sister gagged. It looked like Fred and Daphne from Scooby Doo were having sex. From then on, cartoons were never the same. I promised myself I would handle it differently.

"What do you know about sex?"

Kendal finds a piece of hair on the side of his head and twists it until it can wind no more. "Not much."

"Do you know what you call a woman's—" Pause. I

was confused at the proper word. I know what I called it when I was with my boys. I know what to call it when I am with my girl, but with a son is much different. I clear my throat and try again. "Do you know what you call a woman's . . . ?" Pause. "Thing?"

Visibly uncomfortable, Kendal drops his head. "*Vagina?*"

I slowly nod my head and smile the same tense smile he does. "I guess that's the word. Tell me what you know about," pause, "vaginas."

During his hesitation he seems to wrestle with whether to tell me everything he knew, or part of it. "I do take health class, Dad."

"What do they teach you in health class?"

"They teach us about the reproductive system."

"And?"

"I know where's babies come from, and how they get here."

This is the answer I have been waiting for. "How?"

He stands up and digs into his pocket. "First you give a woman this," he says handing me a dollar.

"What the—"

He grabs my shoulder and laughs. "Just joking, Dad." He sits back down getting a good chuckle out of my near heart attack. "I know about how men and women make babies. I know that you're supposed to wait until you're in love."

"Married. Until you're married," I corrected.

"That's what I meant," he says.

We continue our talk about love, and then we switch to basketball, grades, and the new school he is attend-ing.

* * *

Deanna hobbles into my office. "Mind if I sit?"

I look up from my work and offer her the seat across from my desk. She looks like she had just come in from a war. Her energy isn't right.

"Coffee?" I ask.

She declines. With each passing minute, she regresses. "I need to speak with you."

I shuffle my papers together and place them neatly in front of me. "OK. What's going on?"

Her chair moves closer. She slides to the edge and gets even closer. "I don't know how else to say it."

I move back. "English works." My stare was apprehensive. "Yep. English works."

She stands. "I think I love you."

My head jerks back. "What?"

She stops swinging her hands. She forces more courage. "I think I love you."

"Love me like?" I start. I wait for her to complete the sentence.

Her mouth opens, but nothing comes out.

"Love me like what?" Pause. "You mean, like a brother?"

She looks to her right and completely ignores me.

I try again. "Like a father?"

She shakes her head again.

"Like your grandfather?"

She purses her lips, sits on the edge of my desk and grabs my tie. She strokes it from the knot to the end. Her skin glistens against the cream silk tie. "I think I love you like my man." She pulls my tie close to her. My neck follows. "Like my male friend." She smells my tie and exhales. "Like my lover." Her free hand runs from my collar to the inside of my shirt. "Like my provider." Her fingers trail a line that leads straight to my pants.

She pauses at my bellybutton. "Like my drug." She grabs my outline that sticks through.

I jump up. "Like a fired employee," I inform her.

She laughs and nods toward the crotch of my pants. "He don't want to fire me."

She's working me over, and I can't let her think she's in charge. No matter what my friend says.

The knock at the door makes Deanna jump.

Mr. Amsterdam adjusts his thin burgundy suit jacket and walks toward Deanna. He placed his stubby fingers on her shoulders and asks her to excuse us.

Without verbal acknowledgement, she answers with a slow ascent as if the bailiff has yelled, "All rise!"

Once the door slams, Mr. Amsterdam digs into his suit jacket pocket and pulls out a Havana cigar. He unwraps it, puts the butt into his mouth, and slowly spins it around until it is saturated.

He takes two quick puffs, throws his head back, and a flurry of halos emit from his lips before disintegrating in the air. The stale office air is now blessed with the familiar aroma of cherry wood. It always lingers long after he leaves.

"Jaw-don, let me get right to it. I'm concerned about Deanna."

Two more halos are born. "Her attendance has been going downhill and her tardiness is on the rise, not to mention Jaw-don, I think you've been covering for her."

Covering? My body braces and my brain locks. "Covering up? How so?"

His penguin-like body shakes from left to right as he prepares to sit up. Three grunts later, he is at my desk, cigar in one hand while the stubby index finger of his other pounds my blotter. "Yes, covering! How many times has she been late during the past month?"

I open my mouth to explain, but he interrupts before I can continue.

"You don't know, do you? Well, I'll tell you. She was late ten days during the past month."

Suddenly I don't feel so good. His cruelty is blatant. His mission is clear. He wants Deanna out, and there is nothing she can do to stop him. Out of anger, my eyes glaze over. "You say that you hired me because I had the same fire and drive that you did, right?"

He remains standing in front of me, staring, not wavering. "And?"

"The point is that if I see someone's behavior is becoming an issue, then I'll get that squared away. You pay me to do this. If you feel you can do it, do it yourself and send me home."

We both stand, guns drawn.

He twirls his gun around his finger. "Something's got to give, Jaw-don." He reaches the door, opens it, and slams his gun into the holster. "Now!"

Once he walks out, I collapse into the soft brown leather. I was getting of his antics of trying to do my job for me. At one point, he wants me to shine. On the flip side, he wants to tell me how to shine.

Deanna's head appears.

"Can I come back in?"

"I'd better come out there. Don't know when the boss will try to be the boss," I say. I walk out and sit in front of her desk. I sit back and watch her watch me. She is and rightfully so. As of late, her work ethic is horrible. It is clear that she doesn't know how to maintain her workload with the time she's given. The only thing presentable is the way she dresses. With everyone else on lunch, I feel it's safe to talk openly. She needs it from both angles. A friend and a boss.

"Mr. Amsterdam is watching you," I tell her.

She doesn't look surprised. "I know. He watches me all of the time." She looks up and gives a synthetic smile. "But honestly, I think he likes you."

"What?"

She smiles and nods to me and the direction that Mr. Amsterdam just left.

Inside, instant anger presses. I don't play the gay card and hate when people even refer to it.

"The way he comes in and gets that glistening in his eyes. I overheard him telling someone that you are his prized possession and without you in his life—" Her voice trails off. Her smile has more authenticity. "Just joking."

It takes me a few seconds to calm down. Obviously Deanna doesn't know that gay jokes aren't high on my list. "I know you're joking."

She changes the subject and pleads her case, "Don't you think we're meant for each other?"

Yeah, I thought. She was meant for the nuthouse. I was meant and destined for greatness. We would feed off of each other. We were meant to work together. We were meant to give off sexual energy at the workplace. We weren't meant for togetherness in any sense of the word together. My look lets her know we're not on the same page. "You're funny."

"Not funny. In love." Her mood changes to a peaceful serenity. "In love with my boss," she sings as she gets up and dances, swaying her hips from left to right. She walks near and pulls my tie. She gets closer than she needs to and teases my memory with her soft hands and eager lips. She whispers so close that her lips touch my ear. *"And* I'm fucking his boss, too." She puts her finger to my nose. "And pussy is power." Her laugh is sinister.

* * *

I imitate her voice. "And pussy is power." I flip over on my stomach and lay across the table. The masseuse, a tiny Oriental lady with a bright red kimono, tucks my towel underneath me and begins her slow massage.

"Her pussy *is* power," Tony says. He has more trouble turning over than I did. His white towel looks like a little piece of toilet paper stuck to his ass. His masseuse is an older white lady with big breasts and huge hands. He told me that he always requested someone that had some weight to them. He joked how I always loved the women with tiny hands. "They probably make you feel more adequate sexually with their tiny hands," he said.

It seems like every time we get massages at the same time, the masseuses are synchronized. We turn at the same time. My rubdown is a little longer at the end. Sasha, I call her, always rubs my thighs last. Her English is choppier when tip time comes. I think she feels that if I get an authentic Oriental off of the bus, I'll tip more. There is no difference between broken Chinese and Ebonics as long as the hands press the right way.

Tony lets out a moan as his masseuse digs into his back. "And she said she was fucking *your boss?*"

"Yeah," I answer dryly.

"Yeah. She's got it backwards, though. She's working her way down."

I laugh and comment that his jokes are not as funny as he thought. I lift myself from the table and explain how she told me about her and Mr. Amsterdam.

"She said that she met him at school and he gave her a way in. She said that he told her that he loved her style. She said she loved his drive. And then he went on to tell her all the things he could do for her as an older man. She said she told him that she didn't want a Sugar Daddy. And dig this," I pause to pull my pants up, "he said that he would give her everything she needed and all she had to do was lay with him naked."

Tony stops pulling his pants up and laughs, almost falling over. "He said all he wanted her to do was lay naked with him?"

"Yep."

Tony jumps into his pants. "You think he's impotent?"

I shrug my shoulders. "Don't know. If he is, that's his business. All long as his hand works to write my check, I'm cool."

"What about Deanna?"

"What about her?"

"You sure you can handle her?"

"Nothing to handle." I dig in my pocket and pull out a twenty. I place it on the table and tell Sasha goodbye. She smiles, quickly scoops up the money before retreating to the back. I watch Tony gather his things and walk toward the door. "You ain't tipping her?"

"The massage costs enough." He half-heartedly checks his wallet and peruses through a few crumpled bills. He unravels a five and throws it on his table. "We tip everywhere but where we should."

We walk out the door and are temporary blinded by the afternoon sun that punches our eyes as we walk out. Tony points toward the left.

"Let's grab some pizza."

We argue for a second about which pizza shop is more authentic. He loves the thick crust, and I love the thin crusted pizza with little sauce and lots of cheese. We go for the thick crust.

He finishes his thought from earlier, "How many educators do we tip?"

I don't answer, instead choosing to check my phone for missed calls.

He answers his own question. "We don't tip teachers. And they spend more quality time with us. Our kids."

"You ain't got no kids."

"I mean ours, as in our black kids."

I nod my head. It amuses me when Tony attempts to show he has been reading the local papers. He makes points, even at the most inopportune times.

He looks at me with disgust. "And look at you. Tipping the Chinese masseuse. Have you ever tipped one of Kendal's teachers for doing a great job with him?"

For once, Tony actually begins to make sense. I have never tipped anyone except people who were paid to do a service. And if I was paying for the service, then why should I tip? If they did a great job then shouldn't I just keep coming back and give them my business?

"We do pay extra for perfection," I admit. "Even though we are paying for perfection." I stop walking and acknowledge his point. I tell him that afterward, we should go to the hospital because I am starting to sound like him.

Chapter 18

Traci

"Your twelve o'clock appointment is here," Traci's secretary yells through the intercom.

Traci has been expecting Mr. Critchlow. He's a prospective parent with a high-energized three year old. He is well off and attitudinal. Traci prided herself on taking the children that no one else could. In three years, her program had received write-ups in the local paper and received accolades as one of the only day-cares in Upper Marlboro to prepare their students for kindergarten. Traci knew that education would separate her from the others.

She presses the intercom button. "Send him in."

She removes a couple scattered papers from in front of her and takes a quick sip of water. As the door opens, she stands, then falls back into her seat.

Solomon speaks casually. "Hello, Ms. Johnson."

Solomon walks into the office and takes a long look around. After fifteen seconds of nodding his head, he turns. "Not bad, Ms. Johnson. Not bad."

Traci's body aches. Her head pounds and her temples beat uncontrollably. All she can do is sit deeper into her chair and watch him walk around the office.

"Can I sit?" he asks.

She closes her eyes and rocks slightly. She silently curses herself. She takes a few deep breaths and mentally lets a few things go. "Go right ahead." She points to an empty chair that sits in front of her desk. She asks herself how she could've gotten caught up in his shit again. She decides that she will maintain what little dignity she has left. He wasn't going to affect her today. Today would be the first day of his last.

"What do you want, Solomon?"

Their eyes play an intense game of chess. No one seems to want to make the first move. It's a battle of wills. A battle of power. A battle of first love verses true love.

After a moment of silence he asks, "Does he understand you?"

Traci feels her energy turn negative. She feels pins prick her skin. She ignores his question and stares. She gives him the blank stare he hates. He hates when she zones out and pays no attention to him. In fact, he has it all wrong. She is paying attention to him. She is finding all of his little flaws so she won't be overcome by his quick wit and charm. In this instance, she stares at his shitty smirk. She hates it. His lips curl on the right side and he would laugh and throw his head back. It was his power move when he felt he was right. She stares at the little zit on the side of his mouth. Probably a fucking canker sore. Or since he talks so much shit, a few particles probably trickled to his lips. She stares at his eyes. She remembered the angry version of them when he went off. She remembered his eyes when he stared at other women in her face. She remembered how they grew wild and disoriented. They changed from burnt brown to fiery red in five seconds.

Solomon loosens his tie and folds his legs. "Does he understand you?"

Traci begins to feel herself losing control. *"What?"*

Solomon casually points to the coffee maker in the corner of her office. "Is that a fresh pot?"

Traci looks at the coffee and can't believe that he talks as though they are best friends coming together after a summer apart.

She musters up a silent yes.

He gets up, strolls to the corner, and fixes himself a cup of coffee. He turns to her and asks, "You still take yours two creams and four Equals?" He knows she did. He sees the Equals. He also knows she doesn't want to let him know that he did anything right.

Her silent answer is vocalized.

He returns to his seat and hands her a cup of coffee. "Just in case you did still take it like that." He was cocky *and* observant.

She hated both. It was a deadly combination.

"How are we going to do this?" he asks. *Sip.*

Traci stares at her cup of coffee. She had just made the pot and needed some badly. She doesn't want to drink anything that he brought her. It's her coffee, she convinces herself.

Sip. She exhales.

He watches her perfunctory reaction to his gesture. He passes yet another test he takes. He knows from her exhale that remembrance isn't usual. Another thing Gordon doesn't do.

"What do you want?"

"I want us to make this happen." Pause. "For Indigo."

"Really? For Indigo?"

Solomon's a bastard, Traci thinks. None of this is for Indigo. Well, maybe a piece is for her, but the rest is for him. He wants her back and she wants absolutely no parts of him. Last night she cried because she didn't feel a strong connection between her and her daughter. Solomon came out of the blue and showed up with a picture hoping it would bring her back to him. Part of the lack of connection with her daughter had to be that Indigo was connected to him. She was part of a package deal and it's hard for her to come to grips with moving back to a place she didn't want to be.

"I want to see her."

Solomon stops sipping. He puts his cup on the ground and inches closer. "You want to see who?"

"My daughter."

"No. You want to see *my daughter.*" He relaxes, picks up his cup and sits back. *Sip. Sip.* His tone is condescending. "You gave up the rights to *your daughter.*"

Traci begins to fight the two sides within her. A year after she gave up her rights, she went regularly to a psychiatrist. She beat herself up mentally. Destroyed her own self-worth. Almost ended up with a backwards white jacket in a solid white room. She tried to contact Solomon, but he wanted no parts of a part-time mother. He wanted no parts of someone casually entering and leaving *his daughter's* life. She tried to put the shoe on the other foot, but that only made her feel like shit about her own self. Mothers all over had learned how to juggle career, marriage, and kids. All those mothers didn't have to deal with Solomon Pernell Jackson.

He spit his words out. "How bad do you want to see her?"

Traci presses the intercom and tells her secretary to hold all of her calls. She pauses and whispers, "Yes, even his call." With that said, both knew they were getting down to business. Traci would see where she was emotionally with the whole situation.

She speaks confidently, "I want to see her."

Sip. "And what are you prepared to do to see her?" he asks.

Her voice is businesslike, "What do you want Solomon?"

"I want you to come out with us. Your visit would have to be supervised by myself, and then you would stay with us for the night."

"I can't do that!"

His voice remains calm. "You are in no position to tell me what you can and can't do." He stands and walks toward the window. "Let me tell you what you're in position to do." He turns around and counts on his fingers. "One. You're in position to do what I ask. *You* gave up custody. *You*, legally have no rights. If I don't ever want you to see her, then you don't. Won't. But, on the other hand, if you were compliant, then we could possibly do some things."

She holds her position. "I don't agree to anything without a guarantee."

He laughs "What guarantee?" He speaks slowly, walking toward her. "What could I possibly guarantee you?"

She backs up in her seat. "You could guarantee me that I will see her."

He sits on the edge of her desk. "Show some good faith."

She plays his game. She warms and attempts to combat evil with niceness. "And what is good faith?"

He puts his hands on hers. "Spend the night with us." His tone warms. "No sex. Just spend the night with us."

"And why is me spending the night so important?"

"Indy needs to see some solidarity."

Traci grips her cup tight. "Solidarity?" Her voice rises. Anger hits instantly. "Fucking *solidarity?* Are you out of your mind?"

Still leaning on her desk, he acknowledges her anger with a lick of his lips. He backs away and sits back in his seat. He shakes himself out of his brown blazer. His smile is seedy. "I may be out of my mind, but that's not up for you to judge." He smacks her desk hard with his hand. He almost hits hers in the process. "Is it?"

Traci knows he wants to bring her to his level. She won't allow it. She remembers more yoga. Does a few mental exercises and deals with his demons. She controls a few of hers in the process.

"I'm not spending the night," she declares.

"I'm leaving this weekend." He stands and finishes his coffee. "And I kid you not, I will *never be back*. This is your only opportunity to make it happen." He walks to the door and grabd the handle. "We will expect you around eight o'clock Friday. That gives you two days to tell Gordon the deal." He opens the door and walks out.

Traci's trembling hand picks up the phone to call Jordan.

Chapter 19

Jordan

"Dad?"

Shit! My puffy red eyes widen as I search in vain for Halle. Only seconds ago, her beautiful, bronze tits bounced in my face as I gripped her ass.

"Dad?"

I close my eyes and her face flickers in the dark as I wait for her to appear again. Two more screams from Kendal, and Halle is gone for good.

"What?"

"Traci just called. She said it was important."

I don't budge. A vacation is meant for me to sleep as long as I want.

He continues his interruption of my sleep. "You guys getting married or something?"

I bark back out of irritation. "No. Nobody's getting married."

He brushes my comment aside and moves to the next subject. "You promised to take me to the YMCA today."

I growl, swing my feet to the edge, and ease them into my grandfather slippers.

By the time I get dressed and walk into the kitchen, he is already rustling through the cereal boxes.

"You cooking?" I ask.

"Nope." He holds up a box of cereal. "I can make you a side of nada," he jokes. "If you don't want that, there's a bowl with cereal in it on the table."

His sense of humor warms me. It surprises me at how much he was beginning to turn out like his old man instead of his mother. Serene didn't have a sense of humor and never encouraged his crazy antics, so he suppressed them when he was with her, and became rigid like her. But with each passing hour with me, he seems to be coming into his own. His natural bubbling personality is starting to take over the withdrawn young man I picked up from the bus station.

I sit down and wiggle my bowl of dry flakes. "What happened to the Frosted Flakes?"

"We ran out, so I fixed you some Corn Flakes."

I lean over and look into his bowl. "Are you eating Corn Flakes, too?"

"Nope. There's frost on my flakes. There was only a few left and I figured we both shouldn't have to suffer."

"You got me," I tell him. I dip my spoon into my dry bowl of Corn Flakes. "Where's the milk?"

He smirks. "There was only a little bit left and you had so many Corn Flakes that I didn't want to spoil your breakfast with it." He points toward the counter near the sink. "I opened a can of Carnation Milk so you can enjoy a full bowl of cereal." He starts nosily munching on his. "Or I'll be finished in a minute, then you can use the rest of my milk. And Mom lies; I don't back-wash."

*　　*　　*

Another drive with Kendal means more tape popping, more music switching, and more hearing loss. I don't usually play ball on Wednesdays due to work, but Kendal was eager to play, and I was just as eager to show him who was still king. I called Tony and invited him to join us. He said he would stop by after twelve. He had an early appointment with some lady who worked for the president. I didn't bother to ask.

We stopped at the store and picked up a few bottles of Gatorade before heading to the YMCA. When we arrive, there are two basketball games going on. The really old men play farthest away, while the younger crowd played at the court near the door.

"Which court do you want to play on?" I ask.

Kendal looks at both sides for a second before letting out a distraught sigh. "It doesn't matter. I really wanted to play you in some one-on-one."

"We don't have to stay here."

"Where's the closest park?"

"It's downtown. It'll take us about forty minutes to get to, but if we go now, we can play for about an hour or so before everybody gets there."

"We're here now. We might as well stay. And isn't Uncle Tony coming?"

"Yeah."

Kendal grabs the ball and yells, "I'm going over there and warm up. You can stay and stretch before you pull a hamstring. If you need to score any hoops, call me over and I'll save you."

I put my bags down and stretch, I watch a few minutes of the game while I work my groin area. When they finish, I saunter toward a few of the players that are getting ready to play.

An older black man with tiny red shorts and thick green goggles says, "We need one. Wanna play?"

When he points to the rest of his teammates, I know we're doomed. The other three have to be over fifty and look as if they have been playing all day. I introduce myself to the rest of the guys. "You been playing for a while?" I ask.

The eldest of the tribe coughs and grabs his chest. "This is our first game. We'll be leaning on you to carry us to the Promised Land."

It was going to be like playing against the Los Angeles Lakers with Moses, Methuselah, Jonah, and Job on my team. I knew that it was going to be a workout that was welcomed, but not expected.

The team we're playing looks at us, smiling confidently. One guy I played against last summer looks at me and shouts, "Watch out for his jumper. We can let the other guys shoot."

They check the ball in and tell us that we were going to play to eleven.

After ten minutes of running and sweating, we are losing seven to two. We look like crap. I look over at the sideline and notice about ten guys waiting to play next and if we lose, we'll have to wait another hour to play again.

The big guy on their team misses a shot and I grab the rebound. I dribble the ball up court and scoot past a defender while another flails at the ball wildly. I dribble between my legs and past another before spotting Moses under the hoop. I throw the ball behind my back and Moses catches it and throws a wild hook shot toward the rim. Their big man jumps in the air to block it, but Moses has lofted the ball high in the air, and seconds later, it comes swooshing through the hoop. The hecklers on the sideline whoop and holler as we run back down court. Score is now seven to three. Three more bad shots by the other team, one jump shot by me, two lucky shots by Jonah, and we are in the game. Score is now seven to six. While they score the next two points, my old Bible members are running out of steam. I purposely throw the ball out of bounds to get them some well-needed rest.

"You can get 'em, Dad."

I turn around and see Kendal on the sideline cheering us on. While someone retrieves the ball, Kendal throws me my Gatorade. The cold drink cools my temperature and replenishes what little energy I have left.

We score the next two points, and the score is now nine to eight and we were still losing. The heat in the gym continues to beat down and sap our energy. We have possession of the ball and need the next point to tie the game. I get the ball at the foul line, fake like I'm taking a shot and get their chubby player in the air before driving to the hoop for an uncontested lay-up. Nine to nine.

"We ain't letting these old men beat us," the feisty young one with the large Afro pipes.

I let out a sarcastic chuckle and prod the elders on. We trade baskets during the next three minutes, making the score tied at ten apiece. The heat takes even more precious energy from our aged bodies. The crew of guys on the sideline maintain their heckling as our younger opponents feel us wearing down. The chubby one fakes Methuselah and has a clear lane to drive in for the lay-up, but decides to take a fifteen-foot jump shot. The ball circles the rim before spinning out. Job grabs the rebound and is fouled hard by Feisty Afro.

Feisty Afro stands over Job and yells, "Get up, old man. I didn't hit you that hard."

Job clutches his ankle and spins over before letting out a loud groan. Jonah sprints toward Job and ties his sneakers tightly to avoid further damage to his ankle. Feisty Afro looks at me and slides me a slick grin. "You gotta pick one from the side."

Before I could select the tall guy that stands on the side, Kendal steps forward and says, "I got a basket for you, Dad."

A year ago, he wouldn't have wanted to play, but now his confidence is high. It's a beautiful sight.

I dribble the ball at the foul line and look Feisty Afro directly in his eyes. "I'm about to take you to school."

"Nigga, please!"

I dribble and throw the ball over his head. He spins around to intercept my pass, only to find that I never let it go. He turns around with a look of bewilderment as I throw it off of his head and catch it. Before he realizes what I did, I am on my way to the basket. As their big man rushes toward me, I give Kendal a head nod and I loft the basketball toward the hoop. Kendal leaps high in the air, catching the ball. He keeps rising with the ball and slams it through the hoop with authority. The sidelines go crazy as Feisty Afro rips his shirt off and storms off the court.

"Your son sure did save your ass," Tony yells.

I turn around and see Tony hugging and congratulating Kendal.

I point at the elders and correct him, "I saved their asses is what you meant to say." On the sideline, Job continues to nurse his swollen ankle as the others crowd him, reveling in what appears to be their only moment of glory at this court. By the round of applause they receive from the hecklers; winning really doesn't come easy for them.

Kendal runs toward me, grinning from ear to ear. Enthusiastically he asks, "How'd you like my dunk?"

I admit I was very impressed, but we had more work to do on the court. I hoped at least one of my prehistoric teammates would quit. My teammates didn't seem like much, but they put up a hell of a fight. We prepare ourselves for the next battle.

Tony says he'll watch some of the game before he leaves to take care of some business. "You got your hands full this game," he says.

I quickly size up the four guys that walk on the court. The leader of the pack is a new guy that stands all of five feet, five inches. He has on long red shorts and a white T-shirt with white tube socks that reach his kneecaps.

My team assembles at the free throw line and matches up against the people opposite of them. They're one short.

I tell Tube Socks he has to get another guy.

"He's coming in a second," he grunts.

Aware that it is only getting hotter in the gym, Jonah complains that it's time to get the game started. He tells them to pick someone off the sidelines until their savior came to help them out. I shoot Jonah a cold stare. It's always the ones that have no game that initiate all the shit.

Tube Socks looks in the direction of the hallway stairs and shouts, "Here comes our fifth man."

Methuselah adjusts his weathered basketball jersey, taps me on the shoulder, and displays a worried look. He points toward the door and utters, "We got our work cut out for us. I used to play against that guy in a league down in D.C."

I turn around. For a second, everything goes deathly still. I do a double take. I look over at Tony as he casually converses with a few hecklers while Kendal stretches for the next game.

Tube Socks greets their savior as if he is the next Jesus. "What's up, Solomon?"

Solomon throws his jacket to the side and greets the rest of his teammates. "What's up, fellas?"

Tube Socks informs him, "What's up is that we almost had to pick up a guy from the sideline. You bring your game?"

Solomon jumps up and touches the rim with ease. "Your mother still have teeth?"

"Enough of the chitchat," Moses yells. He points at me and continues to scream, "We don't care who you got because my man right here is going to give you more than you bargained for."

Solomon quickly looks in my direction and does a similar double take. He steps back and sizes me up before checking out his surroundings. He's preparing for something.

All of his teammates jump in front of the four players on my team, which leaves Solomon in front of me. He attempts to impose his size and will with an intense glare. No one knows or understands the magnitude of the match-up that's about to take place. He stands at six feet, seven while I am five inches shorter. He is muscular, but thin, while I have a more natural weight and thickness going for me. I know I have an advantage, which is Traci. He wants what I have. With his confidence brimming, I start to wonder whether I have what he doesn't want. Either way, I am ready to force my presence on him.

He checks the ball and throws me an underhanded smirk. "Didn't know you played ball, Poet!"

I look at him with a haughty stare that chops him down a few inches. "Didn't know you enjoy being strangled."

Instinct tells me to run up on him and bash his head in right there, but Kendal is next to me, and I definitely don't want any trouble while he's there. I put the beef on the back burner and decide to make the best of the bad situation.

For the next ten minutes we go back and forth. Solomon is better than I thought, but nothing I can't handle. When he scores, the hecklers let me have it. With Tony watching the onslaught, I decide to step my game up another level. My teammates aren't doing so well against the stronger players. Even Kendal is having trouble guarding the speedier Tube Sock.

I check the ball in. "What's the score?"

Solomon wipes his bald-head clean and rubs his sweat on the ball before hurling it directly toward my chest. "Seven to three, Poet!"

I catch the ball before it knocks the wind out of me. "Been lifting, huh?" I heave the ball back at his chest with the same force.

He catches it and his mouth curled into another sly grin. "Don't have to lift for you guys." He bounces the ball three times and tucks it underneath his arm. "Put your money where your mouth is, Poet?"

He was putting me in a position where I had to defend my manhood, my integrity, and myself. I look at Moses, who was doubling over and grabbing on his shorts, then at Methuselah, who was leaning against the wall, and realized I couldn't do it with them. While I assess the situation, Solomon assemble his teammates together to talk.

Tony walks over. "Damn, Styles. I told you that you were going to have your hands full. What's the hold up?"

I nod toward Solomon. "Homeboy wants to play for some money. I know we can take these guys."

Tony peeks around me, looks at my teammates, and shakes his head. "Not with them dead ass dinosaurs. And not to mention, homeboy is eating your ass alive out there."

Tony didn't hesitate to throw salt in my wound. "He ain't eating me alive. He's only got two baskets and I've made all three of ours."

"What you gonna do, Poet? We playing or what?" Solomon yells.

The hecklers become restless. I need more time to make this decision and the prehistoric dinosaurs need more time to heal.

I make an executive decision based on pride. "Let's do it for twenty-five!"

Solomon chuckles as though I mean twenty-five cents. "Twenty-five? I wouldn't play hard for twenty-five. What about a buck?"

I knew one hundred dollars was a lot and it probably wasn't a good idea, but I had pride knocking again. "Let's do it!"

Solomon dribbles the ball a few more times before letting his players know it was on.

"One more thing," I say. "We start from scratch and I get to pick my own players."

Chapter 20

Traci

Inside the living room, Kendal fidgets opposite Traci. Traci is unsure where to take the conversation. Kendal, aware of the thick cloud of boredom that lingers above their heads, grabs the remote and turns the channel.

"You watch Springer?" he asks.

She wrinkles her nose and shakes her head.

Just as he reaches to change the channel, she interjects, "I don't mind though."

Jerry Springer looks into camera and smiles, "Today's show is about women that can't let go." Kendal quickly finds the remote and they watch Emeril cook up a Curried Shrimp dish.

During a commercial, Kendal blurts, "I make my own decisions."

Traci's brow furrows.

Kendal notices her look and repeats, "I make my own decisions."

"Oh. OK." Traci has no clue what he's talking about.

Kendal jumps up and walks toward the kitchen.

"Want something to drink? We have soda, cranberry juice, orange juice, and water."

"I'll have cranberry juice."

Kendal disappears into the hallway. A minute later he emerges with a tall glass of juice and sits across from her, tapping his foot nervously.

"What were you just talking about, if you don't mind me asking?"

His mouth twists like his father's as he searches for the right words. "My mother said a lot of things about you and my father," he confesses, "but I'm old enough to make my own decisions."

Traci's soul warms. She needed to hear that. She gives him a hug. "Thank you, Kendal."

The front door handle trembles. A combination of the heat and uncertainty causes a bead of sweat to glide down her forehead. The past year flashes before her eyes. The trembling of the door conjures up feelings and many emotions that lay dormant. While her passion races to greet him, her feet remain idle. She always maintains total control of her life, but her heart did its own thing. She knows she has things to talk about. She needs to be upfront about everything. It's do or die.

The lock clicks and the door swings open. Traci hears the rustling of plastic bags and then watches Jordan slip into the kitchen without noticing her.

Kendal leaps from his seat and disappears into the back, leaving Traci to sit nervously and watch the paint dry on the walls.

In the kitchen Jordan rustles bags and slams cabinets. He yells, "Kendal, you hungry?"

"No!" A few seconds pass. "Dad?" Pause. "Traci's in the living room."

The cabinets quiet, the bags rest comfortably against

the linoleum, and everything in the house remains hushed. Traci thinks about going into the kitchen, but decides against it. She doesn't want to wear out her welcome before she even gets a chance to speak.

Jordan takes a few deep breaths and clears his throat. Traci pushes herself to a standing position and takes slow calculated steps toward the kitchen.

She calls softly, "Jordan?"

Silence answers.

"Jordan?"

He responds weakly, "I'm in the kitchen."

Traci proceeds to the kitchen cautiously, not knowing what to expect. She inhales long winds of dry air before turning the corner.

She forces a grin and walks into the kitchen. "I was just stopping by to see—" Her voice trails off and her brows draw together in an agonized expression. A muscle in her jaw quiveres. Her steps are dawdling as she approaches. "What happened?"

An unspoken pain is alive and glowing in his swollen blue-black left eye. "Nothing," he replies nonchalantly, leaning on the opened refrigerator door.

"Are you sure? Did you go to the doctor?"

He forces a grin of his own. "Just a little war injury."

"What happened?"

After putting the remaining items into the refrigerator, he leans against the counter. "I was playing basketball earlier and got elbowed."

She moves closer and her fingers lightly traces the swell of his eye. "Did the guy at least apologize?"

Jordan snatches his face away. "I'd rather not talk about it."

Traci gives a curt nod and follows him to the living room. Jordan puts on a jazz CD, throws his head back against the black leather couch, and blows exasperation into the air.

Traci doesn't know what to do. She doesn't know whether to explain to him what transpired with her and Solomon or to just live for the moment. The only thing wrong with the moment was that it was temporary.

She sits across from him and clears her throat a few times. She excuses herself and blurts, "Solomon came by today." She watches Jordan's eyes.

He blinks. He looks everywhere but in her face.

"And what did he say?" he asks.

Traci isn't sure what to say. She decides to come semi-clean. "He wants me to go by his hotel and—"

With negativity, Jordan perks up. "And what?"

"And, um—"

"Um, what? Do you want to go?"

She fiddles with her fingers. "I feel I might need to go."

"And all he wants is for you to come and see him." Pause. "And her, I presume."

She gives him no eye contact. Jordan is asking all the right questions, and she can't come up with the right answers. She pauses between questions and stumbles with the answers. She knows he can see past her bull-shit. Or at least he should. Solomon could easily pick up on her wrongdoings.

She answers, "He wants me to come and see him at his hotel. And she'll be there." She smiles at the end of the sentence like it makes her statement valid.

"He didn't make any other request?"

Traci is getting more agitated because she lacks the strength to tell him what really transpired. She grows tired of the little game her and Jordan play with infor-mation. She wants to get up and shout everything she ever thought. She wants to tell him what she felt for him and Solomon *and Indigo.* Something keeps her silent. She opens her mouth and speaks for her daughter.

She huffs. "He said he loves me. Said he wants me to be a part of his life. Now." Pause. "And forever."

Jordan looks dumbfounded.

She continues, "He said that if I didn't go, I would never see my daughter again. He wants me to get back with him. To marry him."

"And what else?" he asks.

"You mean sex?"

"Of course."

Traci is angered by the reference. She spits, "Yeah. I bet he does. He wants to fuck me tonight. I know him. Sad thing is that he knows me too. Knows that I would do incredible shit for an incredible moment." Pause. "And this is an incredible moment." She continues to stare at Jordan, who continues to look in another direction. "I am going to see her." She grabs Jordan's hand and comforts him. "No matter what?"

He finally looks into her eyes. "No matter what?"

Traci grips his hand tighter. "No matter what!"

"At the cost of us?"

A tear slithers down her cheek. She shakes her head. "At the cost of me."

Jordan yanks his hand away. "And what about me?"

She points to the back room where Kendal remained. "You're in there."

"Part of me is in there. I'm right here," he says. He stands and points to himself. Emotion has taken over and his voice gets shaky. "Part of me is in front of me."

She shakes her head and corrects him. "No. That is all of you. Parenting isn't part-time. He is someone you created. Someone you and Serene created." Emotions gets the best of her and tears burst. "And you wouldn't do anything for him?"

He tries to grab her hand and pull her back to the couch. He isn't quite sure how to calm her storm. Never seeing her in this situation, he is completely lost.

"I would do everything for him," he shouts.

"And why would I do anything less?"

Jordan's head falls. He begins to understand her words and feel her pain. "You shouldn't do anything less. But—"

She screams, "But what? But I shouldn't go? But I shouldn't try? Maybe I should just say *fuck it* and let him leave."

Jordan stands and brings her to him and instead of her falling into his arms, she fights. "Don't do this. Not like this. There's other ways."

She breaks away. "What other ways? Do you not understand that I signed papers and I have no say in anything?" She begins to tremble with fear of never seeing her daughter. She gags like she's about to throw up. "He can walk away."

Jordan watches her heave and does nothing.

"Could you walk away?" she asks.

Jordan voice elevates. "I couldn't walk away! I could never not see my child again. I could *never* understand what you're going through, but I can understand that I love you and it's hard to let you walk anywhere by yourself."

She knows she's taking anger and resentment of Solomon out on him, but he is opposing and not helping. She needs him to understand and support. He is fighting, and she's tired of fighting.

She wishes he would think more realistically. She is angered by his inability to understand without further explanation. Her tone screams resentment. "And you think going with me would be helpful?"

"It might help," he answers.

"And it might not. What are you afraid of, Jordan?"

He remains silent. Exhausted, he slumps to the couch. "I'm not afraid of anything."

"Well, if you're not afraid, then please help and support my decision." She revisits his past. "Remember you told me of the things you had to do to keep the peace with Kendal's mother?" She quiets down, realizing Kendal is still in the house. "Remember how you said that you sometimes had to *service her* to hold it down?" Pause. "And you didn't want her. You told me how you hated her guts, but the sex straightened her ass right up." She throws a tantrum without stomping. Her voice is satanic. "Respect my decision. Fucking learn to coddle, embrace, and under*fuckingstand my decision.*" She's losing control of the conversation and doesn't know how to regain composure.

He shakes his head in disbelief. It was something scripted from a bad movie. He hates his part. Her part isn't right either.

"I understand what you're trying to say, but I don't understand why you have to do it," he says. He tries to calm her with reason. He doesn't see that reason is not reachable. He goes the wrong way. "I'm a guy. I know how to fuck and keep the feelings away. I've been doing this for some time now. You ain't built for this."

"And you are?"

"Not anymore."

"I need you to understand," she pleads softly. "I gotta go."

"I can't understand!" He grabs his head and massages his temples. "I can't understand. I don't want my conscience to get the best of me. If he lays a finger on you, I don't think I can understand."

"I need you to understand."

Kendal walks out. He stops short of the living room and tells them that he's going out to play. Traci and Jordan stop talking and wait for his exit. Kendal looks at them with concern and asks if they need something while he's out. They decline. What they need can't be taken care of by him.

As soon as he walks out, Traci continues, "Please understand me."

"I'm trying like hell."

"I need an answer. A truthful answer." Pause. Her words stagger drunkenly. "If I go, will you stay?"

A laugh if followed by a slow movement of his head. Disbelief. Despise. "I don't know."

"I have to go."

"I can't promise anything." Pause. "I can tell you that I'll try like hell to believe in you, but I don't know how far the belief will take me."

She walks over to him and gives him a hug. She has more courage than before, but still not enough to conquer all that is to be conquered. "Thanks for trying," she says.

"I'll try," was all he can muster. He tries to secure her in his weakened hug.

"That's all I need to hear," she says. She tries to snap out of her mood, but it was now ingrained. She wants to rush out and leave well enough alone, but she is sure he won't let her off so easily.

He breaks off the embrace. "When is this to take place?"

"Friday."

"Where?"

Traci sits down next to Jordan and puts her hands on his legs. Her rub is not normal. She strokes his leg out of guilt. "At the hotel."

Jordan gathers power and doesn't let her off so easily this time. He asks, "What if he wants to resolve things by sleeping with you?"

Traci remains silent. She doesn't want to answer, but this is her time to let it all out. She'll be as truthful as she's ever been. "If he wants sex, then I'll give it to him. I might have to do what I do for the sake of something." Her head falls again. "Haven't you ever felt you had to do something you didn't want to for love?" She whispers, "For love?"

Jordan hears what he doesn't want to hear, but knows it was coming. He answers, "I'm not sure I can get past that, but if that's what you gotta do, then I can't stop you."

Traci knows it's a chance she is going to take with or without him in her corner.

Chapter 21

Jordan

It is Thursday and one more day remains. Nothing seems right. My boss was sexing the help. The help was trying to help himself to me. My woman's ex was causing a whole lot of havoc. And Traci and I weren't seeing eye to eye.

Mr. Amsterdam pokes his head in my office as I day-dream about everything but my life.

"Jaw-don, I need to speak to you. Got a second?"

My pen falls. "Sure, Mr. Amsterdam. I've got a second."

He waddles in and sits in front of me, eyeing me suspiciously. His floral tie falls short of matching anything he wears. He unravels a cigar from his pocket and begins wetting the butt of it. I say nothing, instead choosing to wait for him to speak. I'm not offering conversation to anyone.

As he speaks, the fragrance of scotch tickles the air. It will soon be met with the sweet melody of a good cigar. It stinks to me. "It's time to make some changes," he says. His feet find the edge of my desk. He lights his cigar and decorates the room with disintegrating grey rings. They rise to the wall and break apart. Mr. Amsterdam seems to take pride in making the perfect halo. He always admires them once they leave his mouth.

I sip my coffee and watch his feet wiggle from left to right on my desk. I remove a computer printout from underneath his soles and ask, "A change with what?"

"My niece." He watches me through his microscope. He wants to see what I'll do or how I'll react when he mentions her.

"Oh."

His feet hit the ground with a thud as he continues to smoke like a chimney. "All you say is *oh?*"

"With all due respect, sir," I begin. "What can I say? It's *your* niece and *your* business. It's not up to me what goes down."

"Aren't you the slightest bit curious?"

"Once again sir, it's—"

"I know, I know. It's not your business." He flicks his ashes on the corner of my desk. I cringe. I want to get up and punch him in his fat fucking mouth, but I don't. I remain calm, cool, and collected. He was about to test my patience. "I'm more concerned about you," he says.

I shoot him a surprised look. *"Me?"*

"Yeah, you." He scoots to the edge of his seat and points at me with his finger with the cigar stuck in it. "She's told me of some inappropriate behavior involving you two."

I laugh. He's absurd. He has some wrong facts, and I am just the man to correct him. I stand up and pull my suit jacket off. I walk around my desk and sit on the edge. I look down and talk even lower. *"Inappropriate behavior?* You gotta fill me in on this one, sir."

His expensive silver lighter blazes and eases his face

to it. After birthing more circles, he starts with animosity, "Inappropriate like having a staff member at your house."

My stomach roils. I cough out of embarrassment. *Shit!* "M-m-my house?"

He recites my address, smokes more cigar and tells me the layout of my living room. I listen intently. I can't deny it if I wanted to. I quickly think about Deanna and want to run into the other room and kick her ass. I don't hit women, but I will definitely shake the shit out of her. She ain't right in the head. I saw her popping pills on several occasions. At first I thought they were medication, but maybe not. My eyes roll when he asks if the layout of my living room was correct.

"I guess so."

"No time for guessing, Jaw-don. Is it correct?"

I hate him. "It is correct."

"And why was she at your house?"

I have to come clean. Covering up for her did nothing for my job security. I shake my head and think that if he wants what I know, I would give it to him, but on my terms. It's time to have fun with the old man. I just hopes he can keep up. "She said was having problems with her man," I say.

A halo gets caught up in his throat. He hacks. I temporarily lose my memory about CPR. "Problems? Man?" he asks nervously.

I gain confidence and the upper hand with knowledge he needs. I can see him scrutinize my every move. My movement will be vaulted. He wants to know what I know. I won't give him the inside information. I'll hold onto something. "She said she was having problems with her man," I say. "And she told me what they were."

His interest is piqued. I have him chasing the cheese.

His voice is uneasy. "What were the problems, if you don't mind me asking?"

More chuckles erupt inside. "That's the one thing I've always liked about you, Mr. Amsterdam."

He puts his cigar out. "What's that?"

"I like that you care enough about your staff to want to know what's going on with them. Not many bosses go that far."

"W-w-well, I go pretty far," he says.

"Oh, I'm sure you do," I mumble. "Anyway, she told me that her boyfriend was having—" Pause. I scratch my head and snap my fingers to jar my memory. "He was having trouble because he was not well endowed."

Mr. Amsterdam's white skin turned cherry red. He doesn't look my direction for quite a few seconds.

I move my head in his direction, searching desperately for eye contact. His baby blues are elusive. "Fucked up, ain't it?" I say.

He peeks at me out of the corner of his eye. "S-s-she divulged that?"

"Sure did. And a host of other things. That's why I'm surprised she didn't mention any of that. Funny how people only reveal what they want to."

Mr. Amsterdam agrees. He adds nothing.

"So, what do you think I should've done?" I ask. "Being that I'm just like you." Pause. "Caring and all. It's tough not to answer the call of someone in need."

Mr. Amsterdam is becoming more and more uncomfortable. I want him to leave humiliated.

"So, Mr. Amsterdam, if you think I was inappropriate because she came to my house to talk about her man and his little problem," I pause and hold my finger to display a little penis. "Then I was inappropriate."

He shuffles to his feet. "I-I-I can understand your position." He saunters toward the door. He grabs the handle and tells me that he will speak to me about the remaining reasons she is leaving the establishment.

I give him an underhanded smirk. "As a matter of fact, she said that he was short and stubby. Kinda like the cigar you're smoking now."

He disappears in a cloud of smoke.

I wonder what her angle is. At this point I don't care what it was as long as it doesn't include me. I open my door and can see Mr. Amsterdam walking out in a huff. Deanna remains at her post pouting and looking at the screen.

"I need to see you, now!" I bark. I can see her taking deep inhales in an attempt to get herself together. I leave my door open and wait.

She bounces into the office as though nothing ever happened. She sits down, smiles and whips out her paper and pad. "I've got a ton of work to do. Where shall we start?" she asks.

I play her game. My oration is believable. "Dear Dr. Peterson." Pause. She jots the information down enthusiastically. I continue, "I am writing to inform you that we need your help." Pause. *Sip.* "I have a worker who will be coming to your office for a psychological evaluation." Her pen movement isn't as zesty as it had been. I continue, "She has been suffering from mood swings and severe cases of amnesia. She has also made up stories to appease others and is effectively causing mayhem at everyone's disposal but her own." Deanna's pen falls to the tablet. Her head remains bowed. I finish, "I believe she is suffering from a bad case of something that I cannot put my finger on. She is cheerful one day and a moody bitch on others." Deanna's chest puffs out as she holds her emotions in. I continue, "I think she's having a personal relationship with a higher-up official in the organization. She tries to perpetrate as though she is not, but I have reason to believe that there is more to her story than she lets on." I watch a tear fall in slow motion from her eye to the paper. My heart is impervious. I continue, "I humbly request your service because I cannot sit and watch the decline of a woman who seems to have it all, but doesn't realize she is showing negative behaviors that affect people's lives and will in turn affect hers."

Deanna looks up, her makeup running down her cheeks, and forces a smile. "I'm sorry."

My head movement shows disproval. Sorry isn't good enough. This is my job. My life. My career, and I wasn't about to let someone who never had shit come in and piss on my territory. I was beginning to realize that she wanted to fuck with whomever was on top. Traci would've said that she knew that from the start. I had to find things out for myself.

"Sorry ain't good enough." I remain calm. My voice is no louder than a whisper. "Why?"

"Because I-" Her words fade.

"Because you what?" I can't hold my tone in anymore. The bitch came out. My octave rose. "Because you what?" Pause. "Do you know that my boss just came in here and told me that he knew my *secretary* was over my house?" I put my ear towards her. "Do you know that I can get fired for some stupid shit like that?"

"I'm sorry," she wails.

Tears of stupidity have no affect. "None of this, I'm sorry crap. You put everything I've worked for in jeopardy."

Her head rises slowly. Her voice is deeper and slower. "Don't-do-this-to-me."

"Do what?"

She speaks slower. "Please-don't-do-this-to-me."

"You are doing it to yourself." I point in her direction. "You! Not me."

She starts to panic when my anger doesn't subside. Her hands start shaking and trembling. She stands, paces, and wiggles her fingers while she bounces around. I had never seen her go into this zone. I figure it's all an act.

"Too late to shake now. Finish taking dictation," I snap.

She stops and whirls around. Her voice seems dug up from a grave. "No."

My laugh incites more anger. I present her seat to her as though she had just walked in for the first time. "Have a seat."

She turns her head. "I said, no!" Her tears are dry. She shows psychotic behavior I hadn't seen prescription for. I dealt with a crazy chick or two in my day, but they were easily handled.

I figured it was in my best interest to slow my roll. "You can forget about the dictation."

Her hands are still shaking as she put her hands to her face and runs out of the office yelling, "I told you not to fuck with me!"

It amazes me how people crossed paths and don't know the path the other had just come off. I talked to Deanna and hadn't realized that maybe she had mental health issues. I put my job in jeopardy all for some cute conversation and support when my girl wasn't acting right. At the very least, I knew what Traci was bringing to the table. She knew most of my past and I didn't have to spend time wondering if she was going to accept me. With every new person I met, I had to sell myself. I presented my situation. I gave them my energy. I dug into their past. And then I made a choice. Deanna was cute. Sexy. Inspiring. Funny. And crazy as all hell. The 'crazy' put everything into perspective. The one thing that had me whirling about Traci was that I thought I knew her past. I thought I knew what she was all about. This Solomon situation altered my outlook on her. What started out as a temperamental woman with great judgment and a hard work ethic turned into a woman who held secrets and bypassed truth. The only thing that made it difficult to judge was that I couldn't remember if I *ever* asked her if she had kids. It was an assumption. She said she wanted one. I couldn't recall if she said she *always* wanted one. Either way, I felt duped.

I needed to feel better about something, so I figured I'd better stay close to the situation.

Traci picks up on the third ring. "Hey Traci."

"Hi." Pause. "Listen, Jordan. About the—"

"I didn't call for that."

Happily, she let her thought go. I can tell she doesn't want to speak on it, but the fact that she is going to is enough for me to let her go . . . today.

I continue, "I called to make sure you were doing OK. How's the day going?"

"Fine. I guess." Pause. "I changed the day," she blurts.

"What?" I know what she means, but I wasn't prepared to talk about it. Wasn't prepared to find out more information that might cause me to shut down completely. I want to know, but not everything. Just enough was just enough to keep me on her team. At one point I felt my anger was selfish. On the flip side, why shouldn't I be angry? I was tired of playing devil's advocate.

"I changed the day," she repeats. I can hear her tone weaken. "I couldn't take waiting another day. And something in me is telling me to go now. I want to thank you for at least being able to talk about it with me." She sniffles and blows her nose.

I can tell she's been crying, and, knowing her, praying over the decision. I don't want to add to her problems. I have to take one on the chin. I gather strength for her. "Not a problem. Anything for you," I tell her. Actually it was anything but more of this drama that I can't control. This situation is stifling my growth. I feel like I can't move forward with life until I find out what the issues are. *My life* is on hold for her life. *She shouldn't have this much control over mine.*

At the same point, I feel that I can show just a little more compassion. It is her child. And no matter how disturbed Solomon is, he holds a position in her life and I have to accept it or walk. Something in me is not ready to walk away. I just don't know if I'm hanging around to find out the truth before making my decision. Either way, I am here. And so is she.

"What time are you going?" I ask.

"I haven't made that choice yet. I'm trying to deal with one choice at a time."

"Take your time. Do you need anything?"

"I need for you to tell me that every thing is going to be OK."

I wish I can tell her that sincerely. I can't. I tell her anyway. Her laugh seems genuine when she expresses a desire to see me. I don't know if it's a good idea. She doesn't need any distraction from me so I tell her that I'm busy.

"I've got to take Kendal to an appointment," I tell her. I explain that there was a pain shooting through his leg every time he jumps.

For the next five minutes we share small talk. She

talks about the lunch from hell that the Chinese man delivered. I speak about needing to eat better. My cholesterol was on the rise, and I still tried to find ways to trick myself into drinking water. I hate the taste and need something to jazz it up. It feels like the beginning to the end. I see our paths widen and go in opposite directions. I need stability. She seems to feed off of chaos. I know where I'm going. She has no clue. I want to stay for the long haul. She doesn't know about any haul.

It isn't until she utters something about a girl at another daycare who had almost lost her life, that I realize the severity of her dilemma. Kendal almost lost his life with a high fever seizure when he was two. Sharp pains jab my heart. I thought about my fight for his life. What I would do? What I *did* do? Ran every fucking light I could to get there. When he needed me, *everyone and everything* was in my way. The long ass light on Thurgood Street. The red Subaru with the old white lady that ran out of gas a block away from his daycare. The fire hydrant at the only spot out front. The police officer who told me he would tow me. The front door at the daycare that jammed when I pushed it. The nice lady at the desk who asked me to calm down. My phone that rang and splashed the wall when it hit it out of frustration. The ambulance. The paramedic. The spoon. Serene. And my inability to do a thing. Even the good was annoying. I realized that all Traci knew was her daughter not being here and it hit me that she wasn't herself. I couldn't even imagine her trying to be herself. It made me see that her antics were merely her way to survive.

I now understood that her bizarre behavior is motherhood eating her alive. Sporadic is normal. Nothing makes sense. Her world is upside-down, and there's nothing that a shrink, a boyfriend, or anyone else can do about it. It was her fate. She'll resent me if I oppose, and kick me while I stay, because even the good is annoying. I have to grow or be gone.

"I'll be here when you get back," I say.

She pauses and gathers herself. Her voice wavers, "I may not be the same person when I return."

I knew this. "I believe that. I'm sure I'll love the woman that returns."

Chapter 22

Traci

Twice she picks up the phone, only to slam it back down. She left work early and slept for three hours, and that is where she remains. Stuck underneath the heavy, multi-colored Afghan that holds everything in. She loves her room dark, the music light with water trickling in the back.

She rolls over and snaps on the nightlight. She changes the rhythm to jazz. She doesn't need to hear words about old love, new love and unattached love. She needs sexy saxophones, filtering bass lines, and horns that are alive. Redman's sultry sax always gives her energy in the morning. Tonight won't be any different. She needs assistance with her energy. She feels more alive than she has in years, even though she knows rough times are ahead. For the first time since she can remember, she has fight. Be ready to take on the world by any means necessary. She closes her eyes and thanks God for the strength she knows didn't come by itself. She also asks him for the strength to get through the day. She needs assistance just in case she tumbles. She also thanks him for sending Jordan.

She chooses casual. The casual black skirt. Her face remains free of makeup except her lips, and her top reveals she is all woman. She rids her pocketbook of everything except her necessities. She needs ID, money and lipstick. Her phone will wait in the car. She checks the message one more time to make sure she's going to the right place.

On the answering machine, Solomon spoke slowly, "Hey. Glad you could make it. The Marriott near you. Room 112. You gotta give a little to get a little." His laugh is sinister. "I'll be expecting you at 8:15. And eat before you get here." Another sinister laugh erupts.

Chapter 23

Jordan

Thursday came quicker than expected. The twenty four hours seemed to shoot by. Mr. Amsterdam walked in as he had been the past few days. His attitude was becoming progressively worse.

This is the first time he didn't come with his celebratory cigar. His walk is still full of machismo. I entertain his authority by getting up to fix him a cup of coffee. He stops me and tells me that he has what he needs. He pulls out a flask. Solid silver with gold trimmings. He sips like he's a guy in the westerns named Billy Jack Something.

"What happened yesterday, Jaw-don?"

I rub my chin and think about the events. I wasn't into the sugar coating for anyone. I take my time and get myself a fresh cup of coffee. He watches me. I know he's pissed off that my sense of urgency doesn't match his. He'll have to wait. The attitude he shows of late shows me that he needs an adjustment, and I was just the man to give it to him. I wasn't worried about the job because knowing him, he would respect me more, the less I let him get away with.

I sit down and swing around to face the window. "What were you saying?" I kick my feet up on the window sill.

I can hear him unscrewing the top and taking another sip. He swallows hard and clears his throat.

"I said, what hap—"

"Yeah. Yeah. Yeah. I heard that part. I was wondering if you had anything different to say." I swing back around and place my mug on the desk gently. I give him all the eye contact he can handle. "Did anything happen with you two that I should know about since yesterday?"

He almost falls back in his seat. He rocks backwards just to lift himself from the chair. "I think you've got it all wrong, son." He finally stands. He shovels his flask into his suit jacket and wipes his mouth. *"You* are not here to make choices or ask questions." His fat finger pound the desk. He stands over me and grills, "Are you messing with Deanna?"

I jump up. I'm not going to be pushed around by anyone because of their insecurities. If my job performance was in question, then I would have to 'man up' and listen, learn, and apply. Deanna has nothing to do with my work. She wasn't listed on my performance evaluation.

My speech is slow and sounds rehearsed. "Does she have anything to do with my work, sir?" Pause. "If not, then I request that we not speak about her without her being present. If you want to discuss something involving her, please give me something in writing, because all of this barging in and making demands for information is getting me a little pissed."

Mr. Amsterdam stands while he listens.

Deanna buzzes in over the intercom. "Jordan?"

Mr. Amsterdam glares at me. He has never heard her call me by my first name. In fact, she has never used it at work.

She continues, "Mrs. Amsterdam is in the office and would like to speak with you."

I remain calm. She ain't *my* wife. "Send her right in." Pause. I turn back to Mr. Amsterdam, who now is a crimson red. "And you were asking me about—" I snap my fingers to help him with his memory. It fails.

Mr. Amsterdam cuts his eyes at me and scurries back to his seat. He doesn't care that I know now that his wife owns and wears the pants. I laugh at his suit and wonder why he doesn't keep it real and wear a kilt.

There is a long pause after he sits. We both watch the door. Our anticipation is different. He sweats. I feel relief. His eyes dart from side to side. Mine remain glued to the door, only twice sneaking his direction to see his perspiration multiply.

The door creaks and Mrs. Amsterdam walks in, springing through the door like the Queen of Somewhere. Her cream colored hat is larger than life. It flops and dances as she moves gracefully toward me. Her cream pearls match her suit, which matches her shoes. As she breezes in, her floral scent overwhelms the stale alcohol odor that Mr. Amsterdam has left. She approaches me with a wide smile. Mrs. Amsterdam is regal. She calls herself the most powerful housewife on the coast. She once told me that she gave up her dreams of being a fire chief. She wanted to save the world. Now, she utilizes her free time to work for the world. She fills her time with countless hours at the Red Cross. She says they think the world of what she has to contribute so they put her in charge of fundraising. She is frugal. Mr.

Amsterdam is loose with who he gives his money to. That is evident by him paying top dollars to a psycho who just left college with a huge set of breasts and a small sense of business. Mr. Amsterdam doesn't realize that her being the 'Administrative Manager' to his business gives her the ability to look through all of the paperwork. She has access to everything he built.

"Nice to see you, Jordan."

We shake hands, and then she sits next to Mr. Amsterdam. They are cordial as she nods his way.

"How are you?" she asks him.

His movements in his seat are unnerving. He shows defiance when he reaches into his pocket and pulls his flask out. He watches her as he unscrews the top. As the top hits his lips, Mrs. Amsterdam faces him. Her glare ss evil.

"Not here, Philonius."

I guffaw. *Philonius?*

Mr. Amsterdam quickly looks my way before addressing his wife. "I need to speak with you in private."

She gives me a courtesy smile, spins his way and strongly suggests that they not deal with anything other than today. She says her head is not feeling the greatest and he isn't helping matters any.

Once Mr. Amsterdam twists the cap back on and returns the flask to his pocket, she begins slowly, "I have a few concerns regarding staff."

Mr. Amsterdam closes his jacket up and fiddles with the buttons. He remains silent.

I take the lead on this one. "Mrs. Amsterdam, what is the concern?" Even though she doesn't control the hiring and firing, I knew there is plenty table talk at dinner with who stays and who goes. I didn't want my life determined over a piece of baked chicken.

"My concern is that the young lady out front is not being treated fairly," she states.

Not being treated fairly? I knew we were about to go everywhere I never knew existed.

"Can I say something?" I ask.

She puts her hand up, quieting me. "You can speak after Philonius does," she says. "He has something to say on the matter. I can feel it."

"Oh. I've got something to say," Mr. Amsterdam murmurs.

"Excuse me?" Mrs. Amsterdam asks.

Mr. Amsterdam tucks his tail between his ass and says nothing.

"She expressed to me a concern that she isn't getting her fair shake."

"F-f-fair shake?" Mr. Amsterdam stammers.

"Yes. She feels that the men here are not being forthright with information on her performance evaluation so she can get a raise. She says that she has inquired about stock options, but nothing has been done." She smiles broadly. "And she says that she knew that me being the wonderful woman behind the scenes, I could get something done."

My look is smug as I wait for the rest of the storm to hit.

Mrs. Amsterdam sits back as though she is finished.

Deanna has me confused. I don't know what she wants, but I know that whatever it is has nothing to do with me. Mr. Amsterdam, on the other hand, was stifled. Water pours from his neck and saturates his collar. He needs a drink. His dick led him somewhere his pocket had to dig him out of. I know he wants to fire her, but with her knowing everything she did, his hands were tied, behind his back.

"Well, I've got nothing to do with this, Mrs. Amsterdam," I say. "I have always promoted a healthy work environment. I cannot do anything that your husband doesn't give the OK on." I hand her an envelope with facts about the business. "And if you look closely at my statistics, I can only help the company rise. I've spoken to Mr. Amsterdam about relieving him of some of his duties, but he loves the work." Pause. "Or, at least that's what he says." I walk over and put my arms around Mr. Amsterdam, whose sweat is beginning to give off an alcohol odor. "I would love for him to take some time and take you to Bermuda. He always says that you love to travel." I shake Mrs. Amsterdam's hand before I depart. I never look back as I leave for my late lunch. Deanna isn't outside at her post, but that doesn't surprise me. I am beginning to realize that she is untouchable as long as she had Mr. Amsterdam by the balls. And those aren't balls that anyone should want to hold.

Chapter 24

Traci

Traci double checks her face in the mirror. She has an epiphany. It is like she sees herself in the mirror for the first time in a long time. She strokes the length of her face. It has matured. She grew into her nose. She turns to the side. Her nose is sleek, not long. She lifts her chin. Her lips are full, not big. She lowers her face. Her eyes are amazing, dazzling, and full of energy, not wide and innocent. She smiles. It shows her character lines. It shows she won't lose. It shows her that in the midst of turmoil, she still has herself. She is the only person that can make herself smile the widest. Many made her frown. She thinks of a few. The names don't matter. Her mood plummets. Her features wither. Her eyes grow amazingly wild, and her look is uncultivated. The lines of her smile remain, but the smile is gone. She tries unsuccessfully to wipe away the worry lines on her forehead, but no matter how hard she wipes, they remain. She wipes again. Success won't come without work or effort. She thinks of happy things and watches her face. *Her career. Jordan. Cheesecake and the little kids at her job* warms her soul. Her face transforms right before her eyes. She can't hide hurt. Can't hustle the pain away. She thinks of how she watches Jordan when she wants to know if he was telling a lie. Never once has it occurred that she watch herself and find out her subconscious. She was an excuse maker for everyone including herself.

She slams the car door shut and walks toward the hotel. She sings *We come this far by faith, leaning on the Lord* as she walks. She doesn't remember the rest of the words, but it doesn't matter because the message is clear. She pauses at the door and quits singing. Everything she was taught in church and in life will come into play tonight. People all over are scared to put their faith to test. She used to be that way, but today she will find out where she is in this crazy world of life. She questioned herself earlier in the day if she was doing the right thing. She thought of her mother and her mother's mother and realized that she was doing what every mother should do. Who gives up children for careers? Who gives up dreams? What was more important? She was learning about life on the fly. Learning to deal with growing up and remaking choices. She knows now that you can't go back, but you can do things to rectify a situation. It isn't perfect, but no one is. If Jordan doesn't understand, then he will have to go. He has to understand. He has a child.

She reaches into her pocket and jingles her keys out of nervousness. It's amazing that after the first step into the hotel, her mind eases. She follows the signs to room one-twelve.

He opens up on the first knock like he's been waiting for hours. For years.

"Glad you could make it," he says.

She freezes. Everything she thinks of before she came to the door disappears. The smiling in the mirror and the touching of her face is gone. She can't remember what she talked to herself about to calm down. She can't revive any of her pep talks. Her hands fill with a wealth of sweat as she remains stuck in the doorway.

Solomon, always knowing what to do, invites her in by grabbing her hand and pulling her in.

She wants to run. Her heart hurts, and the onset of a massive headache is appearing out of nowhere. She wants to pop ten extra strength pills, but that will make her appear weaker than she is. She doesn't want Solomon knowing how he affects her, even though she feels he has a good idea. She musters up all the courage she owns and walks to the living room and sits on the couch. She looks around the hotel room and nods her head to the music. She can't hear the words, but the melody soothes her. He plays jazzy Luther. She wants to tell him to turn it off, but that may show another sign of weakness. She knows she has to play it his way before she gets it her way. She rehearsed how she was to tell him that it was impossible for them to be together on any level except Indigo's mother and father. Just the pairing of them together made her shake. She closes her eyes when he asks if she wants something to drink. She declines. She needs nothing from him except some papers stating she can see her daughter. In her perfect world, Solomon would flip on the lights and bring her out and tell her that it was a birthday party and then she would take Indigo in her arms and hug her all night long. She looks at Solomon and knows that is impossible. His sits across from her. His suit, freshly pressed. His tie, matching. His shoes, shiny. His hair, freshly cut. His eyes, constantly roving. His smile, dazzling. His taste, immaculate. His attitude, brass. She hates all of it. So what Jordan doesn't dress this way? His ties sometimes matched nothing he wore. His hair was rumpled, and his taste wasn't always appealing. She and Jordan were different, but that was OK. It was OK that they shared different dreams. They shared differences of opinions, but that was OK. He didn't know what she liked to drink, but was that all important in the long run? Maybe. Maybe not.

"I'm ready," she says. She doesn't know what she was ready for, but she was sure that the statement will get the party started.

"You sure?" he asks. He moves to the edge of his seat. She can see his mind working overtime. Today, she was going to accommodate his overtime. She was going to know either way where she stands. "I said, are you sure?" he asks.

She huffs silently and rises. "What do you want from me?"

He stands and closes the gap between them slowly. "I want it all." He opens his arms to her.

She denies his request.

It doesn't matter to him that she doesn't want what he wants. He moves close and pulls her near. His hug feels sincere. She feels his pain by the way he holds her. Strong around the waist. Clutching her neck with a soothing massage as they rock. Wrong as it seems, she feels safe. They are old souls meeting again under different circumstances. She thinks of the embrace and how it feels so rightfully wrong. She closes her eyes tight. A host of memories tear at her sense of right. It rips into the heart of what's wrong. She holds onto the corners of his elbows as he rocks her. Crying is supposed to release pain. The first tear releases the shakiness. She grabs tightly, burying her head deeper into the nape of his neck. He smells familiar. He holds her the way she needs to be held.

She lifts her head and starts to speak. He quiets her with his finger to her lips.

She allows him to quiet her. She doesn't want to speak, but feels the need to. Here she is, in a room full of candles, thoughts and memories, about to be led by Solomon, again. The Promised Land is Indigo. She doesn't know how to bring up the subject, or what type of agreement they'll come to, but she is making sure she does her part.

"Follow me," he whispers. His arms fall as he lets go of her and walks casually toward the back room, never looking back.

She stands like a pillar. Her feet won't allow her to go any further as she watches him disappear into the back. She is supposed to be right on his heels, but something tells her not to. She shuts her eyes, looking to self for answers. The picture is dark, but a light shines through. People have done stranger things to take care of business. She whispers to herself, *by any means necessary.* It is her motto. Her creed.

She watches the back light go on and off. She finds a rhythm in the song and taps her foot. The familiar music is her only sense of connection. It gives her strength and feeds her energy. It always has. From the time she was young, she cleaned every Saturday to Bobby Womack. She remembered his thick white goggles and the way he talked to his women in the songs. Yesteryears substance was the difference in the music. Nowadays, the singers didn't mention anything without sex. She remembered when Marvin was shot and Teddy's limo crashed. The older singers sang about issues. The singers of today sing about problems. The classics remained the classics because problems are temporary while the issues remained constant and relevant. She needs to talk about the issues of motherhood. She knows of a higher love that doesn't quite exist. She persuades breath to leave as she walks toward the back room.

Within ten steps she changes her mental state and crosses over. She is a new woman, ready to do anything for her family. She walks into the room.

"I'm here," she says. Her stance shows strength. Her confidence barges in before she does. She stands with her hands on her hips. Her smile is authentic, as far as he was concerned.

The room is comfortable. Solomon sits in the swiveled chair and rubs his chin. She feels like a piece of meat as he combs her body. He moves to the edge of the bed looking into the mirror. His mood is carefree.

"So, you really don't want to be with me, huh?" he asks.

She watches him, speaking with confidence. "Not at all."

Solomon slowly licks his teeth, giving her a smart-aleck smirk. "What would you suggest?"

"It's your show." She talks as though she doesn't care, but she doesn't know how long she can keep up with the counterfeit conversation.

His cockiness is beginning to wear off, but he still remains true to his plan. "I love you," he begins. "And I think we should try." Pause. "For her." He walks behind her. "And you *know* you still feel me." He sounds convincing until he ends with an unsure, "*Right?*"

Her words are punctuated with truth. "I don't." She lets him remain behind her. She wants him to know that while he examines her body, she's in another world. She feels filthy, like *she's* done something wrong. Someone else takes over her emotions and reacts for her. She wants to say so much. She feels the need to beg. She has no desire to get back into his good graces, but knows she has to. Being with him forever was out of the question. As plainly as she can, she asks, "What is it going to take, Solomon?"

He stops his rubs and hugs her as though they were still dating. "You. Can you give me what I need?"

She needs so much. She can't fathom herself trying to give him the world when he wasn't willing to give her a county. "I could give you a lot, but don't you want it given with a smile?" She tries to appeal to his human nature.

"Maybe." He lets her go and stands in front of her, infiltrating her personal space. She accepts with disgust. "Then again, maybe I don't need you to feel anything."

She says nothing.

He grabs her shoulders and massages. His tone is sarcastic. "You feel numb?" His hands don't feel warm or comforting.

"I'm fine."

"I need something from you." He moves her back and looks into her eyes. "I need for you to look at me. No time for bullshit." His is very businesslike. It makes her feel better.

She looks at him. His stare penetrates, but she doesn't waver. She looks him directly into his eyes. She searches for compassion. She wants to find an inch of decency, even though she may have not showed him that she cared for years. She was here. She showed up. Deep down she knew that wasn't enough. Retribution would come at a high cost. She knew he would raise the stakes until she put an end to it. Solomon always fought her to her limits. She just never knew her limits. Now she did. She fucked up for years and she was willing to pay with all she had to offer. A piece of her.

"What do you want?" she asks. "Money? Blood? Sex?"

Solomon's eyebrows raise. He turns his head to the side. "We could start with that."

"What?" She maintains eye contact. She wants everything laid out. She had sex for worse, even though it was always with a boyfriend who knew they had her on the ropes. Once it was for the lights to be turned on. Another time it was for the chance to shop for necessities. It was always a simple statement like, "Before we go shopping, would you mind giving me some?" She knew men shopped better after sex. Men always bartered with sex. She knew the power she had and she used it, as long as they offered first. Today would be the last day she ever bartered with her body.

He moves uncomfortably close. There noses almost touch. He begins his bartering with Indigo. "We could start with you giving me what I want," he says.

She doesn't back away. "No games. What do you want?"

"Sex."

She moves forward. "Sex?"

"Of course."

"And then what?"

"And then I'll give you what you want."

She waits for him to make another move. She waits for the punch line. After a few moments, she realizes there is no punch line. Solomon hasn't changed. Sex rules him even when it comes to their daughter. She nods.

"If we do, I won't have any involvement."

He smiles. "And?"

"You want it like that?"

He smiles. "You don't have to be involved now. You might come around." He moves close and wraps his arms around her. "You don't have to do a thing. I just want to be with you one more time."

She allows him to hug her. Her body tenses. Her jaws clench. His cologne smells like shit! She thinks of nothing.

"Where?" she asks.

Solomon clears a path to the bed with his hand. "Right there."

She makes a decision and accepts her fate. If this was what she has to do, then so be it. She walks to the bed begins to undress. He shifts his posture and watches her begin with eager eyes.

After her shoes fall from her feet, she thinks of her daughter. She begins to take her shirt off.

"Wait right there," he says. "You're moving too fast." He walks over to her and lifts her shirt off himself. He puts his hands around her neck. He remembers she likes that. He kisses both sides of her neck. She closes her eyes tight and tries to replace him with someone she used to love. No one comes to mind. She opens her eyes and watches the dim light hit the ceiling.

"You don't want to like it, huh?" he says.

She bites her lips, holding all of her comments to herself.

Her silence angers him.

"You don't want to talk?"

"I don't have to talk," she informs him.

He removes his hands and steps away. "And I don't have to do shit, either!"

She knows she won't get anywhere with shit, so she tries honey.

"Sorry." The word stings. Why was she apologizing? She remembers why she is here. She goes to the bed, turns over and begins to take her pants off. It's easier to undress while she faces the wall. Walls don't have personality and they don't make her feel bad.

He returns to her. Her back faces him. He admires how she's grown. His hands travel the length of her back. He stops at her lower back and tells her how much he has missed her. She says nothing to encourage his affection. He pushes against her and kisses her neck. Her flinch angers him. "Look," he says, "you don't have to do any of this."

She turns around and tells him in a nice way, that she has to do all of this, no matter how grimy it is. Men and women are just different, she says. She would walk to Europe and back if that was what she had to do.

"Thanks for not making it tough on me," she adds sarcastically. She wants to be crass, but not offensive. She wants this over. She knows what Solomon wants. He wants her to feel good about it or fight. It might even ease his conscience. She cannot hold everything in. Her attitude peeks out. "You want it like this, then take it!" She bends over the bed and lets her arms flail to the side.

"Don't patronize me," he says. His temperature rises. "It's your fault that we're in this predicament." He lifts her from the bed. "If you were half a fucking mother, then we wouldn't be in a fucking hotel. We would be in our own house making love." Pause. "Do you think I want it like this?"

She remembers their past lovemaking and wants to desperately emulate the mood, the motion, and the passion so her job will be done more efficiently. She says nothing; instead, she shakes free from him and lies on her back and watches the ceiling.

He wants to argue, but there's nothing to argue about. She is doing exactly what he wants her to do, without him telling her.

She hears his zipper unzip. She flinches again.

"I don't want to argue, Solomon." She gets into role. She takes her panties off and lies them next to her. "Make love to me, please."

He takes his clothes off and sits on the bed next to her. He fumbles with his condom as he takes it out. His mood is apathetic. He throws the wrapper to the bed and looks at her. His fingers travel the length of her naked thigh. She pays no attention. She parts her legs slightly.

"You want to do this?" he asks.

She knows it's a trick question. She forces her answer out. "I do."

"It'll all be worth it," he says as he rolls over on top of her.

Traci's heart shudders as he climbs on top of her. She tremors at the touch of his body on hers. It had been so many years since she last lay with him. Motherhood killed the idea of her getting up and punching him. She remembers how he loved for her to spread her legs wide and hold them open with her hands. She re-enacts. He fumbles with the condom as he positions himself directly over her.

His hand slides to her clitoris. What used to be a magical strumming of her spot now feels like a hardened rub of skin on skin. She wonders how she put up with this for so long when they were together. She closes her eyes and thinks of the brook near her grandmother's house. The water trickling off the rocks. She used to sit on the grass with her feet in the water. She begins to relax with each passing minute. "You don't have to do this if you don't want to," he says.

She knows it's another trick statement. She goes forward and brings him near. He moves to kiss her lips. She turns her head and allows his lips to fall to her neck. Once his head is down, her facial features tell a horrid tale. Her stare toward the ceiling is angry. She wishes he would get off of her, but what's done is done.

The idea of never seeing her daughter again rocks her soul. Passion overtakes caution. She brings him close and holds him tight. She knows his Achilles Heel is his hair being rubbed. He also loves to be licked. She knew she wasn't going to be performing her whole show, so she prepares herself for the side show.

She says, "I am glad you're back," and grips his back tighter.

His hug has feeling. He reaches around her back and pulls her up to him.

She wants him to get this over with so she can move on with her life. She doesn't need the loving atmosphere for completion. He was getting too emotional and she needed closure.

She pulls him near. She grabs him firmly and helps him guide the tip of his head to her. She prepares for the hurt. Physically she's not moist. She doesn't care. He'll have to get it however he can. "You ready?" she asks.

He jumps up from the bed. "No!"

She sits up and reaches for his hand. She is so close to finishing her part of the bargain. "What's wrong?"

He sneers. "Nothing. Just need a break."

She unsuccessfully tries to pull him near. She grabs his legs and pulls him close. He fights her touch and stands. He paces around with the condom hanging from his limp penis.

She wants him to rise, get on top of her and give her what she needs. She doesn't need the penetration for pleasure. She needs it to move forward.

She feels like a slut with her legs open and a man walking around deciding whether or not he's ready for her sex. She makes a decision to force the issue. She stands and walks to him. He remains in the mirror watching himself and rubbing his own hair. She enters the picture in the mirror and wraps her arms around him. He doesn't move. He doesn't even look up at the picture. She coaxes him to take her back to the bed by kissing his neck. He remains unresponsive.

"Hey, baby," she says. The words flow easier. She acts. Something inside her triggers her role of a despondent mother doing any and everything to get her man to leave. She thinks of what a woman would do if she knew a man wanted sex and wouldn't leave until he received some. She would make him receive her.

"I'm ready," she says.

He spins around. His role is undefined. He plays the part of a barbarian. His anger elevates to levels she cannot understand.

"You ready?" he yells. He grabs her shoulders and lifts her and brings her to the bed. She falls to the bed in a heap.

For reasons unknown to her, she isn't scared. This is what actresses do. Was the actress that played Tina Turner scared when the fake Ike put his hands up? She figures she'll get her fucking Oscar when it was all said and done. Her trophy was her daughter.

"I'm ready," she screams back. "I've been thinking about this all day," she says with venom.

"Yeah?"

She sits up on the bed quickly. "Yeah!"

He pushes her back down. His condom is now filled with malice. She knows he doesn't like it presented on a platter so she makes him take it.

He forces himself on top of her. No kisses. No hugs. No love. The viciousness of his entry is unnerving. She jumps. She takes him as though he had two inches. In reality, his girth far exceeds comfort.

He pushes with his body. It is for his purpose. He intends harm. She remembers child birth and opens wider. She accepts all of him as her head moves uncontrollably upwards. She stares at the ceiling.

"So," *Push!* "You've" *Push!* "Been Wanting" *Push! Push!* He yanks her hair. "This?"

She looks in his face. Her eye contact is out of character. "Yes. I have been wanting this."

He pushes himself to her hilt. He moves aggressively from left to right.

She continues, "As a matter of fact, how bad have you wanted this?"

His strokes intensify. He kisses her neck with a wet opened mouth. He bites her nipples. "For a while, bitch!" He gives her three hard pumps for the road. "Turn around!" he commands.

She complies instantly. She's into her role. She sees the end. She turns around and gets on her knees. She lifts her ass in the air and allows his entrance. He spreads her and enters with wild abandon. His first stroke sends her toward the headboard. As he pushes himself in, he pushes emotion and memory out of her.

Push! Indigo. *Push!* Failure. *Push!* The director forcing himself on her. *Push!* The call. *Push!* Waiting for her father on the porch. *Push!* He never comes. *Push!* Jordan.

Her memory overwhelms her. She watches the headboard while he does his business behind her. He shouts something about him not wanting her to forget this moment. She wants him to release. She needs him to collapse on the bed. She promised not to touch him.

She reaches underneath her body and plays with his balls. When he slams into her, she caresses.

"You want me to come?" he asks. The penetrating blows never stop. His pace quickens. "Do you?"

Traci puts her head down and shakes it from side to side. She feels no pleasure. She doesn't even feel pain. It felt as though someone was probing her at the doctor's office.

"This is mine," he shouts. He grabs her shoulders and pummels her from behind. "This is mine," he repeats. Then he stops. Her body shudders as she expects more blows that never come. He leaves his hands on her shoulders and presses deep. He shakes as he normally did when he comes.

She wonders if he's done. She still feels him inside of her. He goes limp. He pushes her to the bed and falls next to her. She's exhausted. Below, she throbs. Her walls feel like have been tormented and tortured for hours. Her mind is totally blank. A numbness appears and takes over. She can't cry. Can't talk. Can't feel.

Solomon stretches out and puts his arm across her chest. She has no energy to tell him she was finished and needs her part of the deal fulfilled. She wants to leave, but the music still plays. She hopes it's the last song. She can't hear the melody, only words that speak of pain and heartache. She sings.

"I hate you," he says. "I fucking hate you."

Traci says nothing. Her heart melts at the cruelty, the timing and the tone. He sounds as though she were a cheap trick that charged him too much for nothing.

"Did you hear me?" he says. When she doesn't respond, he lifts himself and walks to the mirror. As if nothing had just transpired, he buttons his shirt. He looks angry, yet calm. His cufflinks are next. He inspects the buttons and talks as though he doesn't know her. "You made my life miserable. Just to think that I wanted *you.*"

She turns to her side and suddenly she realizes something is not right. She heaves.

"I wanted you to feel the pain I felt for all of these years when you weren't there."

Traci rolls over and leans over the side of the bed. She knows something is way off.

He walks over to her. "Don't throw up now. Indigo died two months ago. She always wanted you to have this." Solomon throws a gold necklace at her. It lands in the vomit.

Jordan opens his door. Traci collapses on his doorstep.

"Baby," he yells. He instantly falls to the ground and cradles her. "What happened?" He rocks her. He rubs her hair and waits for her to respond.

Slowly she opens her hand and reveals a stained necklace with a heart encrusted with the words *# 1 Mom.*

"I told you I won't be the same."

He puts his hands over hers and closes her hand around the necklace. "I'm not the same either," he says. "I'm not the same, either."

About the Author

Gerald K. Malcom was raised in Atlanta, Ga., and he now resides in Albany, New York. Malcom fell in love with writing after successfully writing and publishing his book of poetry, The Naked Soul of a Man. After touring the country, he released his debut novel, *After the Games Are Played*. He has also developed a program, Books By Us, where he teaches young students how to publish and write their own books. In the summer, he devotes countless hours to ACID (Asset and Character and Individuality Developement Through Writing), a program for students in summer camps in NY. In his spare time he enjoys spending time with his family and cooking soul food.

Acknowledgments

To the man upstairs . . . thanks for giving me the courage and strength to continue to do what I do. Without our late night and early morning conversations, I would be a total loss. I would like to thank my children for allowing their precious "daddy time" so I could complete this book. To my children Warren, Davion, Denzel and the little princess Zoe . . . ice cream for everyone, but me. It's a lactose thing . . . ya'll wouldn't understand. You are my heart and soul. I would like to once again thank Mercedes by getting on my knees and kissing the ground she walks on. Fighting through the struggles and still giving head rubs, now that's love! To my immediate family; my mother Peggy, my brother EB, my sisters, Rochelle, Aqueelah and Bendelia. I'm trying to make the doughnuts. To my other moms, Joyce and Alma, thanks for supporting me as though I was your own.

Now for the book world and those who have helped me through this rough process. Echo Soul. Thank you Kim for supporting me from day one. I love you. I can never leave home. Or you can never get rid of me. It's the same thing. Echosoul.com.

My sister and homegirl, Jamise L. Dames. I love that we can talk about everything. Keep hitting those best selling charts. My other sister, Nakea. Philly? What? I love you guys. Can't forget about our traveling voice and fellow night-on-the-town girl, LaShon.

Q-Boro Books, what can a brotha say? I would like to thank Mark Anthony for taking a chance and bringing me out to the party. So this is how it looks? LOL Candace . . . thanks for helping me not go crazy and with your editing.

To my silent group of friends that are the voices for some of the craziest characters around. My brothas from the heart, J-Cob, Court, Juan, K-Will and EB.

I would like to thank Saundra for being an ear, a friend and a great listener.

Super shouts to Glinessa and Ty for taking care of my woman.

To the few authors that I've met and were so gracious to give me a little time and information about the biz...Eric Jerome Dickey, Jamise L. Dames, Shannon Holmes, Terri Woods, Timm McCann, Angie Daniels, Brenda Jackson, Beverly Jenkins, Tony Cheathem, Zane, Marlon Green, Trustice Gentiles, Doreen Rainey, Michael Pressley, Iyalna Vanzant, Gayle Jackson Sloan, Will Cooper and any other author I may have forgotten in my quest to give thanks.

I cannot forget Janice Aaron from Odysseys Book Network in California. I appreciate your raw opinion of the book when it was in its rawest form.

Super shouts to my editor Shelley Rafferty for teaching me once again all about the literary world. I've learned so much from you over the past few books and I love that you are not afraid to tell me that something is not my best work.

Shouts to Kenny Braswell with Urban Voices. Soul Kitchen for providing me that poetic food. My other brothers, Aaron, Morgan and Jordan. To Mantic Records,

Angel, Wakalak, J Swan, Matthew and all the others who continue to work from the ground up.

It's been two long years since this book was supposed to be released, but because of things out of my control, it wasn't. It was a blessing in disguise. I wasn't ready to give the world what I was blessed with.

To all of my readers that stuck with me throughout the rewrites . . . thanks for the support. Way to stay hungry for my words and accepting of my stories. To those who are forgotten . . . you truly are not.

It's been hard, but worth it. I struggle to find my voice at times, but I am steadily recording so I can perfect the pitch. I am here, world, I am here!

Gerald K. Malcom

LOOK FOR MORE HOT TITLES FROM

Q-BORO BOOKS

LOOK FOR MORE HOT TITLES FROM

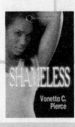

LOOK FOR MORE HOT TITLES FROM

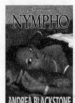

NYMPHO - MAY 2007
$14.95
ISBN 1933967102

How will signing up to live a promiscuous double-life destroy everything that's at stake in the lives of two close couples? Take a journey into Leslie's secret world and prepare for a twisted, erotic experience.

FREAK IN THE SHEETS - SEPTEMBER 2007
$14.95
ISBN 1933967196

Librarian Raquelle decides to put her knowledge of sexuality to use and open up a "freak" school, teaching men and women how to please their lovers beyond belief while enjoying themselves in the process. But trouble brews when a surprise pupil shows up and everything Raquelle has worked for comes under fire.

LIAR, LIAR - JUNE 2007
$14.95
ISBN 1933967110

Stormy calls off her wedding to Camden when she learns he's cheating with a male church member. However, after being convinced that Camden has been delivered from his demons, she proceeds with the wedding.

Will Stormy and Camden survive scandal, lies and deceit?

HEAVEN SENT - AUGUST 2007
$14.95
ISBN 1933967188

Eve is a recovering drug addict who has no intentions of staying clean until she meets Reverend Washington, a newly widowed man with three children. Secrets are uncovered that threaten Eve's new life with her new family and has everyone asking if Eve was *Heaven Sent*.

LOOK FOR MORE HOT TITLES FROM
Q-BORO
BOOKS

DARK KARMA - JUNE 2007
$14.95
ISBN 1-933967-12-9
What if the criminal was forced to live the horror that they caused? The drug dealer finds himself in the body of the drug addict and he suffers through the withdrawals, living on the street, the beatings, the rapes and the hunger. The thief steals the rent money and becomes the victim that finds herself living on the street and running for her life and the murderer becomes the victim's father and he deals with the death of a son and a grieving mother.

GET MONEY CHICKS - SEPTEMBER 2007
$14.95
ISBN 1-933967-17-X
For Mina, Shanna, and Karen, using what they had to get what they wanted was always an option. Best friends since day one, they always had a thing for the hottest gear, luxurious lifestyles, and the ballers who made it all possible. All of this changes for Mina when a tragedy makes her open her eyes to the way she's living. Peer pressure and loyalty to her girls collide with her own morality, sending Mina into a no-win situation.

AFTER-HOURS GIRLS - AUGUST 2007
$14.95
ISBN 1-933967-16-1

Take part in this tale of two best friends, Lisa and Tosha, as they stalk the nightclubs and after-hours joints of Detroit searching for excitement, money, and temporary companionship. These two divas stand tall until the unforgivable Motown streets catch up to them. One must fall. You, the reader, decide which.

THE LAST CHANCE - OCTOBER 2007
$14.95
ISBN 1-933967-22-6
Running their L.A. casino has been rewarding for Luke Chance and his three brothers. But recently it seems like everyone is trying to get a piece of the pie. Word of an impending hostile takeover of their casino, which could leave them penniless and possibly dead. That is until their sister Keilah Chance comes home for a short visit. Keilah is not only beautiful, but she also can be ruthless. Will the Chance family be able to protect their family dynasty?

Attention Writers:

Writers looking to get their books published can view our submission guidelines by visiting our website at: www.QBOROBOOKS.com

What we're looking for: Contemporary fiction in the tradition of Darrien Lee, Carl Weber, Anna J., Zane, Mary B. Morrison, Noire, Lolita Files, etc; groundbreaking mainstream contemporary fiction.

We prefer email submissions to: candace@qborobooks.com in MS Word, PDF, or rtf format only. However, if you wish to send the submission via snail mail, you can send it to:

Q-BORO BOOKS Acquisitions Department
165-41A Baisley Blvd., Suite 4. Mall #1
Jamaica, New York 11434

*** By submitting your work to Q-Boro Books, you agree to hold Q-Boro books harmless and not liable for publishing similar works as yours that we may already be considering or may consider in the future. ***

1. Submissions will not be returned.
2. Do not contact us for status updates. If we are interested in receiving your full manuscript, we will contact you via email or telephone.
3. Do not submit if the entire manuscript is not complete.

Due to the heavy volume of submissions, if these requirements are not followed, we will not be able to process your submission.